C000099270

DARK OPERATIVE A GLIMMER OF HOPE

THE CHILDREN OF THE GODS BOOK 18

I. T. LUCAS

FOLLOW I. T. LUCAS ON AMAZON

Also by I. T. Lucas

THE CHILDREN OF THE GODS ORIGINS

THE CHILDREN OF THE GODS

DARK STRANGER

DARK ENEMY

KRI & MICHAEL'S STORY

DARK WARRIOR

DARK GUARDIAN

DARK ANGEL

DARK OPERATIVE

DARK SURVIVOR

PERFECT MATCH

SETS

THE CHILDREN OF THE GODS BOOKS 1-3: DARK STRANGER TRILOGY—INCLUDES A BONUS SHORT STORY: THE FATES TAKE A VACATION

THE CHILDREN OF THE GODS: BOOKS 1-6—INCLUDES CHARACTER LISTS

THE CHILDREN OF THE GODS: BOOKS 6.5-10 —INCLUDES CHARACTER LISTS

TRY THE CHILDREN OF THE GODS SERIES ON **AUDIBLE**

2 FREE audiobooks with your new Audible subscription!

COPYRIGHT

Dark Operative: A Glimmer of Hope
is a work of fiction!
Names, characters, places and incidents are products of the author's imagination or are used fictitiously and are not to be construed as real. Any similarity to actual persons, organizations and/or events is purely coincidental.

Copyright © 2018 by I. T. Lucas
All rights reserved.

No part of this book may be reproduced in any form or by any electronic or mechanical means, including information storage and retrieval systems, without written permission from the author, except for the use of brief quotations in a book review.

CONTENTS

"Fuck!" The young man tore the headphones off his head.

The operative was still alive.

Even if he weren't so familiar with Turner's voice, he heard Sandoval call the fucker by name.

With another curse, he hurtled the expensive headphones against the wall of the shed he'd been hiding in—his camouflaged command post, or rather listening post, because he commanded no one.

Watching the expensive set shatter, pieces of broken plastic bouncing off the floor, brought no satisfaction. No remorse either. He could afford new ones. Hell, he could afford anything money could buy, but nothing was going to fill the big hole in his heart.

Xavier was gone, and no amount of worldly riches was going to compensate for the loss.

Someone had to pay. The burning need to avenge Xavier was the only thing that kept him going, but the idiots he'd hired hadn't done their job.

Fuck, he sucked at this.

Xavier had been the brain of their operation. He would've

known the right people to hire for the job, and he would've demanded proof of execution.

A sob escaped the young man's throat.

He was such a failure. Avenging Xavier was the singular goal in his life, and yet he'd messed it up because he had no fucking clue what the hell he was doing, and there was no one to teach him. It wasn't as if he could've learned this at the fancy university he'd gone to.

Xavier was gone.

It had been Xavier who had come up with what had seemed at the time such a simple plan, foolproof. The ransom money could've set them up for life. But they hadn't counted on Sandoval hiring Turner, or on the hell the operative would unleash upon them.

Xavier's people were good, rough and tough gangsters who hadn't been easy to take down, but Turner's people were better. Ex-commandos, trained professional killers who as civilians were selling their murderous skills for money.

What carnage. The blood and lifeless eyes were still vivid in his nightmares.

After securing the hostage, there had been no need to go on a killing rampage. But the commandos had been instructed to make an example out of Xavier and his men so no one would dare mess with Sandoval again.

Turner's instructions, not Sandoval's.

The fucker was going to die even if it took years. The right opportunity to avenge Xavier would eventually present itself.

It was karma.

CHAPTER 1: RONI

*R*oni wasn't sure what he'd expected to feel right out of transition, but it sure as hell wasn't an underwhelming sense of sameness.

He was still the old Roni. Same skinny arms peeking out from the sleeves of the hospital gown, same bony knees tenting the thin blanket, and the same flabby middle even though he was underweight. Without looking in the mirror it was hard to tell, but he had a feeling he'd lost even more weight and was scrawnier than ever.

His hopes for waking up with an amazing new body were crushed.

Except, if nothing had changed, why the hell was he so sore?

Roni ached all over as if he'd spent days stretched on the rack. Skin, muscles, tendons, they all felt too tight for his skeleton.

"You're awake." Dr. Bridget stated the obvious as she walked in and handed him a cup of water with a straw. "Congratulations. Welcome to immortality."

He looked at the paper cup. "Shouldn't a toast be made with champagne?"

"Pretend that it is."

Pushing himself back on the hospital bed, Roni gulped greedily, moistening his dry throat. He still hadn't asked the most important question. "How long have I been out?"

"Almost three days."

He whistled. "That long?"

She nodded.

"Fuck, Sylvia must be worried. Where is she?"

"I sent her up to get some sleep."

Disappointing. He had fantasized about Sylvia watching over him throughout the transition.

His expression must've revealed his thoughts because Bridget added, "We knew you were doing fine and that there was nothing to worry about."

"How did you know that I was? Three days in a coma doesn't sound okay to me."

Bridget smiled. "You were growing. That's an excellent indicator that your body was working hard at transitioning. It needed to divert all its energy to the rapid growth."

Grimacing, Roni lifted his arm. "Does this look bigger to you?"

She whipped out a measuring tape, wrapped it around his bicep, and noted the measurement on her tablet. "You lost three-quarters of an inch of muscle."

He let his arm plop at his side. "That's what I thought."

"But." Bridget lifted her hand. "You gained an inch in height, bringing you to an impressive six foot two. Your shoulders are also wider by nearly one and a half inches."

That explained the aches and pains. "No wonder I feel like I've been stretched on the rack. Everything hurts."

"I can give you something for the pain."

"Please, but none of those mind-bending drugs. Plain ibuprofen will do. I'm the ultimate anti-macho guy, and I welcome pain relief whenever possible, but I hate mental fog. I'd rather suffer than compromise my brain."

She patted his hand. "I wasn't going to offer you anything

stronger than that. There is no need. Do you want me to call Sylvia?"

Duh. "Please."

Bridget picked up the bedside phone and dialed. "Your guy is awake, and he is asking for you."

There was a happy squeal on the other side. "I'll be there in a minute."

It took him a moment to realize that Sylvia sounded as if she had been talking on a speakerphone, but he knew she hadn't. The phone was right there where he could see whether the button was lit. "Unbelievable. The hearing, I mean."

Bridget nodded. "Do you want to test your eyesight?"

"Sure."

She pointed to a chart on the wall. "Can you read the small print at the bottom?"

Even though the lights were dimmed and the writing was small, he could read it easily. "Amazing. Can you dim the lights even more? I wonder if I can still read it in near darkness."

Bridget did as he asked, lowering the switch all the way down. "Give it a go."

He squinted a little. "I can still read it."

"What about smells?"

He sniffed. "I like your perfume. What is it?"

Bridget chuckled. "Not this kind of scent. I meant the more subtle ones. What do I smell like under the perfume?"

Roni closed his eyes and concentrated. "Happy. You smell happy and excited."

It was so weird to be able to detect the smell and even weirder to recognize it for what it was—kind of like taste. You knew sweet when you tasted it.

The other scent, however, was not something one mentioned to one's doctor. Roni felt his cheeks heat up but went ahead anyway. "And horny. I'm sorry, but you asked."

He was quite sure the doctor's arousal had nothing to do

5

with him. After all, she'd seen him in all his unimpressive glory. Besides, it would've been uber awkward otherwise.

Bridget was hot, but he was taken.

Her laugh was as happy as her scent. "You are right on both counts."

She didn't elaborate, which left him with an uneasy feeling. He had to find out. "Who's the lucky guy?"

Bridget lifted a brow. "Do you need to ask?"

Wow, talk about a big surprise. Roni didn't know whether he should feel flattered or threatened. On second thought, he was definitely flattered. Maybe that extra inch was what made all the difference.

But then the rush of excitement helped clear the last tendrils of fog from his brain, and he slapped his hand over his forehead. Evidently, the three-day coma had affected his memory.

Turner.

When the guy had gone missing, Bridget had called Brundar, asking for his help. In turn, Brundar had dragged Roni out of bed and asked him to hack into several security cameras. Roni had managed to get the camera feed from Turner's last known location, the entrance to the fancy restaurant he'd dined at that evening.

As they'd all watched Turner exit the place, get stabbed, then pushed into his own car and driven away by a fake valet, Bridget had sobbed openly.

She was way too cool of a chick to cry over an acquaintance. Obviously, the two were lovers.

"Turner, right?"

"And the prize goes to the recently-transitioned guy on the bed."

"How is he doing? All better now?"

"He is. Didn't you see him at your transition ceremony? He was there from the beginning to right after you passed out."

"I was a bit busy being scared shitless and trying to keep

from soiling my pants while reciting slam poetry."

Bridget shook her head. "That stuff was awful. Did you write it yourself?"

"Yes, but most of it was based on gangster rap. Disgustingly offensive stuff, and coming from me it's saying a lot. I have a dirty mouth, but nothing like that."

Roni didn't want Bridget to think of him as someone who even listened to lyrics that insulted women and glorified violence. "It felt bad spouting that crap. But I had no choice. It wasn't as if I could have spurred Kian's aggression with my nonexistent fighting skills. He suggested I use slam poetry instead because he detests it. I forced myself through it, and it worked. I made him angry enough to produce venom. Potent stuff too. Much better than that of the other guys."

As far as he knew, Roni was the only Dormant who'd required four bites from four different immortal males to transition, starting with Andrew, then Onegus, then Brundar, and ending with Kian—whose bite had finally done the trick.

Apparently, that piqued Bridget's curiosity, and she lifted her tablet. "Tell me about the differences. Were the effects produced by the other bites similar to each other, and only Kian's was different? Or was each bite unique?"

Concentrating, Roni tried to remember the details, which wasn't easy given that after each bite his brain had gone on a pleasant vacation to la-la land. But one thing he was sure of —Kian's had been the best.

"Andrew's was the weakest. I don't think he gave me enough before retracting his fangs. This was his first aggressive bite against a male, and he was probably afraid to overdose me, accidentally killing me. Onegus's and Brundar's were almost the same, except Brundar's hurt less, which was a big surprise. The dude is scary, but his bite was gentle and precise. He has incredible control."

"What about Kian?"

Roni smiled. "The difference between his and the others

is what I would imagine the difference between pot and acid is. After the other bites, I had a short pleasant trip to dreamland. After Kian's bite, I soared through psychedelic landscapes and felt one with the universe. That's the best way I can describe it, but it doesn't do the trip justice. His wife is one lucky lady."

Bridget's wince lasted a split second, but Roni caught it. Damn, he should've kept his big yap shut. All the immortal females were yearning for an immortal male's bite, but only a few had been lucky enough to score one.

Actually, there were only three. Kri, Amanda, and Carol. Though only Amanda and Kri had the real deal—a truelove mate. Carol and Robert had gone their separate ways.

Eva hadn't known what she was, let alone about the ecstasy of an immortal male's bite. Syssi had started out as a clueless human, and so had Nathalie, Callie, and Tessa.

Roni would have known none of that if it were not for Sylvia who kept him updated on the keep's gossip. As it was, he knew the stories and the names of the participants but not the people involved. Getting to know everyone in his new family was going to be a slow process. Luckily, he now had all the time in the world, and Sylvia was the fourth clan female to score an immortal male—him.

The full impact of what had happened to him finally hit home.

He was immortal.

"When will I get my fangs?"

Bridget patted his shoulder. "Patience, Roni. Don't expect to bite your girlfriend anytime soon. Your fangs will take a few weeks to grow, and it will take even longer before you'll be producing venom. You can talk to Andrew and Michael. They can share their experiences with you."

Poor Sylvia. She'd waited so patiently for him to transition, and now she would have to wait even longer for the coveted venom bite.

Bummer.

CHAPTER 2: BRIDGET

*B*ridget knocked on Kian's office door then let herself in. "I want to talk to you before Turner gets here."

"About?" He put down his pen and pushed aside the yellow pad he'd been writing on.

"I want Turner to move in with me. It's a temporary arrangement, only until the redecorating of his apartment is done. After that, I'm going to move in with him and leave mine to Julian."

"Define temporary. Few days? Few weeks?"

"Probably a few weeks."

Kian leaned back in his chair. "Is it my imagination, or is the guy slowly but surely worming his way deeper and deeper into the clan? If he cohabits with you, he will need access to the clan's private parking level and the elevators. What is going to stop him from snooping around? He already knows too much."

"It wasn't his idea. He suggested that I move in with him, but I can't yet. I have to wait for Julian to take my place in the clinic."

"How soon is that going to happen?"

"He is coming back next week."

"Can't you wait until Julian gets here and then move in with Turner? I'm sure the redecorating can wait."

"I could, but then it would take too long. First, I need to train Julian before he can start, then I need to be around for at least a few weeks in case he needs me. Besides, I don't want to move into Victor's apartment before Ingrid transforms it into a livable space. You should see it. The place looks as inviting as an insane asylum from the forties. Everything is white with polished metal accents."

Kian arched a brow. "And you're willing to risk further exposure of the clan because of interior decor? That doesn't sound like you."

Bridget crossed her arms over her chest. "I dare you to come see it and tell me that you would've been willing to live in that place."

"Is Turner inviting me?"

"I don't see why not. If he's letting Ingrid do whatever she wants with his place, he must realize that his address is no longer a secret. Besides, what else is there to find out? He already knows most of our secrets."

"He doesn't know how large our Guardian force is, and he doesn't know anything about our other locations."

That wasn't exactly true. Turner didn't know where the Scottish stronghold was, or Annani's Alaskan retreat. But despite the tight security and secrecy around the village project, he'd discovered where the local clan was moving to. Kian would be livid when he found out the location was compromised, and Bridget was bracing for the blowout once he did.

Victor had promised her he would tell Kian, but he hadn't had the chance yet.

Hopefully, he was going to do so soon because she hated keeping it a secret from Kian. "He will know about the Guardian force when our offense against human trafficking starts. And as far as the locations, no one knows where Annani's is, including you. That leaves Scotland, but it's not like we have a map pinned to a wall somewhere. Unless someone tells him, I don't see how Victor is going to find out. Besides, I believe he is trustworthy." Fearing her guilt might show on her face, she'd avoided mentioning the village.

Kian raked his fingers through his hair. "I don't know. I guess he is, at least as long as he thinks you'll approve his transition attempt. It wouldn't be logical for him to betray the clan he hopes to become a part of."

With a sigh, Bridget slumped in her chair. "We both know that I'm going to approve it. I told Victor he needed to get the cancer under control first and convinced him to get chemo. He agreed. But even if that doesn't work, I can't forbid him to go for it. He is an adult, and he knows the risks. It's his choice."

Kian nodded. "I feel for you. That must be difficult."

"It is. But what can I do? When life gives me lemons, I add sugar and make lemonade."

"Good luck with that."

"Thank you. So is it a yes?"

"How can I say no? I'm not going to take away the sugar you need for your lemonade."

"Thank you."

"When we are done, take Turner to William for his parking sticker and a thumbprint for access to the elevators."

"No cuff?"

Kian snorted. "As if Victor Turner would agree to a locator cuff. The guy would chew off his own hand rather than give over that much control."

CHAPTER 3: TURNER

"*I*'ve made room for your things in the closet."
Bridget reached for one of his suitcases.

Turner pulled his arm back. "I don't need help."

She cast him an amused glance. "Right. Follow me."

The woman was strong, but that didn't mean he would let her carry his suitcase. His injury barely bothered him anymore, and even if it did, he would've sucked it up. He was a rational man and all for women's lib, but there was a limit to how far he was willing to go.

As he followed Bridget into her walk-in closet, Turner was surprised to see how little clothing she owned. He hadn't investigated a woman yet who hadn't had her closet bursting at the seams. Bridget's was less than half full.

"Did you get rid of stuff to make room for mine?" He put his two suitcases down.

"I've done some cleaning up. It had been ages since I'd gone through the stuff in my closet. Can you imagine that I still had several outfits from the sixties? I think it's safe to assume those will never come back into fashion."

It was a reminder that Bridget was much older than she looked, and that he still didn't know exactly how old. "Are you ever going to reveal your age? Or is it going to remain a mystery forever?"

She walked up to him and wrapped her arms around his waist. "I'll tell you after your transition. No need to freak you out when you still think of age in human terms."

He dipped his head and kissed her plump lips. "I take it that you believe I'll make it?"

"I have to. Thinking otherwise is going to suck all the joy out of my life."

Looking away, Turner hid a wince. He didn't want to think about Bridget's pain either.

She was an unexpected complication in his quest for immortality. When he'd come up with the idea, there had been nothing overly important he had to consider. Unlike most people, Turner wasn't afraid of dying, and at the time no one would've been too devastated by his passing. Alice might have shed a tear or two, his son would've been sad for about a day, and his staff of independent consultants would've missed the good income he'd provided for them.

Maybe some of his clients would've bemoaned the loss of his valuable services.

That was about it.

His death would not have been a big deal to anyone.

But now there was Bridget. And his death was going to pain her.

When he'd set out to seduce her, Victor hadn't expected to care for her as much as he did. She'd been a means to an end.

His mistake was not taking into account the law of unexpected consequences. He'd fallen into the web he'd so carefully spun to entrap her, and now they were both stuck inside of it—for better or for worse.

Bridget tapped his nose with her fingertip. "What are you thinking about?"

"Of how far we've come. I've never shared a home with anyone before."

"Are you scared?"

"Scared? No, of course not. I'm curious, and I'm looking forward to a new experience."

"Naturally." Her smirk suggested she didn't believe him.

"What should I be afraid of? Do you turn into a monster on nights when the moon is full?"

"Like a werewolf?"

He shrugged. "Any other creatures that turn into monsters on a full moon?"

"Not that I've heard of. But I can turn into anything you want." She waggled her brows. "Do you have anything specific in mind?"

He'd forgotten about that side of the thralling ability. When Turner had first met Kian, the guy had revealed who he was, and Brundar had provided the proof by vanishing himself, Anandur, and Kian from sight, then bringing them back. It was all a mind trick. Brundar had manipulated Turner's mind not to see what had been right in front of his eyes. He could've just as easily projected any other image, like turning the three immortals into chickens or werewolves.

"I don't. Surprise me."

"Close your eyes."

A tingle of excitement rushed up his spine. "Okay."

"You can open them now."

The woman in his arms was still Bridget, plump lips, smiling eyes, and flaming red hair. "I don't think it worked."

She smirked. "Look down."

"Holy shit!" Startled, he let go of her.

Instead of legs, Bridget had a long fishtail that sparkled emerald green. Quickly, he closed his arms back around her. Without legs, she couldn't hold herself up, and if he didn't hold her, she would drop to the ground.

Bridget's laughter filled the closet. "It's an illusion, Victor. I still have legs, and I'm still standing. You can let go."

Experimentally, he did, but just in case he needed to catch her, his hands hovered close to her waist.

Standing on her fins, Bridget remained upright. "How do you like Little Mermaid?" She flipped her hair back. "We have the same coloring."

Logically, he knew that what he was seeing was an illusion, but his mind responded instinctively to the visual stimuli. A fish couldn't stand on its fins, and he couldn't help but hold on to Bridget to keep her from falling.

Catching her around the middle, he brought her close against his body. "The Little Mermaid is a lovely young fish girl. I prefer my Bridget."

"Oh, that's sweet." The tail vanished, turning back into a lovely set of legs.

A thought crossed his mind. "What if the story is based on a mischievous immortal who wanted to play mind games on the young prince?"

Bridget tilted her head. "I'll have to ask Annani. I wouldn't put something like that past her. This is exactly the kind of prank she would've found hilarious."

That was highly unlikely. Surely the goddess, the mother of the clan, was not into playing tricks on unsuspecting humans. "What makes you think it could've been her?"

"Several things. First of all, she is tiny, even smaller than I am, and at first glance looks like a seventeen-year-old girl. Secondly, she is stunningly beautiful, with red wavy hair that reaches all the way down to her hips. And third, she has a mischievous streak the length of the Mississippi River. She drives poor Kian insane. He always worries about what she'll do next."

CHAPTER 4: RONI

"I want a steak." Roni grimaced at the bowl of clear chicken soup Sylvia handed him. He was so fucking hungry he could eat five steaks, and it wouldn't fill him up.

"Bridget said you should only have clear liquids for the first day." She held up the spoon, waiting for him to take it.

"I don't give a fuck about her instructions. I'm hungry and I want to eat something that will fill me up. Steaks, potatoes, and more steaks."

Sylvia put her hand on her hips and struck a pose. "She said you're going to throw up if you eat solids."

"I'm willing to chance it."

Ruth pushed up from the couch. "I'll make you a steak."

Sylvia turned her ire on her timid mother, who was a much easier target than Roni. "Mom! It's going to make him sick!"

"So what? If he wants to eat it, let him. What's the worst that could happen? He is going to throw up? Not a big deal."

"Thank you, Ruth." Roni wanted to kiss the woman on both cheeks.

"You're welcome." She walked to the kitchen and opened

the freezer, which was fortunately stocked with enough meat to last him a month.

Well, not really. It would've lasted the old Roni that long or even longer. The new Roni was going to go through it in less than a week. Bridget had told him that once the queasiness passed in a day or two, he needed to eat a lot to provide his body with enough fuel to grow stronger and better.

Hopefully, he was going to grow some muscle over those protruding bones. He looked like a walking skeleton.

"I'll make you a smoothie," Sylvia offered with a resigned expression on her beautiful face. "I'll stuff it with berries and veggies and nuts."

Roni leaned forward and caught her hand, pulling her into his lap. His new strength, although expected, was surprising given his lack of muscles. During the transition, he'd lost inches instead of gaining them. "A smoothie is still made of solids. It's not a juice. You can make a smoothie out of the steak, but it won't change how it affects my stomach."

She leaned into him, putting her head on his bony chest. "It might. But maybe a liquid is easier to digest."

His fingers brushed through her thick hair, playing with the long locks. "Thank you for taking care of me. Again."

She'd been so good to him, his Sylvia.

The girl had a heart of gold and apparently poor eyesight.

He was a skinny, pimply teenager with a bad attitude when she'd come to him and taken his virginity. She had done it as a favor to Andrew in exchange for Roni's hacking skills, but she could've thralled him to believe they'd had sex instead of actually giving him such an incredible gift.

This beautiful, smart girl had seen in him something that had touched her heart, and Roni would forever be grateful for that. Even though he was a grumpy patient and didn't act as grateful as he should, she'd taken care of him when he was sick with pneumonia, and now she was doing the same after his transition.

Stretching up, she kissed his cheek. "You're welcome."

"I need to thank your mom too. It's so nice of her to come and cook for us."

Sylvia snorted. "Yeah, if you had to survive on my cooking, you would starve."

Roni suspected that Ruth's motivation for coming to stay with them had little to do with her eagerness to cook for her daughter's boyfriend. Lately, Sylvia was spending more and more time at his apartment, and her mother didn't want to be left home alone.

He didn't mind. Ruth was an odd bird, but a good person. The only problem he had with the arrangement was keeping quiet during sex.

Immortals were supposed to be open-minded about that, but still. Having the mother of your girlfriend sleeping in the next room while the said girlfriend was moaning and screaming was not something he was comfortable with—especially since those bloody immortals had such good hearing.

Hell, he was one of those bloody immortals now. Thank God, hallelujah. Gone was the constant worry over whether he was a Dormant or not, and whether he was going to transition.

Roni felt twenty pounds lighter, and only five of those was actual weight loss from his three-day coma.

The delicious smell of cooking meat wafting from the kitchen made his stomach rumble, the pangs of hunger twisting his gut getting worse by the second. "I need to chew on something right now."

He lifted Sylvia off his lap and held her up until she had her feet firmly on the floor. It didn't require any effort. The old Roni would've not been able to pull that off without huffing and puffing from exertion.

"Sit down." Ruth motioned to the barstools next to the counter.

"Yes, ma'am."

"Do you want anything with your steak?"

"Another steak would do."

Sylvia rolled her eyes. "You are so going to barf."

"I don't care."

Ruth took the two steaks off the frying pan, dropped them on a plate, and put it in front of Roni. "Enjoy." She looked at Sylvia. "Do you want one too?"

"Sure. How does the saying go? If you can't beat them, join them?"

Roni felt like an ass. "Here, take this one." He forked one steak and transferred it to her plate.

"I thought you were hungry?"

"I am, but I can wait for the next one. I can't eat while you have nothing on your plate."

Sylvia arched a brow. "Since when?"

He had a fast metabolism and a limited stomach capacity. Roni liked to eat small meals several times a day. His girl, on the other hand, wasn't a big eater and often joined him just to keep him company.

"Since I know you want one too."

"Only because you're eating."

He pointed at her plate. "Stop arguing and eat."

"Yes, sir!" Sylvia saluted and lifted her utensils.

Her back to them, Ruth snorted softly, dropping two more steaks into the sizzling pan. "There is a first time for everything."

Sylvia was busy chewing, which was a perfect opportunity to learn more about his girl. "What do you mean?" Roni asked.

Ruth waved the spatula. "Usually, my Sylvia argues until she wins."

"Mom! That's not true. I only argue when I'm right."

"But you always think you're right."

As mother and daughter went on and on, Roni finished demolishing his steak. "I think those are ready." He pointed at the smoking pan.

"Oh, dear." Ruth turned around, grabbed the pan by the

handle and took it off the burner. "I'm afraid these two are no longer edible."

Roni cast a questioning glance at Ruth. "If you don't want them, I'll eat them. I don't mind that they are overdone."

Shaking her head, Ruth put both on his plate. "I'll make myself a new one. Do you think you'll want more after you're done with these two?"

"I might."

Sylvia shook her head. "When you puke your guts out, don't say I didn't tell you so."

CHAPTER 5: BRIDGET

"*C*an we stay here and watch a movie? Maybe something romantic?"

Bridget snorted. Suggesting a romantic movie was Turner's latest and most desperate attempt to avoid company. But she wasn't going to let him have his way—hiding in her apartment and slinking around like a ghost, avoiding people.

It was time to nudge him out of his comfort zone, or rather widen it a little to include a few friends.

"Come on, I already told the guys we will meet them at the café."

"I thought we were going for a cup of coffee and a Danish. I'm not in the mood to socialize."

She threaded her arm through his and led him toward the door. "Of course you're not. But you're going to do it anyway. Who knows? You might even enjoy yourself."

With the expression of a condemned man on his face, Turner entered the elevator and leaned against the wall. "Who is going to be there?"

"Anandur, Brundar and Brundar's girlfriend Callie. Andrew and Nathalie may come if they can get Syssi to babysit Phoenix, which she loves doing, but sometimes Kian vetoes it."

"Why? Doesn't he like Andrew and his wife?"

"That's not it. He is jealous over Syssi's time. He wants her all to himself. I wonder what will happen when they have children of their own."

Turner rubbed his clean-shaven jaw. "Can't help you with that. I have no clue."

Bridget stepped in between his spread legs and pressed her hands to his chest. "I wasn't expecting an answer. I was just thinking out loud." She kissed him lightly on the lips.

"I get it."

Victor was learning that not every comment required an answer and that not every complaint meant that she was asking his advice.

When they reached the glass partition that separated the clan's private area from the rest of the lobby, Bridget pointed to the lock pad on the door. "Press your thumb right there," she instructed.

Last night, she'd taken Turner to William, who'd scanned his thumbprint and given him a sticker to put on the windshield of his car. Victor would have to remember to take it with him whenever he switched between the many cars he used.

With the first barrier crossed, they continued past the wall of greenery into the café proper. This late in the evening, Carol's station was closed, but that didn't mean the place was deserted. With a press of a button, the Nespresso machine provided coffees or cappuccinos in several flavors, and a variety of pastries and sandwiches was available from the line of vending machines. As long as someone kept the machines stocked, the place could practically run itself.

"Hi, guys." Bridget walked up to Brundar and Callie's table.

She leaned to embrace Callie, but only nodded at Brundar. The Guardian had gotten somewhat better as far as touching people went, but he still cringed whenever someone other than Callie did that.

"Callie, this is Victor. Victor, this is Callie." She made the introductions.

"Nice to meet you." Turner shook Callie's hand.

Victor wasn't big on touching either, and the only one to get hugs from him was Bridget. In his case, however, it wasn't due to an aversion or a phobia, he was just too stand-offish and aloof to initiate or invite physical contact.

"Brundar." He nodded at the Guardian who nodded back.

"Would you like coffee? A Danish?" Bridget asked.

Turner perked up. "I'll get it." He seized the opportunity to get away and avoid socializing for a few moments.

She'd allow him the short reprieve. "I want a cappuccino and a cheese Danish."

He lifted a brow. "Cheese? You told me it's unhealthy."

"It is, but it's okay to sin on occasion. As long as you keep the bad-for-you-stuff to no more than five percent of your daily calorie intake, you're doing fine."

"Are you saying that I can have a steak once a week and it's not going to affect my health?"

"Yes."

"Hallelujah." There was a spring in Turner's step as he headed for the wall of vending machines.

Bridget shook her head. "Men are strange. The one time I hear him utter a word of praise to a higher power, it's for a steak. No thanks for the homeless guy who drove him to the hospital, not for how the knife miraculously missed his lungs and heart, but for a piece of meat."

"Never underestimate the power of a tasty steak." Callie reached for Brundar's hand and clasped it. "That's how I lured this guy in."

Bridget cast Brundar a questioning glance. "Really? A steak?"

"Among other things. And it was more than one steak," he confirmed.

Bridget was still laughing and shaking her head when Turner returned with the cappuccinos.

"What did I miss?" he asked as he put them down.

She waved a hand. "Brundar is also a steak lover."

The guy shrugged.

"I have an idea," Callie said. "We should have a barbecue. Is it okay to grill on the balcony?"

Bridget picked up her cup. "I don't think so. This place is too fancy for that. Perhaps on the penthouse level it's okay. We will have to ask Amanda or Kian to host one."

"Host what?" Carol sauntered into the café and sat next to Callie.

"A barbecue," Bridget said.

"That's a fab idea." Carol looked at Turner, throwing at him one of her seductive smiles.

Apparently, the keep's rumor machine had somehow skipped over Carol and she didn't know Turner belonged to Bridget.

"Turner, this is Carol, the one who manages this café when it's open. Carol, this is Victor Turner, and he is with me." Better to let Carol know he was off limits before she unleashed her full arsenal of feminine wiles. Very few males could remain unaffected, and Bridget had no intention of testing Turner's resistance.

Carol's eyes widened. "The same Turner who found where the Doomers were holding me?"

He nodded. "In the flesh. But from what I heard, you'd saved yourself, and my help wasn't needed."

"I had help from a very decent Doomer. But I'm grateful to you nonetheless. Sebastian needed to die," she hissed, her eyes glowing dangerously. "Without your help, all the other girls they kidnapped would have been still imprisoned, or dead." Carol pushed to her feet and walked over to Turner. "Thank you." She wrapped her arms around his neck and kissed him on both cheeks.

Bridget's ire jumped from zero to a hundred in a nanosecond, but Turner's almost comical response extinguished it just as fast. Her guy leaned away from Carol like a kid trying to avoid a kissy, obnoxious aunt.

"You're welcome." He gave her a gentle push.

Understanding dawning, Carol straightened up and took a step back. "Brundar and you should become best buddies."

Callie chuckled. "I love it that my guy doesn't allow anyone but me to touch him. I'm not a fan of all that hugging and kissing. I'm too jealous for that. Then again, I have nothing to worry about. All the available ladies in the keep are his cousins."

Brundar grunted. "You have nothing to worry about period."

CHAPTER 6: TURNER

*T*he curvy blond finally got a clue and stopped her assault.

Unless a woman was going for sex, Turner was uncomfortable with spontaneous displays of physical affection. Those should be reserved for close family members, and even then they should be limited to a quick embrace and nothing more.

Slobber was not welcome on his cheek. The only exception was when that mouth was on its way to slobber over another part of his body, which meant that as long as he was with Bridget, she was the only one allowed to kiss him.

"I'm glad that you're okay," he said, and meant it.

Without going into details, Kian had hinted that the woman had gone through a brutal ordeal. Her immortal body had obviously healed, but Turner wondered whether her mind had had enough time to heal too. Mental wounds were much harder to recuperate from.

Carol went back to her seat, her curly blond hair bouncing up and down as she plopped on the chair. "I'm tougher than I look." She winked at him. "It's not easy to break me."

From the corner of his eye, Turner caught Brundar

regarding Carol with what looked like a mixture of pride and respect. For a hard, stoic man whose expression softened only when gazing at his girlfriend, that look expressed better than words the Guardian's high opinion of the blond.

There must be much more to her than the cheerful yet empty-headed persona she showed the world. Could Carol be a spy?

The best in the field were the least obvious.

"What do you do, Carol?" Turner asked.

The smile she flashed him transformed her small face, which only moments ago had been twisted with fury at a dead guy, into that of a sweet cherub. "I make sandwiches and coffee."

That was definitely not all she was doing. "What else?"

"Sometimes I train beginner self-defense classes, filling in for Brundar, my sensei." She dipped her head in mock deference to her teacher.

In Turner's opinion, Carol looked too soft and padded for a woman who engaged in rigorous training. His thoughts must have shown on his face because Brundar jumped in to defend her.

"Out of all the trainees, Carol is the best markswoman."

Turner tilted his head. "Are you training to become a Guardian?"

She shook her head, those curls of hers bouncing around her angelic face. If he weren't a taken man, there was no way he wouldn't have been affected by her. Carol was temptation personified. She knew it, and she used it. Definitely spy material.

"No way. Guardians have to obey the law, and I'm a rebel."

"That she is," Anandur said as he walked up to their table.

Grabbing a chair from the next one over, he put it between Carol and Callie but a little way back since there wasn't enough room. "And her marksmanship skills are wasted. She refuses to go hunting with me."

Carol crossed her arms over her chest. "I'm not going to shoot at defenseless critters."

Anandur leaned over her shoulders. "But eating steaks is fine?"

She tucked one side of her hair behind her ear. "We had this discussion before. It's not the same."

"Are we back to talking about steaks?" Bridget asked.

"How about we move to stakeouts?" Anandur offered. "As much as I love a juicy steak or two, I think those are much more interesting." He glanced at Turner. "How are we going to storm those brothels you were talking about? Just show up and boom! Or first reconnaissance, and then raid?"

Startled by Anandur's question, Turner instinctively looked behind his shoulder and then scanned the large area the café occupied.

Bridget patted his shoulder. "It's okay, Victor. Only clan members can come in here, and the glass is bulletproof and soundproof. We can talk freely here. You have nothing to worry about."

Normally, he would have argued to the contrary. Only those on the need to know list should've been privy to the information. Except, Bridget was going to lay it all out for the entire clan, so there was no point in keeping it quiet.

"I already put things in motion. Operators are mapping the places and getting the layout and security measures of each one. The teams on the ground will have all this information before doing their own reconnaissance. The more prepared we are, the smoother the execution, and the fewer the casualties."

Bridget frowned. "Aren't you jumping the gun by starting before the funds are approved? What if the clan votes against it?"

"They won't."

"How can you be so sure? And in the meantime, you're spending your own money."

"I'm positive the vote will be in favor. And if not, I'll find another backer for the operation. This needs to be done."

Carol clapped her hands. "You're my kind of guy, Victor. If you weren't such a prudish oaf, I would kiss you on both cheeks again." She winked. "Maybe even twice on each, like the French do."

"Please don't," he and Bridget said at the same time.

Carol's laughter was as fresh and as sweet as the rest of her.

She was either an amazing actress or had a split personality. One was a carefree young woman who was interested only in having fun, and the other was that of a hardened warrior who could withstand the worst torture and emerge unscathed.

"Oh, you guys are so cute. I should've known Bridget would be a jealous and possessive girlfriend. With that red hair, there was no way she wouldn't."

Bridget glared at Carol. "What's that supposed to mean? Hair color has nothing to do with personality. That's as much of an urban legend as the blood type diet or that blonds are dumb. You shouldn't believe everything you read."

Carol shook her head. "Temper, temper, my dear doctor. According to that same urban legend, redheads are also quick to anger." She put a finger to her lips and tilted her chin up. "I wonder where they get those strange ideas from?"

CHAPTER 7: LOSHAM

*A*ll throughout the long flight home, Losham's emotions had been oscillating between crippling fear and overblown confidence. Now that he was sitting in the vestibule of his father's receiving hall, waiting for his conference with Navuh, he was experiencing more of the same.

An execution was a remote possibility, but demotion and humiliation were not. After thousands of years as his father's lead advisor, losing his position was almost as terrifying a prospect as losing his head.

When Navuh's secretary emerged from the servants' door, Losham's heart kicked into overdrive, the thundering beat so loud he was sure the secretary must've heard it.

There was no way he could go into the lion's den like that.

His father would chew him up and throw what was left for the dogs to finish. Fear was the worst emotion to have when dealing with the Brotherhood's exalted leader.

The servant bowed. "Lord Navuh will see you in a few more minutes."

Losham nodded imperiously. "Thank you."

The air left his lungs in a whoosh as soon as the secretary

had returned the same way he'd come in and closed the door behind him. For once, Losham was thankful for his father's diva antics of keeping him waiting for hours.

Over the next few minutes, he was going to calm down by imagining only the best possible outcomes. Maybe Navuh had a new project he wanted to run by Losham, perhaps his father wanted him to head that project. After all, Navuh had learned a long time ago how invaluable Losham's advice was.

When the door opened again, he was ready.

"Lord Navuh will see you now," the secretary said as he opened the massive doors leading to Navuh's reception hall.

Losham stood up and lifted his chin. "Thank you." He strode in as if he owned the place

"Greetings, my lord." Losham bowed low.

Thankfully, he was exempt from the obeisance the rank and file were obligated to offer Navuh.

His father's throne sat on a tall dais, with the guest chair facing it about seven feet lower. It was an uncomfortable straight-backed thing, designed to keep the guest as uncomfortable as possible, and with a sore neck from having to look up the entire time.

"Losham." His father acknowledged him in the same bored tone as always. "Come, join me in my office." Navuh pushed off the throne and took the short flight of stairs down to Losham's level. The office, which was located off the reception hall, was used for when Navuh wanted absolute privacy. Soundproofing the small room was easier for the son of Mortdh than doing so for the entire big hall.

This was good news.

Navuh's need for absolute privacy meant that he needed Losham's advice on something important.

Losham hurried to open the door for his father and bowed again as Navuh walked by him.

The leader sat in one of the two armchairs and motioned for Losham to take the other.

With another bow, Losham did as instructed. "How can I be of service, my lord?"

"We need more money," Navuh cut to the chase. "There aren't enough wars going around for us to profit from. And aside from the lack of income, it creates another problem. Having an army of mercenaries without a war to fight is like sitting on top of a dynamite keg. We need to find something for them to do before we have a rebellion on our hands."

"I agree. We need to instigate a new war."

Navuh nodded. "I have a few ideas, but I'll leave it up to you to research."

In other words, his father didn't know where in the world was the most fertile ground for pushing existing conflict into a full-blown war, and he needed Losham to figure it out.

"Naturally, my lord. I'll get right on it."

Navuh signaled that he wasn't done. "The drug trade isn't bringing in as much as it used to either. The gangs are difficult to control, there is too much competition, and the prices are going down."

"What about our protégés? That's our biggest source of income."

Navuh cringed. "We lost the biggest one. The current ruler wasn't too happy when he discovered that we were working with his number one enemy, playing both sides."

Losham wasn't surprised. He'd advised against it, expecting exactly this outcome, but Navuh wouldn't listen. As always, the leader was greedy for the money and for the influence.

"We could send Lokan to convince the ruler he can't do without our help. This relationship is decades long. It started with his grandfather."

Lokan was a prick and not too bright, but he possessed a powerful thralling ability and was a master at compulsion. If anyone could convince the powerful ruler to come back into the fold, and more importantly keep paying for their services, it was Losham's half-brother Lokan.

Navuh shook his head. "The current ruler is immune. He has a powerful and suspicious mind. We will have to replace him with someone who is easier to manipulate, but that will take time to organize. In the meantime, we need the money."

"I'll start working on it immediately, my lord."

Navuh nodded. "How did your hunt go?"

Losham's gut twisted, but he managed to control his emotions. "May I speak frankly, my lord?"

Navuh waved, the sleeve of his robes adding royal flair to the gesture. "Go ahead."

"Annani and her clan have been living in hiding for thousands of years, and they are very good at it. I think it's a waste of time and resources to hunt for them. When we seize control of humanity, the clan will become irrelevant anyway."

To Losham's great surprise, Navuh nodded again. "I agree that the way we went about it was a waste of time and resources. But we don't have to wait for humanity's fall to annihilate the clan. The same technologies they helped humans develop will be their downfall. The Internet, security cameras everywhere, drones filming from the air, all of that is making it difficult to hide, and it will only get worse for them."

As it will for us, Losham thought.

CHAPTER 8: BRIDGET

"*Hi*." Julian swept Bridget into his arms and picked her up, hugging her close and spinning her around as if she were a child and not his mother. "I missed you, Mom," he whispered in her ear before putting her down.

Passengers were still spilling out of the same sleeve Julian had just exited, and others were camped in the gate's sitting area, waiting for their boarding calls. Calling her Mom would have raised a few eyebrows even in Los Angeles, the home of Hollywood and the best plastic surgery money could buy.

"I missed you too. You have no idea how happy I am to have you back for good."

Julian lifted his duffle bag from where he'd dropped it on the floor and wrapped his other arm around Bridget's shoulders. "Tell me about the guy you are shacking up with. I need to be mentally prepared to meet the dude if I'm going to cohabit with him."

"Does it bother you?"

"Nah. If you're happy, I'm happy. I'm old enough to share my mom with someone who cares about her and not get too jealous about it."

"As soon as Turner's place is ready, you'll have the

apartment all to yourself. As the keep's doctor, you will probably be one of the last ones to move to the new location."

Julian shook his head. "I still can't believe you're leaving the clinic to me. I don't think I'm ready to go solo."

"You won't. I'll still be there if you need me."

"Good."

They took the escalator down to the baggage claim and waited with everyone else for Julian's suitcases.

"I'm proud of you," he said. "What you're doing is important."

"The whole thing is Turner's brainchild." She didn't want to take credit for something she hadn't done. The truth was, however, that originally it had been Kian's idea, and he'd asked Turner to investigate. But Victor had taken it to a whole new level of complexity.

"I'm still waiting for you to tell me about him."

"What do you want to know?"

"Is he charming? Does he make you laugh?"

Bridget chuckled. "Not really. But he is brilliant, and talking with him is a pleasure. He knows a lot about a lot of things."

"So you fell for his brain?"

"He is also very handsome, but he is not the type I used to go for. Turner is not tall, and he has no hair."

"A short, bald guy? And super smart?" Julian snorted. "I'm going to be sharing an apartment with Dr. Evil."

"Who?"

"The villain from the Austin Powers movies."

Bridget huffed. "Not even close. Dr. Evil was flabby. Turner is all muscle. There is not an ounce of fat on him. He has an amazing body for a guy his age."

"Which is?"

"Forty-six."

Julian shook his head. "An old, short, bald guy."

Offended on Turner's behalf, Bridget crossed her arms

over her chest. "With beautiful blue-gray eyes, an eight-pack, and incredible charisma."

"So more like Vladimir Putin than Dr. Evil. Gotcha."

Bridget rolled her eyes. "I'd better stop responding because you'll just keep going. Turner is like no one else. Incomparable. He is a unique individual."

Julian laughed as he hefted a suitcase off the conveyor belt and put it on the floor next to Bridget. "Just teasing. I'm sure he is a great guy."

He helped a woman with her luggage and then had to chase after his other suitcase, which in the meantime had gotten away from him.

Should she tell Julian more? Prepare him better?

It was true that Turner was like no one else. He required some getting used to, and the first impression he left on people was that of a cold, hard man. He was off-putting to most.

"Turner has some issues," she said as they made their way to her car. "He is not an emotional guy, and at first glance he appears cold." She chuckled. "Also the second and the third. But the weirdest thing about him is that he doesn't emit any scents."

Julian cast her an amused look. "Good, I would've hated to share an apartment with a stinky human."

"I don't mean like that." She took a quick glance around to check if anyone was listening to their conversation. "No emotional scents. I've never encountered any human or immortal who had none. He is an anomaly."

Julian's eyes sparkled with humor. "Maybe he is an alien?"

"Right." Bridget clicked the doors of her car open and got behind the wheel as Julian loaded his luggage in the trunk. "You have that in common," she said as he got inside and buckled up.

"What? Don't tell me my father was not of this world."

Bridget laughed. "Dream on. An illegal alien from another country is the most you can hope for." She eased out of the parking spot. "I meant your fascination with UFOs and aliens. Turner loves stuff like that too. He is always looking to solve one unsolvable mystery or another."

Julian clapped his hands. "Oh, goodie, we are going to be best friends," he said in an excited high-pitched voice.

Her son's quirky sense of humor never failed to amuse her, but the question was how Turner would react to it. Hopefully, the guy's smarts included comprehending jokes and not getting offended by Julian's never-ending stream of funny nonsense.

"Why do you keep calling him by his last name?" Julian asked.

She shrugged. "A habit, I guess. He rarely tells people his given name, which is Victor by the way, and everyone calls him Turner. I bet he thinks of himself as Turner and not as Victor."

"What should I call him? Because I'm not going to call him Dad. I just wanted to put that out there."

Bridget laughed. "You need to be careful with those jokes around Victor. I'm not sure how he is going to react to them."

Julian leaned back in his chair and let his head drop on the headrest. "If he is as smart as you say he is, he'll get it."

"I hope so."

*a*s Turner waited for the heavy door to slide aside and let him into the clan's secure parking area, he didn't feel as if he was coming home. He felt like a visitor, or rather an intruder.

The sticker allowed him access to the section of the keep that non-clan members, meaning humans, were barred from. Not that the building's other occupants were aware of the extensive underground compound, or suspected those residing on the upper floors, where the regular elevators didn't go, of being anything other than richer and snobbier, residing in apartments that were more luxurious than those on the floors below.

After having been treated with suspicion and caution for so long, he would need time to get used to his new access privileges. There would be no more stops by the security station and no more waiting for Bridget or one of the Guardians to come get him. It was straight up to her apartment, which he now shared, and would soon be sharing also with her son.

This was not one of his best ideas. In fact, he should not have agreed to have his apartment turned upside down. New furniture and some colorful rugs would have done the job, and Bridget could've been living with him. He could've invited Julian to a nice dinner at a restaurant, and that would've been the extent of their interactions.

Instead, he was bracing for the awkward first meeting with his lover's grown son. It wasn't that Turner had a problem with new people—he handled new clients and other business associates with ease. The difference was that their expectations of him were limited to his expertise, and they were well aware of his excellent track record. His natural charm or lack thereof had no bearing on their decisions to hire him for a job or join his network of sub-contractors.

What the hell was he going to talk about with Julian?

Bridget's son was a complete stranger, who would probably not regard Turner favorably. Hell, what chance did he have of winning the guy over if connecting with his own son, on any level, was still a struggle?

Douglas possessed average intelligence, was into team sports, and had no hobbies, unless hanging out with friends over beers could count as one. His son was interested in none of the subjects Turner was.

After Douglas had joined Special Forces, they finally had something in common. But then there was very little they were allowed to talk about, so that didn't solve the problem. At their semi-annual meetings, they usually ran out of topics of conversation in less than an hour.

It was painful. For both of them.

And now he would be forced into the same situation with Bridget's son—the difference being that the torture was not going to end with them going their separate ways after one uncomfortable dinner or lunch meeting. They were stuck living together in the same apartment.

Maybe Julian could find a vacant apartment in the keep. After all, Kian was starting to move people to the new place so there should be vacancies.

Which reminded Turner that he still had a confession to make. He hadn't told Kian about discovering the clan's new location yet. Maybe he should go to the guy's office right now and get it done with. If Kian killed him on the spot, he would at least be spared the awkward meeting with Bridget's son.

Right.

With a sigh, he stepped out of the elevator and headed for Bridget's apartment. She'd given him a key, but he still felt uncomfortable using it. Especially today.

Taking a deep breath, Turner schooled his features into an impassive mask and knocked.

The young man who opened the door was tall, handsome, and looked nothing like his mother. Except for the eyes. They were the same color, blue with flakes of green swimming on the perimeter, but where Bridget's were serious, his were smiling. In fact, he looked a lot like Kian sans the countenance of someone who bore the weight of the world on his shoulders.

"Turner, I assume?" He threw the door wide open and offered his hand.

Turner took it, not expecting to be pulled into a bro embrace, complete with rigorous backslapping.

Well, at least the guy was friendly.

"I'm Julian, as you must've deduced. Come in and take a load off."

"Thank you."

Another backslap. "Hey, you're not a guest, you're a roomie. Don't thank me."

"Hi, Victor." Bridget walked into the living room and headed straight for him.

Not knowing how to act around the son, Turner waited for her to set the tone. "Hi, to you too."

She kissed his cheek. "I see that you and Julian have already done the introductions."

He nodded.

"I'm going to whip us up something for dinner."

"How about we order takeout instead? I can go get it." A

round trip to bring food would shorten the time he had to spend socializing with Julian.

Bridget smirked. "So you can get away? I prefer to make something healthy at home."

"I'll help you."

She rolled her eyes. "Fine. Come on."

Turner let out a breath and shrugged off his jacket, then hung it on the back of a chair.

"What can I do?" He rolled up his sleeves.

Pulling the fridge door open, Bridget took out a head of lettuce, several tomatoes, cucumbers, and an onion. "You can chop veggies for the salad." She put down the load on the counter and handed him a cutting board.

"I can do that." Turner pulled out a knife. "Do I need to wash them first?"

"They are already washed."

"Big chunks or small chunks?"

"Small. It's going to be a Mediterranean meal. I hope you like hummus."

"I do."

"Good. I'll heat up the frozen fake meat shawarma."

"Blah," Julian said from the living room. "I hate the fake stuff. One day I have to take you to my favorite shawarma place. Real shawarma is made with turkey and veal, not soy." He walked over to the counter, pulled out a stool, and straddled it. "I've eaten shawarma all over the world, and this place is the best."

Turner lifted the board with lettuce he'd chopped and pushed the small bits into the salad bowl that Bridget had put next to him. "I didn't know medical students got to travel so extensively."

"They don't. I took a year off after high school and backpacked all over. I figured I'd better see the world before diving into studying for eight more years. Then I decided to do it again after graduating college and before starting medical school."

Lucky kid. Only the privileged could indulge like that. For others, like Turner, the only way to see the world was to join the army. "Smart choice, if you have the funds for it."

"My mom is the best. She funded it without me having to beg too much."

Bridget snorted. "He started the campaign in tenth grade. By the time he graduated he'd worn me down. The second time I told him he had to get into a medical school first."

"Naturally, I got in." Julian blew his mom a kiss. "As she knew I would."

Turner finished chopping the tomatoes and added them to the bowl. "You must've been a good student."

"Top of his class," Bridget said. "Julian knows how to work hard, but he also knows how to have fun."

Julian seemed a little uncomfortable with the praise, which made Turner like him even better. For a few moments, the sounds of chopping were the only ones to disturb the silence.

"Mom tells me you're interested in extraterrestrials," Julian said in an obvious attempt to veer the conversation away from his accomplishments and his mother's boasting. "Did you read Jacques Vallée?"

Turner paused his chopping to glance at Julian. "Of course. He is the only one that makes any sense. What sparked your interest in the subject?"

Julian shrugged. "If you think about it, a lot of sightings and encounters can be explained by mind manipulation. I thought that perhaps immortals were responsible for them. I knew it wasn't anyone from the clan, and it didn't make sense for the Doomers to be doing it. Alien theories are not beneficial to their agenda. Except, maybe for the religious apparitions. So if it wasn't us and it wasn't them, then maybe the sightings could lead to other immortals? We were always searching for more survivors. I hoped this could lead us to them or at least give us a clue where to look."

"A logical assumption. What did you find out?"

Julian sighed. "Not much. Unfortunately, I didn't have the resources to launch a full-blown investigation. Kian is too much of a realist to fund something he believes is man-made nonsense. I started reading everything I could about it and found Vallée's theory the most fascinating."

"I agree. And you're right about suspecting immortals. If sightings and encounters are indeed the product of mind manipulation, then your kind is the prime suspect."

CHAPTER 10: BRIDGET

*J*ulian, with his charming, easy-going personality, managed to defrost even Turner. By the time dinner was over, the two had discussed everything from extraterrestrials through to the multiverse and string theory.

"Julian is very bright," Turner said as they retired to their bedroom.

Bridget kicked off her shoes and sat on the bed to pull off her pants. "Coming from you that's a big compliment."

He rubbed his hand over the back of his head. "I enjoyed myself."

"You sound surprised."

"I am. I wish I had as much to talk about with Douglas. It would have made our relationship much easier."

"What is he like?"

"The all-American boy next door. He is a good man, but all he wants to talk about is sports and who won which game. We bore each other. After an hour together we can't wait for it to be over."

No wonder Turner saw his son only twice a year. "Maybe you should make an effort to learn a thing or two about what interests him."

He rubbed his scalp again. "I should, shouldn't I?"

Not wanting to distract him, Bridget waited to pull off her shirt. "It should take you no time at all to learn everything there is to know about sports."

"True. But I'll be faking interest. I don't like doing it in my personal life. I do enough pretending in my work."

She walked up to him and wrapped her arms around his neck. "This is for a good cause. Take your son to a game. Buy tickets to some sports event that is sold out. Who knows, maybe you can find something you both enjoy. Maybe he would like to go to an MMA fight. Or maybe both of you will find wrestling entertaining."

Turner grimaced. "Wrestling is fake. It's all about the entertainment."

"That might be true, but think about the upside. While watching whatever sports event, you guys don't have to talk."

He pulled her close and kissed her lips. "Where have you been all of my life? I could have used this advice years ago. Douglas and I might have been best of pals."

Was he mocking her? Often, it was hard to tell.

"Right. Let's not get carried away. But perhaps you could start afresh and see each other more than twice a year."

"I'll take it under advisement, madam councilwoman." He cupped her butt cheeks and squeezed. "The best ass to ever occupy a council chair."

"Shh, Julian is in the next room, and you know how good our hearing is," she whispered.

By the hard press of his lips, Turner didn't like it one bit. "Can we go to a hotel?"

"Don't be silly. We can be quiet."

"I don't want to. Hell, I don't want you to be quiet. I love those feral noises you make."

She arched a brow. "Feral?"

"You growl like a tigress." He waggled his brows. "It's sexy as hell."

She didn't know that. Did her moans sound like growls?

It was embarrassing. Bridget thought of herself as a lady, and ladies didn't growl or hiss or make any kind of animal noises.

"I'll have to cover my face with a pillow," she whispered.

"Over my dead body. Let's go to my apartment. I don't care if it's messed up. We can take the plastic cover off the bed."

Bridget laughed. "Evidently you haven't checked on Ingrid's progress. She had all the wall-to-wall carpeting removed in the bedrooms, and the marble flooring in the main areas is gone too. Except for the bathrooms, she is replacing everything with hardwood. Not that the bathrooms remained untouched. They are getting new stone and tile. Soft earth tones are going to replace the gleaming white."

He winced. "I had no idea she would go so far. I don't like mess, and I don't really care about the decor, so I preferred not to look. Besides, how did she manage to do it so quickly?"

"That's how she does things. Don't forget that she works for Kian. He wants everything done yesterday."

Victor looked worried, so Bridget continued with Ingrid's update. "She says not to worry about the cost. When she is done, your apartment will sell at a premium price, and she says it will more than cover the cost of everything she is planning to do."

"I'm not worried about the cost."

"So what was that look for?"

"I'm still trying to figure out where we can have sex without worrying about being overheard."

Talk about a one-track mind.

A moment later, Bridget's phone pinged with a new text.

"I hope no one needs me at the clinic," she said as she took it off the charger.

The message was from Julian. *Going clubbing with Ed and Charlie. Will be back late.*

Turning the phone so Victor could see the text, Bridget

46

let him read it. "Coincidence? I think not. He must've over-heard us."

Victor took the phone out of her hands and put it back on the charging dock, then pulled her into his chest. "Whether he did or not, I'm going to exploit this opportunity to its fullest. Who knows when we will have privacy again?"

She put her hands on his shoulders. "What do you have in mind?"

Victor pushed into her, letting her feel how hard he was. "Lots of noise."

She arched a brow. "Yours or mine?"

"Yours." He turned her around and pushed her face-first into the wall, his body enveloping hers from behind. "I want to hear you scream my name as you come," he whispered in her ear.

Bridget glanced at him over her shoulder. "Are you going to frisk me?"

His hand in her hair, he tilted her head to the side and kissed the spot where her neck met her shoulder, his other arm going around and cupping a breast. "I'm going to do much more than frisk you. Put your hands up on the wall."

The tone of command in his voice went straight to her core. It tingled with need, already moistening in preparation for what was coming.

"Higher, above your head where I can see them." He waited for her to obey. "Now take half a step back and spread your legs about two feet apart."

Those were very precise instructions. She wondered what he had in mind.

"Push your fabulous ass out." He kissed her throat before moving back a few inches.

She did, grinding against him.

He sucked in a breath. "Behave." A hard slap landed on her ass.

Bridget opened her mouth to protest, but all that came out was another moan.

His body enveloped hers again, and he leaned to whisper in her ear, his hot breath fanning over the side of her face. "You like this, don't you." He nipped her ear.

"Oh. Fates, I do."

"And I like that you're honest with me." Victor rewarded her with a flurry of kisses down the column of her neck, then dropped down to his knees and unceremoniously tugged her pants down.

"Lift up," he instructed, holding her foot, freeing one leg and then the other, leaving her nude from the waist down.

There was something both vulnerable and erotic in the position, and as his warm palms coasted upward to her inner thighs, Bridget felt herself grow wetter by the second.

But Turner was in no hurry, going slow, deliberately prolonging her anticipation. When he gripped her buttocks, his fingers digging into her flesh almost painfully, she groaned, clenching her sheath in a desperate attempt to relieve the tingling itch to be filled.

When Bridget finally felt his velvety lips on her, kissing softly, reverently, she was rendered undone, and as his hot tongue speared into her, she would've collapsed if not for his hands propping her up.

"Fates, Victor, I'm about to come."

His tongue retreated. "Not yet, I want you to climax when I'm inside you."

Damn, if he didn't want her to come, he shouldn't have said that. Bridget took a deep breath and tried to hold off the impending orgasm by going through the parts of the lymphatic system in her head. But it was no use.

As his fingers replaced his tongue, the orgasm blasted out of her on a scream. She hadn't waited as he'd wanted her to, but she'd given him what he'd asked for—shouting his name as she came.

The sound of Victor's pants coming down was like a promise of a wish coming true, and as he entered her in a single hard thrust, she came again. And that was even before he started pumping into her like a man possessed.

Bracing her hands against the wall, she took the pummeling, backing into him and giving as good as she got. Victor didn't last long, his climax rising fast and pulling another one out of her.

"That was a hell of a lot of noise," he groaned as he collapsed against her back.

Bridget smiled. "Happy to oblige."

CHAPTER 11: KIAN

*A*s Bridget finished her presentation to the assembled committee, Eva clapped, soon to be followed by everyone else in the room.

It was powerful, touching without being melodramatic, depressing, but also optimistic. She'd managed the perfect balance between playing on people's conscience while at the same time offering them a roadmap to a better future.

Would it be enough to lure back the retired Guardians, though? Kian wasn't sure.

"Very well done, Bridget," he said. "But I'm not as confident as you are about the Guardians' response. There is a big difference between abandoning their comfortable lives and everything they worked for to defend their own, and doing so for strangers. For thousands of years we've refrained from intervening directly in human affairs, and for a good reason. Unless they learn to solve their problems for themselves, our help will only be a temporary fix and not a solution. It is much better for us to provide the tools, the progressive ideas and the technology to enable the progress than to go in and fight their battles for them. Even if all the Guardians come back, it is still an insignificant force for such a large scale operation."

Bridget nodded. "I know you're playing devil's advocate, and I can't refute your logic because it's solid, but I believe our work will put the big wheels in motion, and eventually the governments will step in."

"You're an optimist," Eva said. "Show me one politician who is willing to risk contamination by association. No one wants to touch the subject."

Bridget collected her papers into a neat pile. "That's because they don't see a possible solution. Politicians will not undertake what they believe is a lost cause. They need easy wins to get elected and reelected."

"True," Turner said. "And I agree with Bridget that this might push the boulder just enough for it to start rolling."

"The Guardians will come." Bridget leveled her eyes at Kian. "There is a reason these men chose to become Guardians in the first place. It's not an easy job, and although the pay is good, it's not enough of a motivator for dedicating decades to training and risking their lives in defense of others. It's a passion, a calling, and if there were battles for them to fight, they would've still served. No one wants to be idle and feel useless, especially highly trained people whose hard-earned skills are not getting put to good use. It's almost humiliating. No wonder most of them retired."

Bridget rose to her feet and started pacing. "Give these men a purpose, a worthwhile cause, and they will come eagerly. You'll have the large force you want, and the Guardians will have their pride back—the satisfaction of being needed and necessary as they were in days past."

Kian glanced at Anandur who'd been uncharacteristically silent throughout Bridget's presentation and after. "What do you think, Anandur?"

The big guy shrugged. "I'm still here, ain't I? I didn't leave to go searching for other things to do with my life. Being a Guardian is more than a job for me, it's who I am. Same goes for Brundar and the others who stayed. That's why I can't speak for those who left. With that, I'm with you, Kian. I'm not sure what motivates the others, and how they are going to respond to the presentation."

"I don't have a crystal ball." Bridget returned to her seat. "You know these guys better than I do, Anandur. We'll have to wait and see what happens."

Kian was thankful to Anandur for curbing some of Bridget's enthusiasm. If the results ended up not being as spectacular as she was hoping, at least she'd be mentally prepared.

"I'm going to coordinate a convenient time for the big assembly with Sari and Annani. I'm shooting for two weeks from now. Is that enough time for you to have everything ready?"

Bridget nodded. "I want to add a few visuals, and I need to rehearse, but two weeks will do."

"Let's make it three weeks to be on the safe side." Kian looked at Turner. "What about you? Are you satisfied with the presentation?"

"Bridget did a superb job."

"I didn't do it alone. You helped a lot."

Kian lifted a hand. "You can compliment each other later."

"Right." Turner smoothed his hand over the back of his shaved head. "I started mapping the targets. I know the funding hasn't been approved yet, but I wanted to get a head start. I have a partial list of over thirty brothels here in the US and several in the UK. If you like, I can add it to Bridget's presentation. I think soldiers will prefer an actual tactical plan to generalities. It will also drive the point home how widespread this is, and that it is not a problem limited to third-world countries. It took my people only a few days to come up with these. Just imagine how many more there are right here under our noses."

"Can I take a look?" Eva asked.

Turner pushed his laptop to her so she could see the map.

Kian pointed to the large screen behind his desk. "You can hook it up to that so everyone can see."

Several clicks later the map appeared on the large screen.

Anandur shook his head. "Unbelievable. Are you sure those are all brothels? I didn't know there were that many. And how do you know they are not legit? And I don't mean as legal or illegal, just no forced or coerced prostitution."

Turner leaned back in his chair and crossed his arms over his chest. "My instructions were to document all places employing underage girls. I don't give a damn if the girls volunteered for that or not. They shouldn't be there, and I want to get them out. But chances are that they are not there of their own free will."

"He is right," Eva said. "It's one form of coercion or another. There isn't enough awareness, and most are not familiar with the methods the scum use to lure girls into a trap. That's why I started writing a fiction book describing the ordeal of one girl. If it gets enough publicity, it might help girls recognize the signs before it's too late. Unfortunately, it's going slow because I don't have a lot of free time."

Brandon, who until now hadn't taken part in the conversation, perked up. "I would like to take a look at what you have written already. I can give you some pointers. Or, if it's really bad, I can get you a ghostwriter."

Glaring daggers at the media specialist, Eva huffed. "Thanks a lot for the vote of confidence."

Brandon wasn't intimidated. "I'm being practical. Why waste your time? If it's good, I'll tell you, and you'll be motivated to push forward with it, and if it's not, I'll save you a lot of time by providing an assistant."

"So now it's an assistant." Eva made air quotes around the word. "Not a ghostwriter."

"Potayto, potahto. You can get as much or as little help as you want. Don't take it personally."

"What about the charity events?" Kian stepped in before Eva hurled something at Brandon's smug puss, which in her case could be anything from a knife to a bullet between the eyes.

"I'm working on it. I've lined up several stars who are

willing to sing at the event. They will bring in the deep pockets."

Kian lifted a brow. "For free?"

"I promised to list what they would normally charge for a performance as a charitable contribution. Naturally, the sums are grossly inflated, but it will look good for them as well as for us."

CHAPTER 12: TURNER

"*A*re you coming?" Bridget asked.

Turner leaned to kiss her cheek. "I have a few things I need to discuss with Kian." Translation, it was confession time.

Catching his meaning, Bridget nodded. "I'll see you later."

Kian was in a good mood after the meeting, the spat between Eva and Brandon lightening the mood, which made it the perfect opportunity to broach the touchy subject of the clan's new secret location not being as well guarded as Kian believed it was.

"Can I have a few words with you?" Turner asked when everyone else had left.

"About?"

"Security measures." Turner walked over to the office's doors, closed them, and then walked back to sit at the conference table across from Kian, making sure he wasn't within the guy's reach.

"Which ones?"

"The clan's in general. It's not as difficult as you think it is to discover your location. I have a few security protocols I would like to suggest."

Kian frowned. "It was easy for you to find us because you

had me and Andrew followed after our meeting with you. You were in a unique position to do so."

"True. But you're trying to keep the new location secret from your own people, and they can do exactly what I have done—follow your butler as he drives people to the new place."

As he waited for the meaning to sink in, Turner braced for the explosion. Hopefully, his roundabout way of telling Kian that he knew the location of the village would soften the blow.

The moment it did, Kian's eyes blazed. "You sneaky bastard. That's what I get for letting you in? I should've never allowed you to move in with Bridget here in the keep."

Turner raised his palm. "I discovered your new location long before I moved in with Bridget. I knew it even before I came to ask for your help. You made it too easy, my friend. And that's why I'm here, risking your immortal wrath. I want to show you a better way of doing things."

As Kian let out a breath and leaned back in his chair, Turner mirrored the guy's pose. It seemed the explosion had been averted. Or so he hoped.

Kian shook his head. "I thought I was so clever. I can't believe I overlooked such a basic thing. Of course, people could follow Okidu."

He narrowed his eyes at Turner. "But he started taking visitors there only recently. You said you discovered the location a long time ago."

"Your butler also drives the delivery trucks up there. I had him followed from the keep to the warehouse, and from there to the village. Easy."

"Fuck."

"But I can offer a solution."

Kian waved a hand. "Please do."

"Your guy, the one who followed me, I assume he reported his lack of success?"

"Damn. Anandur was sure you didn't see him. He lost you

a couple of times. Did you make all those evasive maneuvers because you knew you were being followed?"

"No. This is standard operating protocol for me. I have enemies, but I don't have bodyguards. I need to be very careful."

"Understandable. Are you suggesting we employ similar procedures?"

"Basically."

Kian shook his head. "People will be coming and going to and from the village every day. I ordered special cars that will self-drive part of the way while their windows lock and become opaque. Or do you know about that as well?"

Turner nodded. "I didn't bother to check the special features, but I know about the shipment. It's a clever solution but dangerous. What if there is a malfunction or an accident and your people are trapped inside a locked car?"

Kian smoothed his hair back. "It's a remote possibility. Do you have a better idea?"

"Not if you want to keep the location secret from its own occupants."

"The Doomers are doing it. Only the pilots who shuttle people to and from the island know the location, and they are under strong compulsion not to reveal it."

"Can't you put a similar compulsion on your people?"

"No. Immortals are immune. Their pilots are human."

"And it's an island."

"Exactly."

"I guess the self-driving cars are the only solution."

"What about your car switching method?"

"First of all, don't let anyone drive straight from the keep to the village. Have your butler drive to a large mall, and not with the limousine, leave the car there and proceed to a different parking structure on foot where another car will be waiting."

"Is that how you do it? You always have another car parked in a mall?"

"Yes, but if I'm followed, I call for a pickup."

"Uber?"

Turner chuckled. "There is a lot you still need to learn about security. Uber is an application, which is very susceptible to hacking. I use transport services that don't display their function with signage and don't use an app. An old-fashioned phone call is required to schedule service."

Thankfully, Kian didn't seem offended. "I might have a better idea than switching vehicles at the mall. We have a tunnel under this building that leads to several of the other ones we own on this street. We can park the cars that are going to the village over there, scattering them between the underground parking lots of the other high rises."

Turner was impressed. "That's even better than my solution. It's less involved." He eyed Kian with new appreciation. "I guess you didn't build the tunnels for that. Those are emergency escape routes."

"You got it."

"Let me give it some thought and come up with the right protocol for using the other buildings. I want to make sure nothing is overlooked."

"Good deal. Let me know as soon as you have it ready."

CHAPTER 13: BRIDGET

"*I* saw Julian today," Amanda said as she grabbed a chair from a nearby table. "He looks good, happy."

The get together in the café had been Carol's idea—a girls' night out without actually going out.

Bridget moved her chair closer to Eva's to make space for Amanda's. "The residency was hard on him. With all the pain and suffering bombarding his senses he was barely hanging in there. Julian is a sensitive soul."

"Are you sure?" Syssi arched a brow. "He reminds me a lot of Kian, who can sometimes be quite obtuse."

Bridget huffed. "Julian only looks like Kian. Personality wise he is more like Anandur. Everything is a joke to him."

"Anandur is a sensitive soul," Carol said.

Amanda put her cappuccino cup down. "He is a romantic, that's for sure, but I don't know about the sensitive part. He is a Guardian, a warrior. He needs to be tough."

"A person can be both," Eva said. "Take me for example. I can be tough and ruthless when needed, but that doesn't make me unfeeling. The opposite is true. I'm ruthless because I internalize the suffering of others deeply and feel compelled to do something about it. I want to be the champion and the avenger for those who can't protect themselves." She sighed. "I miss those days."

Bridget wondered what Eva was talking about. As far as she knew, the woman was a detective who specialized in corporate espionage, and when there wasn't enough work in that, she collected evidence on cheating spouses.

"Aren't you still doing that?"

Eva waved a hand. "No, I gave it up when I became pregnant. Too much darkness for the baby." She rubbed her stomach, which had started to show a little.

"Why? Are you afraid one of the cheaters will attack you?"

Eva regarded her with a puzzled expression on her face, then shook her head. "Right. Yeah, I stay away from the domestic violence cases." She smiled. "The upside is that I have more time to write my novel."

"How is that going?" Amanda asked.

"Slow. Brandon suggested I hire an assistant, meaning a ghostwriter, but where is the fun in that? I want to see if I can do it."

"What is it about?" Syssi leaned closer. "Is it your story? Are you writing about an immortal female who doesn't know why she doesn't age?"

Eva shook her head. "I started the outline on that one, but then Kian decided to really sink his teeth into modern-day slavery, and I thought this was a more important project. I want to raise awareness about the problem. I don't know if my book will end up any good, or if anyone will read it. But if by some chance it takes off, maybe it will help girls and their families to be more careful and know what to look out for."

Amanda patted her shoulder. "Well, good luck with that. I hope you're done before this baby arrives."

"I hope so too."

With a smirk, Amanda trained her intense blue eyes on Bridget. "How are Julian and Turner getting along? You have a full house now."

If she was fishing for gossip, Amanda was going to be disappointed. "Actually, they get along great. You know Julian, he can charm anyone."

Amanda arched a brow. "Even a cold fish like Turner? That's an accomplishment."

The barb hurt even though it hadn't been directed at her. "You don't know the guy. Don't repeat what you've heard from others before you had a chance to talk to him."

Amanda hadn't visited Turner after his injury, which was fine since she hadn't known him prior to that, but still. She should've done it as a gesture to Bridget. They were supposed to be friends.

Unfazed, Amanda shrugged. "You're right. Some men are cold to other males but charming to women. Is he one of those?"

"No, he is not a charmer, but he is not cold either. I think Eva understands. He has a similar attitude to hers."

Eva made a face. "Maybe. He is impossible to read. Is it me, or does the guy not emit any emotional scents?"

Bridget nodded. "He's an anomaly."

"Interesting." Eva lifted her glass of orange juice. "That might be a very useful trait when spying on immortals."

The woman had a one-track mind. "That's not his job."

"Right," Amanda agreed. "What I want to know is what happens at night. It must be awkward to enjoy each other with your son in the next room."

Bridget couldn't help the grimace. "Yeah, that's the only downside to the arrangement. Other than that it's wonderful to have a full house. It's like we are a family."

Syssi chuckled. "Kian was freaking out when Annani was staying with us. We ended up using one of the timeshare apartments on the lower levels."

Amanda clapped her hands. "That's a splendid idea. Julian can move to one of those. Problem solved."

Bridget shook her head. "I can't suggest it. It will sound as if I'm not happy he is back home because I have a man living with me."

"Don't worry about a thing, darling. I have it all figured out." Amanda pushed her empty cappuccino cup away and leaned forward. "We have a situation which Julian can help us resolve." She glanced at Eva. "Sharon and Robert need a place to hook up, but Robert can't leave the keep unsupervised. And for obvious reasons, we can't have Sharon come to his place, not without breaking the rules, that is, and our Robert is a stickler for them. Not that I blame him; he is still on probation as far as Kian is concerned, but I digress. If Julian moves into one of the timeshare apartments, we can have Robert move in with him, and then he can invite Sharon to his place. The lower levels are not restricted, and Julian can act as Robert's unofficial keeper."

Satisfied with her idea, Amanda leaned back in her chair and crossed her arms over her chest. "What do you think, girls?"

Bridget was fine with most of it but not the part about her son guarding Robert. "Julian is a doctor, not a Guardian. He is no match for Robert."

Amanda waved a dismissive hand. "Robert is not going to do anything. Kian is just being paranoid."

"He can have the remote to Robert's cuff," Eva suggested. "If he tries anything, all Julian will need to do is press the button and boom! Off comes Robert's hand." With an evil smirk on her face, she spread her arms to demonstrate the explosion.

How awful. Imagining the blood and gore, Bridget's stomach lurched. The woman was even more ruthless than she'd given her credit for.

Coming from Eva, a very feminine-looking woman who also happened to be pregnant, such a suggestion was very unsettling. But then, after years as a DEA agent and then a private detective, Eva had probably developed a sort of macabre humor as a way to cope. Surgeons often joked most inappropriately, but no one in the operating room took offense. Everyone knew that they were just releasing stress.

"What about privacy?" Syssi asked.

Good point. "Sharon and Robert will have the same problem Victor and I have."

"Not the same, darling. You're his mother. Besides, Sharon won't know Julian can hear them, and I doubt Robert cares one way or the other."

Bridget sighed. "I hate having to be quiet. Takes half the fun out of it."

Across the table, Syssi's cheeks reddened, and she lifted her coffee cup to hide her embarrassment.

Naturally, Amanda hadn't missed it and pounced. "Sweet Syssi. Still can't talk about sex without blushing."

"I wasn't the one talking about it. You guys were."

"And still your ears are red."

"Stop it." Syssi grabbed her napkin and chucked it at Amanda. "It's bad enough that I suffer from this embarrassing affliction that makes me seem like a prude or a virgin. You don't have to advertise it."

Catching the flying piece of paper, Amanda crushed it between her fingers, then glanced at the women around the table. "All I can say is that appearances are misleading. Our sweet Syssi is far from a prude. In fact, she is quite adventurous."

"Amanda!"

"What? I'm just saying. You don't want people to think you're a virginal prude, so I set the record straight, and you're still complaining. I didn't know you were so hard to please."

Syssi threw her hands in the air. "You're impossible!"

CHAPTER 14: TURNER

"*A*re you sure you don't need help?" Turner eyed the heavy suitcases Julian was hefting. The things must have weighed a ton since they were filled with books. Expecting this to be his last move before the one to the village, Julian had emptied his bookcases, but instead of using boxes, he was using duffel bags and suitcases he'd collected from their neighbors.

"I got it. Only one more round and I'm done. Robert is going to help me move my desk."

Julian muscled the suitcases out the door. "Can you close it for me?"

"Sure."

"Thanks. I'll be back in a few minutes, so don't start anything yet." He winked.

Turner was still adjusting to the immortal's casual attitude toward sex. The guy was talking about his mother as if she was a roommate.

"I apologize on Julian's behalf," Bridget said.

"It's fine."

"For a moment, you looked scandalized."

She was getting better at reading his subtle facial clues. "I like Julian, and I don't want him to think he has to leave on my account."

"He does not. I told you, Amanda asked him to do it as a favor to her, and he was more than happy to say yes. I think he is relieved. A guy his age doesn't want to live with his mother. He prefers to share an apartment with another dude. After all, he's lived with other guys for the past seven years. Moving in with me probably seemed like a step backwards to him."

"I'm surprised that he doesn't mind an ex-Doomer as a roommate."

Bridget smiled. "The young find it easier to accept Robert. Dalhu as well. They didn't witness the atrocities the Doomers committed. Knowing about it is not the same as living through it."

"Did you?"

"It's not going to work, Victor. I'm not going to tell you how old I am, so stop fishing."

"I'm not fishing." He was.

It was annoying that she kept her age a secret from him. As if it would've bothered him to find out she'd lived a few centuries. It would've only made her even more fascinating. He could've asked her about events she might have witnessed, events he had a feeling were not reported correctly in the history books.

But if she kept refusing, maybe he could find someone else who was old enough to shed light on some of those events.

"Who is the oldest immortal living here in the keep?"

She arched a brow. "If you're asking whether I'm that person, the answer is that I'm not."

He pulled her into his arms. "Given how touchy you are about the subject, I'm starting to suspect that you're ancient."

She pushed on his chest, but he held on. "I just want to know who could tell me things about historical events I'm curious to find the truth about. That's all. You can keep your secrets."

She relaxed and let him hold her. "Kian is the oldest. But you'll have to ask him how old."

"Is he also shy about his age?"

"No. But it's his choice whether he wants to tell you or not."

"I'll ask him on the trip. Five hours in the air should give us plenty of time to chat about non-business related stuff."

"It's six hours to the big island. But good luck with that. Knowing Kian, he is going to take work with him. The guy never rests."

"In that case, you and I can use the time to make out in the bathroom."

Bridget laughed. "Not going to happen, buddy. You'll have to wait for a commercial flight to join the mile-high club."

"I'll have to charter a private plane just for that."

"You're serious? You would do that?"

"Why not? I want to experience as many things as possible with you." What he hadn't added was the *before I die*.

But he didn't need to. As Bridget's smile wilted, she leaned her head against his chest. "I didn't want to come on this trip, but I'm glad you convinced me to go. There is so much I want to do with you."

He rubbed small circles on her lower back. "It must be difficult for you. You're used to thinking in terms of boundless time, but for me it is finite."

She nodded. "I was so busy with the presentation that I didn't take the time to pause and ponder on life with you. Regardless of what happens, and when it happens, we need to make the most of each day. Do you have a bucket list? Because I want to check off all the items on it."

Turner chuckled. "I don't, but I'll make one." Wanting to lighten the mood that had suddenly become heavy, he added, "Just so you know, though, it's all going to be about where and how we have sex."

With a mock stern expression, she waggled a finger at him. "I don't share, so no crazy ideas about threesomes."

"Wouldn't dream of it. I don't share either. Any other limitations?"

"No."

He arched a brow. "Are you sure?"

For a moment, she looked uncomfortable. "I know that there is some crazy shit out there. I'm not naive. But you don't strike me as a sexual deviant."

He lifted her up and kissed her hard. "I'm not. I have nothing weird in mind, and I'm not all that imaginative either. Besides, we will never do anything you're not comfortable with. In fact, I'm pretty sure you'll have some ideas that are going to shock me and not the other way around."

The little smirk on her lush lips confirmed his suspicions. "I promise not to shock you."

"On the contrary, please do."

CHAPTER 15: ROBERT

*R*obert peered over the recipe he'd printed earlier, then double checked he had everything he needed. The main ingredients were already lined up in the proper order on the counter. All that remained was to measure the exact quantities of spices. As a novice cook, he shouldn't improvise but follow the instructions to the letter.

Julian walked into the kitchen and glanced at the orderly display. "You should have barbecued, dude, or ordered takeout."

Bridget's son was the best roommate possible—easygoing, equipped with a sharp mind and a good sense of humor, and not nearly as messy as Robert's previous roommates. The most Julian left lying around was a book or a magazine or one of his electronic devices. No empty pizza boxes, no dirty dishes, and no shoes in the hallway for someone to trip over.

"I want to impress Sharon. This is our first official date, and since I can't take her out to a restaurant, this is the next best thing. If I can manage a complicated building-supplies order, I can manage a simple recipe."

Julian leaned against the counter and crossed his arms

over his chest. "I can sleep at the clinic tonight. Give you guys some privacy."

That was very gracious of him to offer, but there was no way Robert could accept. "I wouldn't dream of inconveniencing you like that."

"It's not a big deal. I'm used to sleeping on hospital beds, and right now there are no patients in the clinic. I have plenty of beds to choose from."

Robert measured two teaspoons of paprika, pouring the spice onto a small plate, the second in a row of spice plates he'd prepared. "I appreciate the offer, but I can't accept." He looked up. "There is more to this arrangement than us sharing an apartment. You're supposed to keep an eye on me."

Julian uncrossed his arms and pushed his hand into his pocket. "I have this." He pulled out the remote to Robert's cuff. "The clinic is not out of range. I can watch the feed from the security camera out in the corridor to see if you're trying to leave."

"What if I want to escort Sharon to her car? As a gentleman, I should."

"Then I'll watch the feed from the guest parking lot as well."

"You forget that per Kian's instructions, which you've agreed to, you are supposed to stay here when I come back from work, and if you can't make it or need to leave, you have to arrange for someone else to take your place."

Julian rolled his eyes. "I was desperate for a place of my own, but I didn't want to hurt my mom's feelings and ask for it. I love my mom, but she needs her privacy too. When Kian asked me to move in with you as a favor, I was so glad that I would've agreed to whatever. That's why I didn't argue and point out that he was overdoing it. We can bend his rules a little, and no one will know. It's not like I'm leaving the building."

The level of insubordination the clan members were

allowed still shocked Robert. Kian was too lax of a ruler. He ran the place more like a business than a stronghold, which would've been okay if they had no enemies and their existence didn't need to remain secret. To keep the clan safe, Kian needed to rule like a military commander, and not like the chairman of a board of directors.

"You can bend the rules, but I can't. If I want Kian to trust me, I need to obey his instruction and go by the book."

Besides, Robert preferred it that way. He wasn't a rebel. He liked rules. Life was easier when everyone knew their roles and didn't take liberties. Robert's one and only rebellion had been practically forced upon him. Carol's suffering and the need to end it had overridden everything else. He'd had to save her.

It dawned on him then that perhaps he hadn't been the only one doing the saving; in a way she'd saved him too. If not for Carol, Robert would've never left the Brotherhood. He would've spent eternity as a meaningless cog in a machine that didn't give a damn about him.

The clan, regardless of the limitations imposed on him, had given him a new life. He had a job he enjoyed doing, and now he had a shot at love, maybe even an immortal mate. It was a life he would've not dared dream about while in the Brotherhood.

"I understand," Julian said. "I'll stay in my room, listening to loud music with noise-canceling headphones on." He grimaced. "Those are so uncomfortable to sleep with. But whatever."

Robert inclined his head. "I'm grateful."

"One more thing," Julian said. "This time as the clan's new physician and not your roommate."

Robert arched a brow. "Yes?"

"We need to have a talk about condoms. Do you have any?"

"No. I never use them. What for? I'm sure Sharon is on

birth control like all the other human females I've been with. The immortal females never asked for them either."

If the chances of him impregnating a human were slim, they were almost nonexistent with an immortal female. Still, it had crossed his mind that if that miracle happened, an immortal female would not acknowledge his paternity. If he ever had a child, Robert wanted to be more than a sperm donor. He wanted to be part of that child's life.

"You thralled the humans to think you used protection."

"Naturally."

"You should use them with Sharon, at least until you're ready to reveal the truth to her, which you should do only when you're sure she is the one for you and you for her. If she is a Dormant, a venom bite combined with insemination might trigger her transition. If it were me, I would want to spend a little more time with the girl and get to know her before that happened. It's a big responsibility."

It was also dishonest and a generally shitty thing to do to someone without telling her. "What happens when I feel it's time to induce her transition? Should I tell her then?"

Julian sighed. "The moment she knows, she becomes a prisoner like you. Kian might relax the rules for her because of Eva, but that's not a sure thing. That's why I'm suggesting you wait until you're positive it's the right thing to do."

"Do you have any condoms?"

Julian shook his head. "You can order a quick delivery. There are services like that. Someone buys what you need and brings it over. It's expensive, but you don't have much choice unless you can ask someone to go get them for you."

Right. He could imagine the snickering. "Do you have the number for a service like that?"

71

CHAPTER 16: SHARON

*A*s Sharon neared the address Robert had given her, the buildings turned taller, the avenues broader, and even the trees dotting the pavement were greener.

This looked to be a pricey part of downtown Los Angeles. Apparently, her theory about Robert being strapped for cash was all wrong. To afford an apartment in one of those high rises, even when sharing rent with a roommate, Robert must be getting one hell of a salary. The guy had been way too modest about his position in the company he worked for, the one Amanda's brother was the CEO of.

What was his story, then?

Why hadn't he invited her on a date until now?

And why was he preparing dinner at his place instead of taking her out?

It was sweet that the guy was cooking for her, a first for Sharon, but it didn't make much sense. Maybe he'd figured it would be easier to get her in his bed if she was already there. But then it wasn't as if she'd been playing hard to get. Sharon had given him plenty of indications that she was ready to sample the goods.

Robert was such a yummy piece of maleness, and she couldn't wait to undress him. A girl didn't need to have a vivid imagination to picture what he was hiding under his clothes.

Smooth, lean muscles stretched over a tall frame, and a set of shoulders she would love to hang on to while he pounded into her.

Damn. Sharon wiggled to alleviate the sudden itch her naughty thoughts had caused. Better to think of other things than arrive all hot and bothered. She might jump the guy and skip the meal he'd prepared for her.

Not nice.

Besides, Sharon didn't want him to think she was a slut. Except, the ship might have sailed on that. Robert had been so reserved and so shy that he'd left her no choice but to pursue him, and she'd done so, no holds barred.

"You have arrived. Your destination is on the left," the navigation system announced.

"Thank you, Mike." That was the name Sharon had given the computerized voice of her GPS.

The personification of the device was just another indicator that she was spending way too much time alone. Her job was a solo operation, and she didn't have friends other than her coworkers and the poker bunch. No wonder she was talking to the computer.

As she turned into the guest parking, a valet waved her over. Apparently, guests were not allowed to park their cars without using the service. Sharon's eyes darted around looking for the sign with the price per hour, but there was none.

Crap, that was going to cost her. Parking in downtown Los Angeles was expensive.

The valet opened her door. "Good evening, miss."

Sharon ignored his offered hand as she stepped out. "I was looking for the sign with the prices, but I must've missed it. How much is it per hour?

The valet smiled. "The service is complimentary. But tips are greatly appreciated."

"Oh." She reached for her wallet.

He lifted his palm. "Only on your way out."

"But there might be someone else here."

"Don't worry about it." He winked. "We share the tips."

"In that case, thank you, and I hope to see you later."

"Same here." He stepped aside.

As Sharon headed for the glass doors leading to the lobby, her eyes darted around looking for Robert. He'd said he would be waiting for her.

The place was enormous, probably spanning the entire width of the building, with soaring ceilings and sparse modern decor, but other than the two guys at the guard station and Robert, there was no one there.

"Hi, Sharon." He walked up to her, leaned and kissed her cheek. "Did you find the place easily?"

Poor guy. Everything from the kiss to his words seemed rehearsed. He was trying so hard.

"Mike navigated like the pro he is."

Robert tensed. "Mike?"

Crap, she shouldn't have said it. Now he would think she was weird. "My navigation system. I call it Mike."

Robert's shoulders lost some of their rigidity, but his military posture never allowed for complete relaxation. Not that she wanted him to slouch, that wasn't attractive, but it would've been nice if he could loosen up a bit. His innate tension affected her, stressing her.

Or maybe it was sexual frustration.

They'd been meeting over poker for weeks, and Sharon's level of horniness was increasing with each time that ended with no more than a couple of stolen kisses.

"I hope I didn't mess up dinner too much. It was my first attempt." He took her hand and led her to the elevators.

Gosh, that was sweet. She was the first girl he'd cooked for. She would eat it and sing its praises even if it was awful.

"What did you make?" Sharon asked as they stepped inside the lift.

"Two roasted chickens with white rice and baby carrots."

"Two? Who else is joining us for dinner?"

"No one."

"What about your roommate?"

"Not trusting my cooking, he grabbed a sandwich from the vending machine." They exited into a corridor that was lined with a thick carpet.

"I'm sure it's his loss. I can't see you failing at anything. You're too methodical and detail-oriented to mess up a simple chicken recipe."

Robert pushed open the door to his apartment, holding it open for her. "I appreciate your confidence in my abilities. I hope you won't be disappointed."

Sharon walked in and stopped at the entry. "Oh, wow, this is one fancy place." The apartment was spacious and incredibly well-decorated with stuff that was elegant and looked pricey. This was an interior designer's work, not the collection of crap most young guys furnished their apartments with.

"It is." Robert didn't elaborate.

"Did you hire an interior decorator?"

For some reason, he winced. "No, it came like this."

"Must be expensive."

"It's part of my compensation package."

That explained how Robert could afford to live in such luxury even if he wasn't making good money. "You have a very generous boss."

"I know."

"It smells fantastic in here. I can't wait to eat your chicken." Hopefully, that didn't sound like an innuendo.

"Yes, we should dine before it gets cold." He walked over to the dining table, which was already set for two, and pulled out a chair for her. "My lady?"

"Ooh, I like it. My lady. I feel important." She sat down and let him push her chair in.

"You are important to me."

What a nice thing to say, and coming from Robert it didn't sound like a line. Sharon could melt into a puddle of goo.

"Well, hello, Sharon," a man, most likely Robert's roommate, said in a pleasant baritone.

She turned around and barely kept her mouth from gaping. This guy was a doctor? That drop-dead gorgeous panty-melter was also smart?

Some guys got all the luck.

"Julian, I presume?" She started to push away from the table.

He put a hand on her shoulder. "Don't get up."

Sharon craned her neck to look at him. He was even taller than Robert. "Then you have to sit because I can't keep looking up at you without straining my neck."

Julian's smile was blinding. "Of course, how rude of me." He pulled out a chair and sat on it sideways, facing her. "Let's do it properly this time." He offered her his hand. "I'm Julian, and it's my pleasure to meet you."

She shook what he offered. "I'm Sharon, and the pleasure is all mine."

Behind her, she thought she heard Robert growl. It had probably been his stomach because Julian ignored it.

"Robert tells me you're a detective. Must be exciting."

"I'm the fact checker and information collector. My boss is the detective. And yes, sometimes my job is exciting, but only to someone like me who likes to dig for hidden stuff. Nick, my coworker, thinks what I do is boring. He deals with all the surveillance equipment and hacks into encrypted systems when needed."

Julian shook his head. "Both jobs sound fascinating to me. I often feel like a mechanic who instead of machines fixes people. Or at least I try to. There is a reason it's called practicing medicine and not curing."

Robert cleared his throat. "Speaking of medicine, don't you have a load of articles you need to catch up on?"

"Yes, I do. Thanks for reminding me." He pushed to his feet. "It was nice meeting you, Sharon. I'll probably fall asleep with my headphones on and will not see you before you leave." He bowed his head. "I bid you goodnight."

"Goodnight, Julian."

Robert waited until his roommate's door closed. "He is handsome, isn't he?"

Her guy was jealous. How sweet.

Sharon pushed away from the table, sauntered over to Robert, and wrapped her arms around his neck. "He is very pretty. But he is not my type. You are."

Robert arched a brow. "A young, good-looking doctor is every woman's type."

"Not this one. I like my man to be a little rougher around the edges, and I don't want to fight the entire female population over him. I want him all to myself."

Robert's other brow went up. "I'm not sure if I should feel offended or flattered. Are you implying that other women don't find me attractive?"

God, men were just as bad as women at accepting compliments. "You are right that Julian is the type of guy every girl and her mother chases. Which probably gives him an ego the size of a zeppelin and an attitude of entitlement. I don't find those attributes attractive."

"Julian suffers from neither. He is a very nice guy."

"I'm still not interested."

"Good. That's all I wanted to hear. Let's eat."

CHAPTER 17: ROBERT

Sharon pushed away her plate, picked up her napkin, and dabbed at her lips. "It was excellent, but I'm full."

Robert eyed her with a frown. Her scent indicated truth, but she'd hardly eaten anything. "You must have a tiny appetite."

"I'm saving it for dessert." She waggled her brows.

Damn, he hadn't thought of buying anything sweet. The best he could offer was popcorn, one of those ready packs that went into the microwave. "I'm afraid there isn't any."

She gave him a lusty once-over. "I beg to differ."

As her meaning finally sank home, Robert's shaft swelled even more. It had been hard since the moment Sharon had arrived, but until now he'd managed to keep it together. That little lustful remark had done him in, causing his venom glands to activate and his fangs to elongate.

Robert was running out of time. The only way to hide the change from Sharon was to get her to his dark bedroom as quickly as possible.

He was on her in a heartbeat.

She squeaked as he lifted her into his arms, holding on to

his neck as he strode with her down the hallway. "Ooh, I like it. Letting your inner caveman out is hot."

"You have no idea." He chuckled.

Her tone had been happy, her remark full of excited anticipation. Sharon was assertive and knew what she wanted, and yet she was nothing like the clan females who hounded him for hookups. Maybe the difference was that she wasn't jaded. Sharon was full of joy, and having a new lover was still exciting to her. She was also interested in a relationship with him and not just sex.

"It's dark in here," she said as he put her down on his bed.

"I prefer it like that. Close your eyes."

She did as he asked, but a small smirk lifted her lips. "Are you shy?"

"No. But I find that once one of the senses is deprived, the other ones sharpen. The pleasure intensifies."

Sharon stretched her arms over her head. "Then both of us should close our eyes and only use our hands to see."

He traced the curve of her hip with his hand, eliciting a shiver. "I want to pleasure you first. You don't need to do anything, just feel."

Her heartbeat accelerated. "I can't say no to that." Her words came out in a hoarse whisper.

The girl was beyond turned on. It was a good thing human females could orgasm many times in a row because she was going to lift off with the first swipe of his tongue and there was much more he wanted to do to her.

Sitting on the bed, Robert lifted her foot and removed her high-heeled sandal, kissed each toe, and then repeated with the other one, all along careful not to tickle.

Laughter was good, but not conducive to arousal.

Her short dress was stretchy, and he pushed the bottom up until it bunched around her middle, then hooked his fingers in her panties and gently slid them down her long legs.

The scent of her arousal, which had been straining his

restraint throughout dinner, intensified. It took all of his willpower not to dive between her legs and lap up his bounty. Instead, he smoothed his palms over her inner thighs, spreading her wider.

For a split moment, she resisted, but then sighed and submitted to his gentle insistence.

Dimly, Robert was aware that he was doing things differently with Sharon. The sequence was all wrong. He hadn't kissed her, he hadn't palmed her breasts, and he hadn't waited for her to hint or tell him what she wanted him to do next.

For the first time that he could remember, Robert was acting on instinct, somehow knowing what she needed without her having to clue him in. He hadn't known he had any instinctual knowledge of that kind. Apparently, it had lain dormant until now.

Or was he inadvertently probing her mind?

Not that it was likely. He had a hard time getting into human minds deliberately, let alone accidentally.

But maybe the explanation was much less mystical than that, and he was putting a spin on what was a practical decision. With his elongated fangs and glowing eyes, it was safer for him between Sharon's legs. Otherwise, he would have to thrall her, and he didn't want to. Not yet. Unlike with his other human partners, he wanted to save it for after the bite.

As his palms clamped over Sharon's trembling thighs, he swiped his tongue over her nether lips.

"Oh, my God!" Sharon exclaimed as soon as his tongue made contact with her wet center.

To give her a few moments of build up before the inevitable explosion, he avoided the seat of her pleasure, going in gentle circles around it and then spearing into her opening to scoop up her juices.

Her gyrations frantic, her moans keening, Sharon was teetering on the precipice. When her fingers caught his short hair, pulling hard, he knew she couldn't take it much longer.

"Please, Robert, I need to come."

So did he. Her climax was going to trigger his, there was no doubt about that, but Robert refused to erupt in his pants. He wanted to be buried deep inside this succulent woman when he did.

The problem was that to stop now, even for the couple of seconds it would take to sheath himself in a condom, was out of the question. Maybe he could ignore Julian's advice?

Just this once?

No. Julian was right. It would be wrong to induce Sharon's transition without letting her know what was going on. It was different when he hadn't known there was an alternative, but now he couldn't use ignorance as an excuse.

Mind over body. He could do that.

Spearing two fingers inside her, he closed his lips on the most sensitive part of Sharon's body and sucked in gently. The eruption that followed was like a mini earthquake, the epicenter of which was right there between his lips. Sucking and pumping with his fingers, he prolonged it until Sharon pushed on his head to stop him.

"No more. I can't."

He lifted his head and kissed the top of her mound. The feeling of gratitude and satisfaction swelling inside him was mostly about the pleasure he'd given Sharon. But a small part was about the strength of his restraint. It had taken a Herculean effort, but he somehow made it without coming in his pants.

Sharon caressed his head, then cupped his cheeks. "I knew you'd be good, but I didn't expect this. You blew my mind."

CHAPTER 18: SHARON

Hello, Robert.
Wow. Talk about blown preconceptions.

Sharon thought herself an excellent judge of character. In fact, she was never wrong in her initial assessment of people. But she'd been wrong about Robert.

Either that or lust had overridden his reserved and careful attitude, making him into one hell of a lover.

First times were never like that.

Heck, she'd been with plenty of men and had experienced everything from those who were awkward and timid and needed her to tell them exactly what to do, to those who thought that they were all that but had ultimately come up short.

Neither was satisfying.

Accepting that the perfect lover didn't exist, she'd convinced herself that this was as good as it was going to get.

Wrong!

Robert's approach was perfectly balanced—hot male dominance that was still considerate and didn't take anything for granted.

It was as if he was reading her mind.

He'd asserted his will, which was totally unexpected, but hadn't forced it. By going slow, he'd given her the option to refuse or redirect. Sharon didn't doubt for a moment that he would have obeyed her wishes without hesitation and without the disgruntled attitude guys usually threw at her when she didn't want to do things their way.

Robert was the best... and he was tearing the third condom wrapper. The sounds she'd been hearing finally pierced through her hazy, dreamy state.

He'd either gotten a defective batch or was having trouble putting the condom on. Sometimes when a guy was too eager, he became clumsy, and the thing tore.

Feeling for him with her hand, she found Robert sitting on the bed with his back to her. "Do you need help with that?"

It was too dark for her to see, but she felt his back muscles contract as he turned her way. "They keep tearing."

"Let me do it." She lifted up to her knees and hugged him from behind. "May I?" She put her palm out, at the same time finding his hard shaft and giving it a little up and down caress.

It was a shame the room was so dark that she couldn't see anything. Given how the smooth, hot flesh pulsing in her hand felt, it must look magnificent. Maybe next time. It seemed Robert was still a little shy despite his display of assertiveness.

He tore another wrapper and put the condom in her palm. As she rolled it on him, it was obvious that there was nothing wrong with the condom. Robert must be nervous.

Or could it be that he was out of practice? He sure knew what to do as far as pleasuring her, though.

"It looked so easy when you did it." He sounded embarrassed.

She kissed his shoulder. "I already had my orgasm, so I wasn't as impatient."

He turned around and threaded his fingers through her long hair, cupping the back of her skull before smashing his lips over hers.

Yeah, definitely impatient.

A moment later, her dress that was still bunched up around her middle got pulled over her head and tossed away, her bra joining it a second later. Evidently, lust impaired Robert's dexterity only when dealing with rubbers, it didn't affect it as far as getting rid of clothing went.

With one gentle push, he lowered her onto her back and got on top of her. It felt so good, having his big male body blanketing hers. He wasn't too heavy, only substantial, and every part of him that touched her was muscled and smooth. The only hair she'd felt on his torso was a light smattering between his pectorals and a delish goodie trail.

Cupping both her cheeks in his large hands, he kissed her, gently at first, just a little nibbling on her lips, but soon his talented tongue was making love to her mouth the same way she wanted the hard length wedged between her thighs to do below.

Why was he waiting?

Wasn't he desperate to be inside her?

Because she sure was. She'd been waiting for this moment for so long the anticipation was already too much.

He was so much taller than her that she had to stretch her arms to reach his ass. As soon as she got a good grip, she sank her fingernails into the solid flesh and arched up, rubbing her needy center against his hardness.

Robert groaned, lifting just enough to reach between them and guide himself inside her.

Bracing, Sharon closed her eyes, but the hard thrust she'd anticipated didn't come. Robert inched into her as slowly and as carefully as if she was a virgin.

Should she tell him she'd given away her virginity years ago and had never looked back?

The snarky side of her wanted to do just that, but she bit

her tongue. Not only would it have been offensive, but the truth was that she was starting to feel a slight burn as he stretched her.

Apparently, after several weeks without sex, she was back to an almost virginal state. Or maybe Robert was thicker than what she was used to.

He was certainly longer.

As he reached the end of her channel, she had to lift her legs and spread them wider for him to fit all of that inside her. And she wasn't a small woman.

As he kissed her again, the drop of sweat that landed on her forehead revealed how hard he was straining to hold back.

But why?

She was drenched and more than ready for him. "What are you waiting for?" The question left her mouth before she could put a lid on it.

"Patience, my sweet. I don't want to hurt you."

"You won't."

"Patience," he repeated, pulling out a few inches and pushing back.

"That's good." At least he was moving.

He thrust again, harder this time, then pulled all the way out and surged back in.

"Oh, yeah, that's it, baby." She clasped those broad shoulders of his, ready to hold on tight as he pounded into her.

Her words acted as scissors, snapping the line that had tethered Robert's natural instincts to his formidable will, and he went all out.

She wanted a pounding, and she was getting one hell of one. Clutching Robert's shoulders, Sharon tried to meet his hard thrusts with her own, but pretty soon it became obvious that all she could do was hang on for dear life and take the pounding because she was no match for his size and his strength.

Getting taken like that was hotter than hot. But only by

Robert. On some subconscious level, she knew that he was the only man she would ever trust to possess her like that— the only one she would enjoy letting go with and not feel threatened by the potential destructive power of her own lust.

CHAPTER 19: ROBERT

*H*e bit her when she came again.

Robert had wanted to save it for another round, but the impulse had been too strong.

Sharon cried out, fighting his hold on her, but a moment later, as the euphoria hit, all the fight left her. His own climax went on and on, spilling his essence into the condom until he was sure it overflowed the rubber's capacity.

Orgasming again, Sharon milked the last drops out of him and then passed out with a blissful expression on her face.

For a few moments, he stared at her peaceful face, admiring her flushed cheeks, the long lashes fanning over them, and the lips that were still swollen and red from their kisses. She was so beautiful.

With a sigh, Robert retracted carefully, remembering at the last moment to hold on to the condom as he did. Tying it off, he padded to the bathroom where he dumped it into the trashcan. Collecting several washcloths, he wet them with warm water before going back to the bedroom.

Sharon was still passed out, not moving a muscle when he cleaned her and then covered her with the blanket. When he returned from the bathroom after tossing the washcloths in the laundry bin, she was still sleeping.

As he examined her neck, he was glad to see that the bite marks were gone already. She should be waking soon. In the meantime, he could watch her for a little longer, memorizing every little freckle on her beautiful face. He didn't want to forget anything about this. About her.

Tomorrow, or the next day, or the day after that, she might decide he wasn't the one for her and leave. But at least he'd have her features memorized for eternity.

There was a concentration of freckles on the bridge of her nose, shaped like a crescent moon, and a few others dotted the creamy-smooth skin of her flushed cheeks. Her lips were parted a little, revealing a hint of white teeth.

Robert freed a long strand of hair from under her arm and wound it around his finger. It was thick and yet soft to the touch, the deep brown interwoven with a more reddish color—chestnut he believed it was called.

Her beauty wasn't stunning like Amanda's, or tempting and alluring in its fake cherubic innocence like Carol's, but he could stare at her face forever.

Was she going to stay asleep until morning?

He hoped she would. Maybe she would think she'd dreamt the bite and he wouldn't have to thrall her. Spending the night with her in his arms would be the perfect ending to their perfect date.

Gently lifting the blanket, Robert joined Sharon under the covers, pulled her into his arms, and repositioned her head, so it rested on his pectoral.

Perfect.

Sleeping was not on the agenda for him. He planned on staying awake, watching his beauty, and savoring every moment she let him hold her close.

She shifted, making herself more comfortable by dropping an arm around his middle and a leg over his.

Several long minutes passed before her eyelids fluttered open.

"Hi," he said. It was lame, but he didn't know what else to say.

"Back to you." The hand on his torso started moving in slow circles.

"Are you okay?" Another lame thing to say, but he needed to find out if she remembered the bite and if he needed to thrall her.

"I'm awesome." Her other hand reached for the spot where his fangs had pierced her neck, two fingers checking the skin. When she found nothing, Sharon shrugged. "Weird-ass dream."

Robert closed his eyes and let out a breath.

"I want to ask you something," she said.

He tensed. She was going to ask if he'd bitten her. "Yes?"

"Would you marry me?"

The girl was still high on endorphins. "Ask me when you're sober. You're not thinking straight."

"I'm not drunk. I hardly had anything to drink at dinner." She looked up at him with her big hazel eyes. "I wanted to be sober for this, and I'm glad I was. You're the best lover I ever had."

"You're high on endorphins. Orgasms have that effect."

She chuckled. "That's why I want to marry you, silly. I want orgasms like that every night for the rest of my life. And sleeping in your arms is a nice bonus." She wiggled closer and put her head on his chest. "You smell so good."

He was still trying to come up with something to say when the hand on his middle went limp, and her breaths became deep and even.

It was a shame Sharon would remember none of that in the morning, and if she did, she would think she'd dreamt it. Nevertheless, he would cherish the memory of her proposal forever. It was the closest he'd get to being loved.

CHAPTER 20: BRIDGET

"*W*ho is flying the plane?" Bridget asked as soon as she and Turner boarded the clan's private jet.

"I think it's Charlie," Syssi said.

"Ugh, I hoped it was Morris."

"Charles is a fine pilot." Kian dismissed Bridget's concerns. "We are not going on a military mission. Charles is good enough to fly us for a family vacation."

Bridget crossed her arms over her chest. "I don't care what you say, I still prefer Morris. Charlie thinks he is still a teenager. Would you want a teenager to drive your limousine? I think not."

Anandur tapped her shoulder. "The young are better trained. I prefer a teenager who spends most of his days playing video games to fly the plane to some old timer who reads books about aerial battles."

Bridget rolled her eyes. "That's nonsense. It might be true for humans, but not for immortals. We don't lose our reflexes over time because our bodies don't age."

"I was thinking of taking a ballet class," Callie said from behind her. "Before my transition, I thought I was too old to start, but if what you're saying is true, I can take it up at any age."

"Go for it, girl." Bridget high-fived her.

"I will. I'm so excited about Hawaii. It's my first time going."

Syssi looked apologetic. "It's a shame Brundar is going to be on guard duty, but you can hang out with us. Knowing Kian, he'll be working most of the time anyway. You and I are going to have fun on our own."

"I'm just glad to tag along. Brundar and I will go on a vacation together when he can take some time off."

Bridget didn't remember Brundar ever missing more than a day or two of work, but that was before Callie. He wasn't exactly a changed man, but his life was about more than work now.

Anandur slapped his brother's back. "My bro is taking his lady on a romantic getaway."

Brundar grunted and flicked Anandur's hand away.

Callie laughed. "It's not like we made actual plans. Brundar is too busy right now."

"Not more than usual," Kian said.

Charlie poked his head into the cabin. "Buckle up, people, we are taking off."

"I'll probably fall asleep as soon as we are in the air," Bridget said.

Turner looked away from the window. "Do you want to lie down? I can move next to Anandur."

She shook her head. "No way. This is our first vacation together, and we are going to act like a couple."

He wrapped his arm around her shoulders and tugged her closer. "It's not exactly a vacation."

"Questioning the Russians shouldn't take too long. We have most of the weekend to ourselves. Is there anything you want to do? Other than sightseeing that is?"

"Just sightseeing. Parasailing is anticlimactic compared to

parachuting, and riding an ATV behind a tour guide is not my definition of fun either."

"Do you like swimming?"

"I do."

"Then let's plan on hitting the beach. Sunbathing and swimming sounds heavenly to me."

"Add to that a waiter serving margaritas and you have my definition of a dream vacation," Syssi said, reminding them that their conversation wasn't private.

As soon as the plane gathered speed, Bridget felt her eyelids droop. She'd stayed up late last night working on her presentation. So much was riding on it that it needed to be perfect. The problem was that no matter how many times she'd revised it, she wasn't completely satisfied with the results.

The speech needed to be effective, which meant a careful balance. The material needed to tug at the heartstrings but not be so overly dark or dramatic that it would turn people off.

Immortals, just as humans, tended to shut off when things got too hard for them to process. Except, that might be true for the females, but not for the males, especially the Guardians.

The hardened warriors probably needed something more jarring than the rest of the participants of the big assembly. But she couldn't gear her entire presentation just to them. After all, the clan's approval of the project was even more important than getting the retired Guardians to come back.

She needed to test it.

Maybe she should have Turner, Anandur and Brundar listen to her revised version, and then have Syssi and Callie do so separately. It was a crappy testing method. They might be inclined to say things for her benefit, or their familiarity with the project could influence their reactions. But a double-blind study, the kind they used to test the effects of new drugs, was not possible.

No wonder she was driving herself crazy. Perhaps Kian had been right. Maybe she wasn't ready to shoulder that much responsibility. And it didn't matter that she wasn't shouldering it alone, or that Turner and Kian's input had shaped the presentation as much as hers had. Bridget would be the one to stand in front of the entire clan, trying to convince them to shift resources from pushing progress forward to a humanitarian effort.

There was a nagging suspicion in the back of her mind that she was forgetting a crucial component. But what was it?

Bridget had spent every available moment examining all the possible angles and deciding which would work best. What else was there?

The answer came to her out of the blue, just landing in her head as if someone had dropped it there.

Annani.

If she could get the goddess's support, the rest of the clan would fall in line. Why hadn't Kian thought of that? It seemed like such a natural thing to do. Once the plan had been hatched, it should have been the first item on their agenda.

Annani was the one who'd drawn the original roadmap for the clan, she should have been the first one to be consulted about altering its course.

"Kian, did you tell Annani what the assembly was about?"

He lifted his head from his laptop. "I told her we need a vote on a new project."

"And she didn't ask what it was?"

"Of course, she did. But I thought it was best if she heard it from you. My delivery leaves a lot to be desired."

Bridget shook her head. "We should have a meeting with her prior to the assembly. If we can get her support on this, the clan will follow her lead."

"You're right. I should have realized that. I'll arrange a conference call."

"Not good enough. I think we should go talk to her face to face."

Kian grimaced. "Are you sure that's necessary? Conference calls are so much more efficient. It seems like an incredible waste of time to spend a ten-hour round trip just so we can talk to her for an hour."

Syssi put her hand on his thigh. "She will be overjoyed by a visit. It will put her in a much more cooperative mood. Besides, I want to see that paradise you guys have created over there."

Sitting straight, Turner perked up. "Can I come?"

"No," everyone except Brundar and Callie said at once.

"I'm sorry." Bridget cast him an apologetic look. "No humans allowed."

"I figured that much, but it was worth a try. I can't wait to meet her."

"Hopefully, one day you will."

Talk about a mood spoiler.

The idea of getting Annani's support had filled Bridget with excitement and renewed hope for the success of her presentation. But Turner's comment had reminded her of how uncertain their future was.

CHAPTER 21: TURNER

"*I*'ll see you later." Bridget kissed Turner's cheek. "Are you sure you don't want to come?"

"I'm sure. They don't need another spectator in the room. Between you, Kian, Anandur, and Brundar, that's already too many people. The Russians pose no threat. They are human females, how dangerous can they be? I would advise against bringing Anandur and Brundar along, but I know Kian won't do it."

Turner had to agree. Less was more, especially since they were not going to employ any intimidating tactics. To coax as much information as they could from the women, it would have been better if Bridget joined them instead of the bodyguards. Women trusted other women more than they trusted men. Or in the Russians' case, distrusted them a little less.

"I think you should come instead of the bodyguards. The women will feel more comfortable with you there."

Bridget shook her head. "I'm not good at this. Vanessa would have been perfect, but no one thought to include her."

"She is the therapist, right?"

"Yes."

"I have not met these women, but I know a thing or two about Russians, and a shrink would have raised their hackles."

"You have a point. Anyway, good luck."

He kissed her cheek. "I'd better go. They are waiting for me outside."

"I'll be lounging by the pool."

"Have fun."

Kian and Syssi had invited everyone to stay in their vacation home, but Bridget preferred the hotel, and Turner was glad of it. Kian and his bodyguards were good company for about an hour or so, but he had no wish to spend entire days with them.

As Turner exited the lobby, it took him only a split second to locate Kian's rental even though he hadn't seen it yet. Anandur's unmistakable red bushy hair was visible through the window of an SUV idling a little further down the curb.

"Where is Kian?" he asked as he got into the back seat.

"Buying swim trunks. He claims that he forgot to pack them, but I think he did it on purpose. So does Syssi. That's why he is in the store right now. "

"Why? Is he sensitive to sunlight?"

Anandur turned around and pinned him with an incredulous look. "Are you kidding me? Didn't you see the sunglasses he whipped out the moment we landed?"

"So did you and Brundar and everyone else. The glare here is strong."

"Yeah, but Kian's are not normal sunglasses. He is extremely sensitive. Ten minutes in the sun and he looks like a boiled lobster."

"So why is his wife insisting on him getting out?"

Anandur shrugged. "She said she is going to slather him in the strongest sunscreen protection available. If she doesn't force him out, he is going to spend the entire vacation working."

Turner had no doubt. The guy needed help, as in trust-worthy people he could delegate work to. Except, he knew exactly how difficult it was to find such people, and Kian's pool of prospective candidates was much more limited than his. No one had told him how many immortals belonged to the clan, but Kian had mentioned that the clan wasn't big.

Were there a few hundred? Several thousand?

Turner had a feeling the clan numbered in the mid hundreds. If he were allowed to attend the big assembly, he could figure it out simply by physically observing those gathered locally and those abroad on the screens. According to Bridget, every adult clan member had to vote.

"Okay," Kian said as he pulled the passenger door open and climbed inside. "Mission accomplished."

Holding a large shopping bag, Brundar joined Turner in the back seat.

Judging by the rattle coming from the bag, there was more than swimming shorts inside.

"What's in there?" he asked.

Brundar put the bag on the seat between them. "Vodka."

"Good thinking."

Anandur chuckled as he eased into the road. "The fastest way to a Russian girl's heart."

"You should know," Kian said.

"I can't wait to see Lana."

Kian lowered the window shade and took his sunglasses off. "Don't hold your breath. She probably snagged a new guy by now."

"Very likely."

The rest of the drive to the captain's house passed in silence. Kian read reports, Anandur was deep in thought, probably thinking about Lana, and Brundar did his usual impersonation of a statue, thinking about who knew what.

Turner itched to investigate the guy just to figure out what his deal was. It wasn't as if Brundar was an important member of the clan with major decision-making responsibility. He and his brother were simple soldiers acting as body-guards. Turner knew the type well. But the Guardian was a mystery, and as such he piqued Turner's curiosity.

Besides, he preferred speculating about Brundar's secrets than thinking about his upcoming chemotherapy.

He'd postponed it as much as he dared without incurring Bridget's wrath, with the Hawaii trip providing a good excuse not to start yet, but he could come up with no more reasons for delaying it. Monday afternoon, Turner was meeting with his regular doctor to start the treatment.

Bridget had offered to accompany him to his appointment. He'd turned her down as gently as he could, but her feelings had gotten hurt despite his best efforts.

Nevertheless, it was something he needed to do alone. Like an injured animal that nursed its wounds in hiding, Turner preferred not to be seen in a weakened state.

"You have arrived. Your destination is on the right," the navigation system announced.

The house Anandur parked next to was a modest dwelling in a middle-class neighborhood. Apparently the dinner-cruising business was not very profitable, or it was but the captain was a frugal lady.

The four of them got out, with Anandur leading the procession and Brundar guarding the rear.

"Are you expecting trouble?" Turner asked.

Kian adjusted his sunglasses, pushing them further up his nose. "Not at all."

Anandur knocked on the door, which was opened almost immediately by a tall blond who looked like she spent hours lifting weights at the gym. The span of her shoulders was wider than that of most men.

She embraced Anandur, kissed him on both cheeks, then shoved him aside to make room for the others.

"Good to see you, Lana," Anandur said.

"You too, deck boy." She dipped her head at Kian. "Hello, boss man." She opened the door all the way then glanced at

Brundar and Turner. "This one I know," she tilted her head at Brundar, "but I don't know this one." She pointed at him.

"This is my business associate, Turner," Kian introduced him.

"Nice to meet you, Lana." Turner offered his hand.

Hers was calloused and strong.

Inside, five pairs of suspicious eyes zeroed in on him. As they pushed to their feet and stood in line to shake hands with Kian and the brothers, he noted that the other five were just as muscular as Lana. Except, she was pretty enough to still look feminine, while the other ones were not so lucky. Except perhaps for the brunette with the intelligent grey eyes.

She approached him first. "I'm Geneva, the captain."

"I'm Turner." He shook her hand, which was just as calloused as Lana's.

"And your designation?"

"Consultant."

She lifted a brow and glanced at Kian.

The guy smiled. "If you want Geneva and her crew to tell you anything, you'd better tell her exactly who you are."

Turner nodded. "I'm an ex-Special Ops strategist who is currently working in the private sector. I specialize in complicated rescue missions."

That seemed to satisfy Geneva who motioned for him to take a seat next to Kian on the couch. "Please continue," she said when he was seated.

"Kian asked me to investigate the worldwide trade of human slaves, the majority of whom are young women and girls who are either abducted or manipulated and then forced and coerced into sexual servitude. When I told him the problem was much bigger than I originally believed it was, he asked me what could be done about it. I had a few ideas. We are here because we need insider information about the nitty-gritty of the operation."

Geneva nodded. "I'll tell you what I can. But I don't know

how much it's going to help you. We only saw a small part."

"I'd appreciate any information you can provide."

CHAPTER 22: ANANDUR

"*A*lexander lured the girls in with his good looks and his charm," Geneva said.

"Did he have a specific type he went for?" Turner asked.

She nodded. "College girls. He liked blonds, or maybe they sold for more. I don't know."

Listening to Turner as he threw one question after another at Geneva, and then to her dispassionate answers, Anandur found it challenging to keep his cool. It was essential that he did if he wanted to stay in the room, which he had to because it was his job not to leave Kian's side.

The anger bubbling inside of him was manifesting as it usually did, with his fangs elongating and his venom glands priming for a fight. The problem was that there was no one to fight with, and no one to take his aggression out on. Next to him, Brundar was having a similar difficulty. If they could step outside for a few moments, they could beat each other up to calm down.

Unfortunately, that wasn't an option either. They were both stuck inside Geneva's living room, forced to hear every vile crime their clan mate had committed against innocent human girls. They'd rescued only a few, while countless other victims had no one to help them and were doomed to a horrible fate.

Impotent rage was the worst.

Somehow, Kian managed to look civilized. The guy either had remarkable self-control or was distracting himself by going over balance sheets in his head. It was probably the second one because Kian had a really short fuse.

"He hypnotized them and drugged them, so they didn't put up a fight. Sometimes he gave them sleeping pills and hid them behind the fake wall in the closet. I don't know how they reacted when they woke up because he transported them still sleeping. Not all, but some. The others went willingly because of what he did to their heads."

Turner nodded, keeping up the pretense that Alex was just a rotten human who knew how to hypnotize people.

Anandur had to give it to the operative. The guy was very professional in his questioning. He never sounded condescending or accusatory, and little by little Geneva and the others were warming to him. They were practically talking over each other to give him the answers he sought.

It was evident that the girls' English had improved significantly since the last time Anandur had talked to them. Back then, Geneva had been their spokeswoman, now those who'd been practically mute before were confident enough to speak up.

Lana rose to her feet and walked over to him. "Come help me in the kitchen. We've been bad hosts, and we didn't offer drinks or snacks."

Thank the merciful Fates.

He lifted the shopping bag off the floor. "Lead the way."

"What you got in there?" Lana asked once they entered the galley style kitchen.

He pulled out a bottle. "Good vodka." He showed her the bottle of Grey Goose, then pulled out the other four. "Do you think it's too early to drink?"

102

She huffed. "Not for us. How about you?"

"I'm good. You know I prefer whiskey, but I can handle vodka too."

Lana eyed the bottles with an appreciative expression on her pretty face. "Good stuff. I'll get the shot glasses." She pulled out a tray from one of the bottom cabinets and shot glasses from the one on top.

"How are you doing, Lana?"

"I love my new life. The boat is a lot of hard work, but the money is good. But what I love the most is not being afraid. We run a legitimate business, and no one is after us." She took out a bag of pretzels, popped it open, and poured the contents into three small containers.

"Speaking of love, do you have someone?"

Her smile was radiant. "I have a boyfriend."

Anandur leaned against the counter and crossed his arms over his chest. He was a little disappointed that his plans would have to exclude Lana, but he was happy for her. "Tell me about him."

She shrugged as if it wasn't a big deal. "His name is Jack, and he runs ATV tours with his brother."

"Does he treat you right?"

"He is wonderful."

Anandur arched a brow. "Do I hear wedding bells?"

She shrugged again. "Maybe."

"Get out of here. Seriously?" He uncrossed his arms and pushed away from the counter.

She handed him the tray. "He didn't ask me yet, but we spend all our free time together."

"Your English has improved a lot." Anandur followed her out of the kitchen.

"I listen to tapes, and Jack corrects me when I make mistakes."

"Excellent."

Lana distributed the shot glasses then poured Grey Goose

for everyone. The small containers with pretzels went on the coffee table.

"Do you know where he picked the girls up?" Turner asked Geneva.

"Mostly at his club. They were excited about going to see his yacht. I don't think anyone ever noticed that the girls were disappearing right after that."

Turner rubbed the back of his head. "A talented hypnotist can affect a crowd. If you watch a good performance, you can see how it is done."

Damn, the guy was a good actor. Not that what he was saying wasn't true, there were some damn talented hypnotists out there, but Turner knew that Alex had used a thrall. And yet, the operative managed to lie with a straight face that looked absolutely sincere. Even his scent didn't reveal anything.

The guy was like an automaton. Not even Brundar could mask his emotions that well. Anandur always knew when he'd really pissed his brother off. The scent of his anger permeated the air. It was the subtler emotions that Brundar had under such tight control that not even his scent hinted at them.

Lana tapped his shoulder. "I need more help in the kitchen."

Anandur followed her, glad to get away from the living room.

She leaned against the counter. "Tell me about you. Did you find anyone?"

He shook his head.

"Why not? You're handsome, and you have a nice smile. I'm sure you can get any girl you want."

"I didn't find the right one yet."

"Pfft." She waved a hand. "You're too picky. You know what happens to guys who keep looking for perfection?"

He had a pretty good idea what she was going to say. "What?"

"They turn into old bachelors. They lose their hair, grow a beer belly, and the number of women interested in them shrinks to very little." She showed how much with her fingers. "You need to lower your standards and catch a nice girl while you still look good."

He chuckled. "I'll take it under advisement. Any nice ladies you can hook me up with? I'm the only one without a woman on this trip, and I feel like the seventh wheel."

Lana made a face. "Marta is available."

"The one with the unibrow?"

She nodded. "We took her to a beauty salon, and she has two now. She looks better."

Anandur peered into the living room and took another look at Marta. The unibrow was gone, but she still looked like a female Neanderthal, stocky and square with a protruding forehead. He wasn't that desperate.

"Maybe next time I'm here."

Lana laughed. "You're a nice guy, Anandur. I wish you luck."

Right. Not really. If he were a nice guy, he would have taken poor Marta on a date and showed her a good time. But he wasn't that nice. "Come on, let's get back."

By the relieved expression on Geneva's face, the questioning part was done. She refilled her shot glass with the Grey Goose and offered to refill everyone else's.

Turner accepted.

Kian shook his head. "I've had enough."

Brundar hadn't drunk the first one.

"I want to thank you again for your help, Kian," Geneva said. "Our dinner cruises are booked for weeks in advance."

"I'm glad."

"I want you all to come on one. How long are you staying here?"

Kian rose to his feet. "We are going back Sunday."

"Then maybe tomorrow?"

"You said you're booked for weeks."

She waved a hand. "For you, I'll cancel a few reservations."

Kian shook his head. "Don't. I appreciate the offer, but I don't want unhappy hotel guests whose reservations were canceled for no good reason. It's not good for business."

"Yes, boss." She saluted.

CHAPTER 23: BRIDGET

The guys returned from questioning the Russians late in the evening, going straight to the hotel's restaurant to join their ladies for dinner.

"How did it go?" Syssi asked.

Kian raked his fingers through his hair. "They did the best they could, but we didn't learn anything new."

Turner's impassive expression revealed nothing. "Perhaps we should do what Anandur suggested and question their boss. The crew didn't know where the buyers came from and how he contacted them. This could be valuable information."

Anandur grimaced. "I don't want to spoil everyone's dinner and get into why that's a bad idea."

"I agree," Bridget said.

There were no eavesdroppers in the private room Syssi had reserved for their group's dining enjoyment, but talking shop was sure to spoil the languid mood from a day spent getting pampered at the spa.

Callie sighed. "We had a wonderful time at the spa. I got my nails done." She wiggled her fingers in front of Brundar.

He looked but didn't comment.

Rolling her eyes, Callie sighed. "You don't like it."

"I didn't say that."

She waved a dismissive hand. "Why do I even try?"

"Your nails look nice." Anandur came to his brother's aid. "But they looked nice before too."

Syssi patted Callie's shoulder. "Don't get upset. Most men don't pay attention to little things like that."

"I don't see the difference," Brundar finally admitted.

Callie's expression softened. "It's a clear polish. And the manicurist gave them a nice shape. I had my toes done too, but also in clear polish. Next time I'll go for bright red so you'll notice."

"I'm not sure about that," Anandur said. "Maybe if you glued on those long fake nails he would."

Callie looked at Brundar. "Do you like long fake nails?"

He shrugged. "I have no opinion."

"Right." Callie sighed.

Bridget leaned back in her chair and tuned out the conversation. She'd made plans for tonight and was eager for dinner to be over so she could tell Turner all about them.

A smile lifted the corners of her lips as she imagined his response. The little game she'd come up with was right up his street, and it was also the main reason she'd declined Kian's invitation to stay in his and Syssi's vacation home, opting for a hotel suite instead.

"What's that smile for?" Turner asked.

"I'll tell you later."

"Did you have fun today?"

"Oh, yeah. Four hours of pampering. I've never indulged like that before. It's not like facials and massages are going to improve my skin or my circulation. But I enjoyed doing nothing and managed not to worry about all the things I still needed to do."

She'd taken Syssi's advice to let her brain take a break. It would function better after having been barely active for several hours.

He reached under the table and took her hand. "Good.

You needed the relaxation after all the hard work you put into the presentation."

She cast him a hooded-eyed glance. "You're absolutely right."

The tightening of his hand around hers indicated that her meaning hadn't been lost on him. "I'm looking forward to whatever you have in mind."

An hour later, after coffee and dessert were served, Bridget pushed away from the table. "I don't know about you guys, but I'm done for the day. Thank you for a lovely dinner."

Turner followed her lead. "Do we split the bill? How does it work?"

"Don't worry about it, my friend. It's covered." Kian put his hand on the folder containing the bill.

"The clan owns the hotel," Bridget said.

Turner still looked uncomfortable. "So it's on the house?"

"Exactly," Kian said.

Pulling out his wallet, Turner took out a hundred dollar bill. "Let me at least leave a tip for the waiters."

Kian didn't argue. "You can do that if you want."

It had been the right thing to do, but it surprised her that Kian understood Turner's need to share in the expense.

With him it wasn't only about his male ego demanding that he pay, it was about Turner growing up in a house of modest means, and his need to prove that he didn't need anyone's charity.

"So what are the plans for tomorrow?" Bridget asked. "Are you guys done working?"

Kian lifted his brows. "I wish. What do you have in mind?"

"A day on the beach doing nothing is fine. Or we can take a speedboat and go on a little excursion."

"I would like that," Syssi said.

Kian wrapped his arm around his wife's shoulders. "Then that's what we are going to do."

Apparently, the way to get Kian to agree to most anything was for Syssi to ask for it.

"I'll take care of it. Are we buying a boat or renting it?" Anandur asked.

"Renting," Syssi said.

"Buying," Kian said at the same time.

Anandur crossed his arms over his chest. "So what would it be? Buying or renting?"

Syssi cast a hard glare at Kian. "Renting. I don't see us vacationing here for more than a few days a year. Buying a boat for that would be a huge waste of money."

"It's not that expensive," Kian tried to argue.

"No. If you want to throw money around, I can think of a few worthy charities it can go to."

Kian threw his hands in the air. "You're impossible to please."

"On the contrary, my love. I'm very easy to please."

And just like that Kian's irritation was gone, and his eyes began smoldering. Pushing his chair back, he made a move to stand.

Syssi caught his hand and tugged him back down. "I'm not done with my crème brûlée yet," she said.

Bridget stifled a snort. Kian might have huffed and puffed, convincing everyone he was the big, bad wolf, but shy, gentle Syssi had the big guy wrapped around her little finger.

They said their goodbyes, leaving the rest of the group to enjoy their desserts, and stepped out into the breezy open-air lobby.

Turner stopped and pulled her into his arms. "Tell me what that smile was all about. Throughout dinner, it was all I could think about."

So had she. "Did you see the movie *True Lies*?"

"The one with Schwarzenegger?"

"Yes."

"I saw it. Funny movie. I liked the beginning with the wife."

"Bingo. That's the scene I want to play."

He lifted a brow. "You want to watch an old movie?"

For a smart guy, he was sometimes so dense. "No, I want you to pretend to be the super-spy who is waiting for a call girl."

He chuckled. "That's what I thought you meant, but I wanted to make sure."

Okay, so he wasn't dense, just cautious.

"What part are you going to play?" he asked.

Bridget rolled her eyes. "The terrorist."

He laughed, the sound filling her heart with joy. "Are you going to be the pro or the timid wife?"

"Which one do you prefer?"

There was no hesitation. "The one you want to be."

Tough choice. Both options offered some exciting possibilities.

"How about I surprise you?"

The hunger in his eyes was her answer. "I'm looking forward to it."

CHAPTER 24: TURNER

*H*is eyes trained on the door, Turner sat in an armchair in the darkened hotel room and waited for Bridget.

She hadn't told him which part she was going to play, that of a call girl or the timid wife masquerading as one. He knew how to respond to the first but not the second. As good as his acting skills were, they were limited to just a few roles, and the loving husband trying to provide his bored wife with some excitement was not one of them. On the upside, Turner didn't need an actor to record French dialog for him. He could manage just fine on his own.

Still, Bridget might surprise him by coming up with a different game. He hoped she would. Turner's ability to predict people's words and actions meant that he was seldom surprised and rarely excited. Not that he was complaining. Most of life's surprises weren't good, and he would gladly do without them. Except, there was something to be said for the unexpected; it provided spice to an otherwise predictable existence.

The knock on the door pulled him out of his reverie. Should he answer in French?

"Come in." He decided to stick with plain old English.

The door creaked open. "Mr. Turner? Is that you?" The voice was Bridget's, but the tone wasn't.

Bridget spoke with confidence; the tone she was using now conveyed anxiety. Had she chosen to play the part of the wife?

It was too dark for him to see her, but he knew she had no problem seeing him. "I'm over here," he said. "Would you like me to turn on the lights?"

"No. It's better like this." She closed the door behind her but didn't move from her spot.

"Come closer," he commanded.

The woman sighed and took a few tentative steps. "I'm sorry, but Stacy couldn't make it tonight. She's got the flu, and all the others have it too. I was the only one available. I'm sorry."

Bridget was playing the part so well, Turner focused on her voice to reassure himself it was her. Still, which part was it? He needed more clues.

"What's your name?"

"Gena."

"Come a little closer, Gena, and tell me why you think you should apologize."

"I'm not who you were expecting."

As she took several small steps toward him, he could finally see the outline of her body. It was definitely Bridget.

"It doesn't really matter."

"It does." She inhaled as if searching for courage. "I'm new. I was supposed to get training, but there was no time. I'm afraid I'll be a disappointment to you. Perhaps you would prefer a refund? I'm sure the agency will give you back your money."

"I don't want my money back." He extended his hand, and when she took it, he pulled her gently onto his lap.

Bridget didn't look at him, her red hair spilling in thick waves on both sides of her face.

He hooked a finger under her chin. "Look at me."

She did, chewing on her lower lip. "Yes?"

Damn, she was good. But he still wasn't sure if Bridget was playing the role of the wife or not.

"Do you want to be here, Gena?"

She nodded.

"Why?" Maybe she would finally give him a clue.

A timid smile lifted the corners of her lips. "You're very handsome."

"I'm glad you think so. But if I'm your first client, you can still change your mind. In this profession, you don't get to choose, and the next one might not appeal to you."

She shifted in his lap, making herself more comfortable, and wrapped her arms around his neck. "I'm going to tell you a secret," she whispered in his ear. "I'm not a call girl in training. I'm the agency's receptionist." Bridget aka Gena kissed his neck, the soft touch sending a bolt of desire to his shaft.

Nuzzling his jaw, she continued. "When Stacy called in sick, I logged into your account to let you know she had to cancel, but then I saw your picture and decided to take her place." She lifted her eyes to him. "Are you mad? I know I'm not as gorgeous as Stacy, but I've been told I'm pretty."

"You're beautiful."

She looked at him from beneath her lowered lashes. "Do you mean it? You're not just saying it to be nice?"

It seemed he'd been right about Bridget's inventiveness. This was a different storyline.

Was he still supposed to be the secret agent?

The role fit him well, so why not. He could roll with that.

Pushing up, Turner let her feel his hardness. "Trust me, sweetheart, I'm not the type who bothers with niceties. I know what I want, and right now it's the curvy redhead sitting on my lap."

"For real? Are you sure there is no one else you'd rather be with?"

"I would prefer a naked redhead."

She giggled in a very un-Bridget-like way. "That could be arranged." Now that sounded more like the Bridget he knew.

Victor moved her off his lap but kept his hands on her waist. "Stacy was supposed to perform a pole dance for me. Can you dance, Gena?"

He'd been looking forward to that part from the movie. The question was whether the doctor had moves.

"I can try."

"Please do."

She looked down at her shoes. "I need music."

He was ready for that. "No problem."

Turner pulled out his phone and pressed play on the soundtrack he'd prepared. "Is that good?"

"Perfect." Sauntering toward the row of light switches, Bridget moved her hips as if she'd been walking the runway her entire life. She pushed one up a bit, illuminating the bed area and leaving the rest of the room in darkness.

Slowly making her way to the four-poster bed, she pulled her dress over her head and tossed it on the floor.

Clad only in a pair of red heels, a black thong, and a barely-there lacy black bra, she wrapped her arm around one of the posts, lifted her leg, and hooked it around the thing. She then bent so far backward that the ends of her red hair were touching the floor and her ample breasts were about to spill out of her bra.

Turner's breath hitched.

The woman knew what she was doing with that pole. Where the hell had she learned how to do that?

Was it an innate talent? Did all immortal females move like that?

Doubtful.

Bridget was a vision. Her body moving in precise fluidity and perfect balance, she performed acrobatics he would have never suspected her capable of.

When the soundtrack ended, he was tempted to start it again even though it was torture to look at the woman and not touch her. But it was sweet torture, the buildup of antici-pation a pleasure on its own.

He rose to his feet and clapped his hands. "Bravo!"

"Thank you." Bridget smiled, kicked off her red shoes, and climbed on the bed. "I forgot you wanted your redhead naked."

He didn't forget, but dancing in her sexy lingerie had been just as titillating as dancing naked would have been.

Probably more.

Turner knew next to nothing about sexy lingerie, but he knew what looked good.

On her knees, she unhooked her bra with one hand, covered her breasts with her other arm, and tossed the scrap of lace on the floor.

"Are you ready to see what you're paying for, Mr. Turn-er?" She turned around and bent forward, thrusting her luscious heart-shaped ass out as she wiggled out of her thong.

Turner smoothed a hand over his jaw. "Mercy," he groaned.

CHAPTER 25: BRIDGET

The dance had been fun, and by Turner's heated reaction she hadn't messed it up. The only pole dancing she'd seen was that one scene in the movie. She'd used a few of the moves she'd remembered and improvised the rest. As an immortal, her body was flexible and supple without much effort put into exercising, which in her case was limited to occasional walks around the block.

Behind her, the heat from Turner's body reached her before his hand touched her behind in a loving caress.

Maybe loving was too strong of a word for it, but she was going to stick with it. His touch was gentle, his palm warm, and his hand lingered as if he never wanted to sever the contact.

With his other hand, he helped her slide the thong all the way down her legs and tossed it aside to join her bra and dress on the floor.

She made a move to lift her torso, but he guided her back down with a soft push.

"Stay like that," he whispered. "It's a million dollar view."

She chuckled. "Three thousand at least."

"Is that what I'm paying you?" He trailed his hand lower, cupping her mound.

She moaned. "Aha…"

His finger dipped between her folds. "Worth every penny."

"I didn't do anything to earn it yet."

"The view alone is worth that much. From now on you'll be working for your tip." He smeared her wetness around her lower lips but not where she needed it most.

Ugh, he was going to take it slow. "Tell me what you want, Mr. Turner."

"I want everything."

It was hard to think with his finger doing all kinds of wicked things to her, and she meant it literally. Not touching her pulsating nerve center was mean.

A sigh of relief escaped her lips at the sound of rustling fabric. Victor taking off his clothes signaled the end of her torment. The man had formidable self-control, but even he had limits. Staring at her ass was no doubt stretching his resolve to the max. Turner was obsessed with it.

Lucky for him, she had a plentiful backside. Not as in huge, she was too small of a woman for any part of her to qualify as such, but she was curvy, with a fairly big bust, a proportionally sized ass, and a narrow waist.

A classic hourglass figure.

In his usual efficient and economical manner, Turner had promptly gotten rid of his clothes, not tossing them on the floor as she had, but folding them neatly and placing them on the bench that hugged the footboard. The way he'd arranged her, visual information was not available to her, but Bridget's hearing was good enough to ascertain every move he made.

The feel of his muscular thighs against the backs of her own was not a surprise, but it provided a thrill nonetheless. She loved the way their bodies fit together like two pieces of a puzzle.

Palming his heavy length, he pushed it between her folds. Rubbing it back and forth and coating it with her moisture, he seemed in no hurry to feed it into her.

She wiggled her butt in invitation, which earned her a stinging smack on the fleshy part of her right buttock. "Hey! What was that for?"

"As a paying customer, it's my call what I want to do next. Stop trying to hurry things along."

"I'm sorry, but I'm impatient." She wiggled again, intentionally inviting another smack.

Turner delivered, then leaned over her back, covering her with his warm torso. "Do you need more spanking, naughty girl?"

It seemed her stoic lover was getting into the role acting. Calling her a naughty girl, or any kind of girl, was definitely new.

Bridget loved it.

Unlike most men, Turner wasn't intimidated by her. He had no problem with her smarts and her medical diploma and her assertive nature. In fact, he loved those things about her. Well, love was too strong of a word when pertaining to Turner, but she knew he appreciated her and most importantly didn't feel threatened by her.

"No," she said, wiggling her butt again.

Two quick smacks followed, not as strong as the first ones, but they stung nonetheless.

"Are you going to keep swiveling those hips of yours like that, or are you going to behave?" He delivered two more.

The giggle was impossible to stifle. "I can't help it."

"Tsk, tsk. You definitely need more training, my girl." He smoothed his palms over her heated behind. "Being a receptionist is a waste of your natural gifts. This ass is too perfect to be stuck in a chair all day, and those plump lips of yours are made for kisses and not for answering phone calls."

"Are you offering to train me?"

"Yes." He chuckled.

They both knew she was the more experienced and could teach him a thing or two. But the switch around was fun. Bridget couldn't remember ever being so playful with a guy.

Even with Andrew, she'd been somewhat reserved, not sexually, but as far as letting her inner girl out.

It was boring to be the responsible adult at all times. On a gut level, Bridget knew that with Turner she could be whomever she wanted to be at that moment and he would accept each and every facet of her.

It was liberating, and it was intimate in the extreme.

"Then teach me, master. I'm an eager pupil." She shook her ass again, barely managing to stifle a laugh.

Turner groaned, his strong thighs leaving hers exposed to the cool air as he dipped down and licked her from behind.

Sneaky operative. He'd taken her by surprise.

She had been expecting his hard length to spear into her, not his tongue, but she could wait a few more minutes. Perhaps he could treat her to a climax once or twice before moving on to the main event.

"I like that." She moaned, her hips moving even though she wanted to stay still.

Clamping his hands on her ass cheeks, Victor didn't answer. Instead, he proceeded to demonstrate that he could teach her a thing or two as well.

The man had a very agile tongue and knew how to use it on a woman.

For a moment, a surge of jealousy washed over her. Who had he practiced on? Was it common for paying customers to treat call girls to cunnilingus?

Not likely.

Then who had been on the receiving end of his tongue's attentions?

Her sudden flare of unease hadn't gone unnoticed.

"What's the matter? Am I doing something wrong?"

"You're doing everything too right."

"Huh?"

She turned her head to look at him over her shoulder. "Who did you practice on?"

Victor shook his head. "Really? That's what you want to

120

ask me right now?"

"Yes."

He turned his eyes up to the ceiling. "I will never understand women." He looked back down. "I learned from watching porn on the Internet. I wanted to know how to do it right. Then I practiced on several of my paid companions. Satisfied?"

Damn, she was such an idiot. Turner looked embarrassed by the admission she'd forced out of him. Why was she behaving like that? Why did she doubt his story about lack of female companionship other than the paid kind?

Because it was hard to believe that a gem like Victor hadn't been discovered by her human competition. It just didn't make sense, but on the other hand, neither did him making this stuff up.

"I'm sorry, did I spoil the mood?"

He grunted but said nothing.

Yeah, she definitely did.

Turning around, Bridget faced Victor and wrapped her arms around him. "I'm sorry. It's not that I don't believe your story. You have no reason to lie to me. I get those uncontrollable, irrational surges of jealousy because I can't believe you weren't snatched up by some other woman already. You have so much to offer."

With a sigh, he rested his forehead on hers. "I know what you mean. I get those too. The irrational jealousy drives me nuts. That's not who I am."

"Me neither. Why do you think this is happening to us?"

Bridget had a good idea what it was, but to say that to Turner would freak him out.

"I guess it's because we've come to mean a lot to each other. It's a form of possessiveness."

Close enough.

"Let me make it up to you." She gave him a gentle shove, pushing him down to his haunches.

"What do you have in mind?"

CHAPTER 26: TURNER

*B*ridget still didn't believe him, which was insulting and flattering at the same time. Did she really think of him as such a great catch that she couldn't understand why he had no prior relationships?

That was a first.

But then Bridget was unlike any woman Turner had ever encountered, and not only because she was an immortal.

They clicked, for lack of a better term.

Somehow, their odd personalities aligned, or rather his odd one found Bridget's no-nonsense attitude and quick brain refreshing and incredibly alluring. Their interests overlapped, and their sexual chemistry was off the charts.

If he were a believing man, Turner would have thought fate had something to do with it. But his fascination with aliens notwithstanding, he was too rational to believe in the supernatural.

Besides, why would fate favor him? He wasn't a good man. He wasn't bad either, but his good deeds hadn't been altruistic. During his service, Turner had rescued people because that was what he'd been trained to do and what he excelled at. In the private sector, he did it for profit.

A saint he was not. Not even close. Not even good enough to stand in the shadow of one.

Except, a small voice in the back of his head whispered that some very good things were often done by very flawed people, while very bad things were often the result of the best of intentions.

The saintly variety didn't hold a monopoly on good deeds.

Kneeling over him, Bridget pushed on his chest until he was flat on his back. "You'll soon find out." She ran a hand over his pectorals, following the ridges and valleys with her eyes. "You have a magnificent body. I could spend days looking at you and touching you."

He smiled. "Do you want me to walk around naked when we are alone?"

"That's not a bad idea."

"Only if you're naked with me."

She chuckled. "Now you know why people wear clothes inside their homes. It's not because of the neighbors getting an eyeful through the windows. It's because not much would get done otherwise."

Reaching for her, he pulled her on top of him. "We would be like the bonobo chimps. No work and all play."

"Lucky chimps."

"I think they discovered the secret of life."

She arched a brow. "Sex all day long?"

"Exactly. Food is plentiful, they don't have any natural enemies where they live, and they resolve all conflicts with sex."

She flicked his nose. "That's because their society is run by the females. They don't let the males get aggressive."

He closed his eyes. "I can live with that."

"Could you, really? What about your curious mind and your need to solve mysteries? You would be bored in two days max."

Obviously, they were no longer playing the game, but

Turner preferred to make sure. "Just so we are on the same page, you're Bridget now, right?"

Snapping her fingers, she laughed. "Here, I made Gena disappear."

Turner made a face. "What a pity. I was hoping for a ménage à trois. Two redheads are better than one."

That earned him a playful slap. "Watch it, mister. Redheads are known for their hot temper. To rile up an immortal redhead is not smart."

Right. Bridget had a good sense of humor, but it didn't extend to jokes about other women. If he wanted this night to end with a couple of climaxes, for her, he'd better think twice before mentioning anything of the kind.

"I've been forewarned." He lifted his palms in surrender. "I'm still waiting for you to make good on your promise."

With a grin, Bridget pushed back to sit on her shins. "That's right." She palmed his erection that had since recovered from its temporary deflation but not all the way to its former glory.

That was quickly corrected as Bridget leaned forward and put her luscious lips on the crown. In seconds, her hand and her lips and her tongue had him panting for release.

"Please." He put his hand on her cheek. "I don't want to come like this."

Unlike Bridget, who could climax numerous times and usually did, Turner wasn't sure he could rise to the task more than once. Especially after the long day he'd had.

He might be in excellent shape, but he wasn't a young man anymore. At forty-six, he would be lucky to climax more than once in one session.

Bridget let go and climbed on top of him. "I'll humor you this time. But just this once." She kissed him, her tongue parting his lips and swiping lazily against his own.

He could have her mount him like this, but he had something different in mind. Her previous pose, on all fours with him behind her, was etched into his brain.

Lifting her by the hips, he moved her over and got behind her. "A million dollar view."

She chuckled, then moaned as he surged inside her, not all the way in, but almost. Bridget pushed back, impaling herself to the hilt.

"Yes," she groaned. "That's it."

If his lady didn't like going slow and didn't believe in taking it easy, who was he to argue?

Gripping Bridget by the hips, Victor pumped into her, increasing the force and tempo of his thrusts while letting the sounds of passion she was making guide him. Even with the bruising grip he had on her, Bridget was bucking into him, spurring him to go faster, deeper. When he felt he was nearing his peak, Turner leaned over her and reached around their bodies to massage the most sensitive part of a female's anatomy.

They climaxed together, her sheath spasming around his shaft and squeezing every last drop from it. He kept massaging that sensitive nub, prolonging her climax until Bridget collapsed under him.

His hands still on her hips, he pulled her with him to lie on their sides. Kissing the soft skin where her neck met her shoulder, he smoothed his hand over her curves, admiring the way her narrow waist flared into her generous behind.

His Bridget had the body of a goddess.

His red-haired Venus.

Was the original Venus a redhead? He remembered Bridget mentioning the goddess's tresses were red. Was the legend of Venus based on Annani?

He almost made the mistake of asking before reminding himself that it was a bad idea to mention another female while he was still buried deep inside this one. Bad etiquette in any circumstances, and especially where Bridget was concerned.

The doctor had a quick temper and a long jealous streak.

Turner grinned. Who would have thought a woman

would ever get jealous over him? He had to admit that it felt good.

"Did you fall asleep?" Bridget asked in a sleepy voice.

"No."

"What are you thinking about?"

"That I'm a lucky bastard who scored the hottest, most passionate woman there is."

She turned her head around, a satisfied smile on her glowing face. "I hope you don't plan on verifying that statement by sampling others."

He kissed her cheek. "I like your jealousy. But just so you know, you risk inflating my male ego to dangerous proportions."

"As long as I'm the only one doing so, I'm okay with that."

"You are? Wait until I start strutting around like a peacock."

"Pfft." She waved a tired hand. "Join the club. The keep is full of peacocks."

I wish I could, Victor thought as he drifted off to sleep. Joining the clan as one of them was an impossible dream he hoped against all hope would come true.

CHAPTER 27: SYSSI

"*I* feel so relaxed," Syssi said, leaning against Kian's shoulder.

The private jet had just finished its climb, the island of Hawaii shrinking in the distance.

"I'm glad to hear it." Kian didn't even lift his eyes from the laptop.

Syssi sighed. She'd managed to drag him out to the beach a couple of times, and the memory of smearing sunscreen all over his muscular body brought a smile to her face.

Her guy had walked onto the sand fully dressed, with a long-sleeved shirt, long pants, a wide-brimmed straw hat, and his special sunglasses, looking like an old man, but one who was in excellent shape. He'd argued when she'd suggested he take at least his shirt off, but in the end, she'd peeled him out of his clothes and protected his sensitive skin with the highest SPF sunblock available. It had worked for the most part, but his ears had gotten sunburned despite her best efforts. It was good he healed so fast. Otherwise, she would not have heard the end of it.

Turner hadn't fared much better, looking like a boiled shrimp after less than an hour in the sun. Unfortunately, his human body couldn't fix the sunburn as fast as Kian's had.

The guy had started out so white he could've competed with Annani for luminescence.

"There is something special in the Hawaiian air. The breeze, the smells, the sounds of the ocean, it's all so soothing," Callie said.

"We should do it again," Bridget said.

Syssi glanced at Anandur, who was peering out the window even though the island was no longer visible. He seemed unusually forlorn.

"How about you, Anandur? Did you have a good time?" she asked.

Still looking out the window, he shrugged. "I guess so."

"What's the matter?"

"Watching all of you lovebirds was so much fun." His tone was sarcastic.

So that was his problem. As the only one without a partner, Anandur must've felt left out. Except, he hadn't seemed to mind before. What had changed?

"No luck at the clubs?" she asked. He'd gone out one night on his own but returned after less than an hour.

He shook his head. "Full of pimply teenagers."

"They had to be older to get in," Turner said. "Unless there was no alcohol served."

"Not my kind of crowd." Anandur shook his head again. "I'm getting too old for that."

He could say that again. The guy was over a thousand years old, although looking at him and hearing him talk no one would suspect he was older than thirty.

Syssi still remembered how jaded Kian had been when they'd met. He'd been sick and tired of the same old revolving door as well.

"I'm sure there is someone out there for you," she said.

He turned back to the window. "I hope so."

Poor Anandur. He was such a nice guy. Funny, charming, romantic. He would make some girl very happy.

Should she attempt to induce a vision for him?

Syssi hadn't tried that for months. Her visions had been so disturbing that she'd decided not to do anything to encourage them, and thankfully she'd been vision-free since she'd made up her mind to avoid them.

Except, not all of her visions were terrible. She'd foreseen Andrew having a daughter, and she had known Eva and Bhathian were having their boy. In the vision, she hadn't seen who the boy belonged to and had hoped he was Kian's and hers. The disappointment upon discovering Eva's pregnancy had been devastating and one of the reasons she made a conscious effort to block any future foretelling.

She was a coward. Hiding from her visions to spare herself grief while she could be providing valuable information to the clan.

Perhaps it was time to lift the barrier she'd erected in her mind and let the visions come.

"Are you okay?" Kian asked.

Damn. It was impossible to hide her thoughts when her husband could smell them on her. It was good the other immortals weren't as good at discerning scents. Except for Brundar, but he was too busy snuggling with Callie to pay attention.

"I was thinking about my visions."

Kian frowned. "You haven't had any in a long while. Are you scared of them coming back?"

"I learned how to block them. But I feel it's selfish to do so. I should open up my mind and learn how to deal with the visions instead of hiding from them."

Kian closed his laptop and wrapped his arm around her shoulders. "I don't want you to do anything that upsets you."

Sweet Kian, always protective and thinking of her well-being first.

"I was given this gift for a reason. It's wrong for me to avoid my visions just because they disturb me. I need to toughen up and let them come."

He shook his head. "If the visions provided useful information, I might have agreed, but they don't. They are too vague. All they do is make you anxious."

She cast a quick glance at Anandur's clenched jaw. "I could help him."

"Or not. You can't control what comes into your mind. Most of it is not good."

Syssi sighed and put her head on his shoulder. "I know."

But what if there was a way to summon positive visions? What if instead of opening her mind to whatever information was floating in the ether she could focus on what she wanted to learn?

Closing her eyes, Syssi imagined Anandur smiling and happy. *Show me his truelove*, she thought.

It was a long shot.

Thinking of the barrier in her mind, she lowered it just a smidgen and flooded the opening with sunlight, the scent of the Hawaiian breeze, and the happy memories she'd accumulated through their vacation.

Feeling herself drifting off to sleep, she sighed. Well, at least there was that. Instead of a sunny vision she was getting a peaceful nap.

The dream started almost as soon as Syssi closed her eyes. A young girl was crying in Anandur's arms. He looked troubled and unsure as he ran his hand in small circles over her back, trying to provide comfort and whispering something in her ear.

The girl shook her head and cried even harder, the stricken expression on Anandur's face getting worse.

In the dream, Syssi frowned, trying to decipher what she was watching. The girl looked too young to be Anandur's love interest, especially since he preferred ladies in their mid-thirties and the girl looked barely eighteen.

Could she be his daughter?

It was possible. Perhaps one of his dalliances with a human had produced a child. But if she were, knowing her would only cause Anandur more pain. His daughter with a human would not carry the immortal gene.

What was the dream trying to show her?

Syssi looked closer, checking for any familial resemblance between the girl and Anandur, but there was nothing to either prove or disprove that.

The girl was tall, probably close to six feet or so. The top of her head reached just under Anandur's chin, and the guy was about six feet seven inches tall. They had the impressive height in common. But where Anandur was a fair-skinned redhead, the girl's long hair was so dark it was almost black, and her skin tone was deep olive. She looked like a Mediterranean amazon warrior woman who spent her days training in the sun.

"Everything is going to be okay, sweetheart, I promise," Syssi heard him say.

The girl shook her head.

Anandur hugged her closer, kissing the top of her head. "Please don't cry. You're breaking my heart."

Clutching his shirt, the girl nodded. "I'm trying," she said in a shaky voice that was slightly accented.

CHAPTER 28: TURNER

"*H*ere." Bridget spread a towel over her couch.

Turner groaned. He felt ridiculous sitting in the middle of Bridget's living room in his underwear. "We should do this in the bedroom. What if someone comes over?"

He was badly sunburned, and it was entirely his fault. Served him right for being an idiot and not reapplying the sunscreen after each swim. Last night, he couldn't make love to Bridget because his skin had felt on fire. Putting on clothes this morning hadn't been a picnic either. He couldn't wait to get home and take everything off.

Bridget squirted a big dollop of aloe vera into her hand, rubbed her palms together, and put them on his sunburned back.

He sighed. "It feels good." Turner imagined a hissing sound and vapor arising from where the lotion cooled his skin.

"I told you so." She smeared the blue gelatinous liquid all over his back, then reached for the bottle and squirted more into her palm. "Next time when I tell you to reapply sunscreen, don't argue."

He groaned. "There won't be a next time."

"Pfft, don't be ridiculous. You love swimming. And I love watching you swim. All those hard muscles at work, yum." She smoothed the cool stuff over his shoulders.

"You can watch me swim in the pool. Didn't you say that there is an Olympic sized one in the underground?"

"There is."

He pushed to his feet. "Let's go. I bet the water is cold." It would be heaven to submerge in all that water with no sun to spoil the fun.

Bridget wiped her hands on his arms. "I can spare half an hour."

"Perfect."

As he strode to the bedroom to get his swimming trunks, his private phone rang. Turner snatched the thing off the charging station, frowning at the display.

"Douglas, what happened?" His son never called unless it was Turner's birthday or to wish him happy holidays.

"Hi, Dad." He almost never called him Dad either. "Nothing happened. Nothing bad, that is. I wanted to let you know that I got engaged."

That was big news. Turner didn't know Douglas was dating anyone seriously. The last time they had met, his son hadn't mentioned anyone special.

"Congratulations. Who's the lucky lady?"

"Her name is Melanie. We met a little over three months ago."

That wasn't long. Douglas was still young, but not too young to get married. Except, he was still serving in a Special Ops unit, and that kind of a career didn't lend itself to marital life.

"What's the hurry?"

There was a moment of silence on the line before Douglas responded. "When it's the right woman, there is no point in waiting. I knew Mel was the one as soon as I saw her."

Turner thought back to the first time he'd seen Bridget.

Had he known she was the one? Of course he hadn't because he never entertained those kinds of thoughts. The only thing he'd known was that she was special and that he was attracted to her. But then Douglas was nothing like him. Thanks to his mother, the kid was normal.

"I'm happy for you."

"I want you to meet her."

That was unexpected. "Are you sure?"

"Mel is the best. I know you're going to like her."

"I'm sure I will. But the question is whether she is going to like me."

Another moment of silence. "I'm counting on you to do your best. She is important to me."

"Should I enroll in a charm school first?"

Douglas chuckled. "Just try to smile from time to time. I don't expect anything more. I told her about you. She knows you're not the friendly type."

That was putting it mildly. "When and where?"

"I was hoping you can come over here. I'm guessing that you have enough miles to fly for free?"

As if that was a concern.

The problem was that Turner was about to start chemo and had no idea how it was going to affect him. Better to get the meeting over with before.

"I can be there this weekend. Does Sunday work for you?"

"Perfect. Our usual place?"

"Text me what time. I prefer lunch if that's okay with you."

"No problem. Thank you. I appreciate it."

Turner put the phone back on the charging dock and sat on the bed.

"Congratulations," Bridget said as she entered the room.

He was still getting used to that super hearing of hers. No conversation was ever private with immortals around. Not that he was intending to keep it a secret, but a few moments to process the news on his own would've been appreciated.

"Thank you."

"Are you flying there for one day only?"

"Yes."

"Why not stay the weekend and spend some time with your son and his fiancée?"

He shook his head. "We usually meet for lunch or dinner and that's it. I will fly in and out the same day. Unless you come with me, then we can stay the weekend if you want." He looked up at her expectantly.

The whole thing would be much easier with Bridget around. She could fill in the awkward silent moments, saving him from having to come up with things to talk about with Douglas.

"To meet your son?"

"Yes. Why not? I've met yours."

Bridget shook her head. "This is about Douglas and his future wife, not about introducing your new girlfriend to your son."

"Why not do both?"

She sat on the bed next to him. "Bringing me along will detract from Douglas's happy moment. Let him and his future bride be the center of your attention."

"I'll miss you."

She cast him a sidelong glance. "Nice try. You won't miss me if you're coming back the same day. Besides, with you gone, I'll have more time to put the finishing touches to my presentation."

He took her hand and looked into her eyes, hoping to soften her up. "You'll be gone the whole day tomorrow, and then I'll be gone Sunday. That's two entire days out of the week."

Bridget, Kian, and Syssi were flying to talk to the goddess, and Turner was not invited. It shouldn't have stung, but it did, and not only because this project was his baby. Bridget should not be going without him. They were a team.

Fuck, he sounded like a lovesick puppy.

When had he become so dependent on her? Why was the prospect of not seeing Bridget for two whole days so disturbing to him?

After spending most of his life alone, this should be nothing. He should be glad to have some time to himself.

Right. He never wanted to go back to that. It had been okay when he didn't know things could be different, that someone could care for him despite his oddities, or that he could care about someone and enjoy that someone's company more than he enjoyed his own—which had been his default preference before he'd met Bridget.

Bridget lifted a hand and put it on his hot back, her cool touch soothing. "Put your trunks on and let's go swimming." She leaned and kissed his cheek. "Maybe after a nice cooling swim you'll feel well enough for some fun time." She waggled her brows.

Well, that was something to look forward to. He rose to his feet and headed to the walk-in closet. "Are you going to wear that red bikini?"

She chuckled. "No, I only wear it for sunbathing. I have a one-piece for swimming."

"That's a shame. I'm fond of that bikini. Though not while other guys drool over your assets." The good thing about Kian and Syssi's vacation home was the secluded beach the gated community enjoyed. There hadn't been too many gawkers.

She walked by him, swinging her hips from side to side to taunt him. "Wait until you see that one piece. I bet it's not what you're expecting."

He followed her inside. "Show me."

"Take a seat." She motioned to the bench.

"Am I getting a striptease?"

"Aha."

"And you want me to put swimming trunks on after that? You're a cruel woman."

"On the contrary, my dear Victor." She winked. "I aim to please."

CHAPTER 29: BRIDGET

"*I*s this really necessary?" Bridget asked as she spread her arms and let William search her with his bug-detecting contraption.

Kian leaned against the wall and crossed his arms over his chest. "Your boyfriend might have planted something on you. Where Annani's security is concerned, I'm not willing to take any risks."

She rolled her eyes. "Did anyone tell you that you're paranoid?"

"You call it paranoia. I call it caution."

"Do you want to pat me down too?"

"No, but I want you to change clothes. And shoes. Leave your laptop and phone here while you go upstairs to change. William is going to check them."

Damn. This was one of the two outfits she usually wore for important meetings, and the other one was at the dry cleaners. She would have to throw something together.

"How do you know he didn't plant bugs in all my clothes?"

"Just wear something you haven't worn lately."

With a sigh, Bridget lifted her large tote and put it on top of William's cluttered desk. "You'd better check this too."

The guy blushed. "Thank you. I was going to ask you to leave it while you go upstairs."

"Don't forget the shoes!" Kian called after her as she exited William's lab.

"I heard you the first time," she muttered.

Up until she hooked up with Turner, Bridget had been treated as a trusted council member and respected as the clan's doctor and researcher; now she was treated like an accomplice.

Up in her apartment, she changed into a pair of black slacks and a grey blouse that she hadn't worn in years. It was one of the few outfits that had survived the closet cleanup she'd done in preparation for Turner's arrival. Paired with low-heeled black pumps, the ensemble would do. Conservative, comfortable, and blah.

On her way back to William's lab, she stopped by the clinic. If Kian was in no hurry, sending her for an unnecessary wardrobe changeover, he could wait a few more minutes for her to check on Julian.

"Hi, Mom." Her son looked away from the computer screen he'd been staring at when she'd walked in.

Bridget leaned and planted a kiss on his cheek. "What are you reading?"

He pointed at the screen. "An article about genetic mapping."

"Anything interesting?"

"I just started reading it."

"Let me know if you learn anything new. I stopped by to let you know I'll be gone all day. If you need help, call Hildegard."

"Where are you going?"

"A meeting with Annani."

He whistled. "Must be important."

"It is. I'm going to try gaining her support before my speech in front of the big assembly. If she is on our side, the clan will follow her lead."

Julian pursed his lips. "Not everyone, but enough. The younger generation doesn't hold her in the same high esteem."

"Really?"

He shrugged. "You know how it is. This is the age of entitlement. They are asking what's in it for them."

Bridget patted his shoulder. "We will talk about it when I come back. The others are waiting for me."

"Have a safe trip."

"Thanks."

She kissed him again before leaving.

In fact, she took every opportunity to kiss her son. Bridget hadn't realized how much she'd missed him until he'd gotten back. Mothers were supposed to let go of their grown children. It wasn't healthy to cling, and she wasn't going to, but as long as Julian didn't protest, she was going to kiss him and hug him as much as she could.

One day he would, hopefully, find his truelove, and then Bridget would have to step back and let another woman take center stage in Julian's life. She was okay with that, more than okay, she wanted him to be happy, to be loved.

But until then he was hers.

When she got back to the lab, William performed another quick scan before declaring her clean.

"Okay." Kian lifted his briefcase off the floor. "Is everyone ready?"

"Where is Syssi?" Bridget asked.

Kian grimaced. "She is not coming." He followed Anandur into the elevator and held the door open for her.

"Why? I thought she wanted to visit the sanctuary."

"It's my sister's fault. Spouting some nonsense about not mixing business with pleasure, Amanda convinced her that they should go together some other time. She said Annani would be offended if Syssi's first visit wasn't some grand affair which was planned weeks in advance." Kian strode in the direction of his car, with Bridget trotting behind him trying to keep up.

"Amanda is right. I'm glad she thought of that. Upsetting Annani is the last thing we want on this trip." She should remember to thank Amanda later.

Kian waved a dismissive hand as he climbed into the passenger seat of his Lexus. "Nonsense. She would've been happy to see Syssi."

Bridget climbed up into the back seat. "For one hour? While we presented our case? I don't think so."

Kian turned around to face her. "Yeah, I see what you mean. Annani will want to show Syssi around and have her undivided attention for at least a couple of days."

"You should make plans for that. You know it would make her happy."

He nodded. "I should. I'm a crappy son for not thinking of it myself."

"Don't beat yourself up. I'm a mother, so I know how a mother thinks. When you have children of your own, you'll understand."

Damn. She was such an idiot.

Kian's pained expression reminded her that he'd had a child once. A human girl who he'd watched grow old and die.

"I'm sorry. I shouldn't have said that. I forgot."

He nodded. "I didn't get to be a father to my daughter. I watched as another man raised her, and it was centuries ago. I have no idea how a parent thinks."

That wasn't true, but Bridget wasn't going to correct him. The sooner this conversation was forgotten, the better.

Kian had taken care of his daughter the best way he could under the circumstances. Faking his own death had meant that he couldn't show himself to her, but he'd found ways to provide for her and her children and then their children. He had kept them safe for as long as he could.

As they arrived at the clan's airstrip, Annani's jet, which

had been flown in by one of her Odu servants, was already waiting for them, fueled and ready to go.

Kian, always the gentleman, motioned for Bridget to climb aboard first. Anandur waited until Kian was seated to close and lock the door.

The jet had four passenger seats, and with Syssi not joining them, Kian could've brought Brundar along, but apparently, he'd decided to leave his other bodyguard behind. Though in truth, even Anandur wasn't necessary on this trip. Annani's sanctuary was the safest place on earth for immortals. Kian didn't need his bodyguards at all.

As she buckled up, it crossed Bridget's mind that Kian wanted Anandur on the trip to keep her company. The Guardian's job was to save Kian from having to talk to her on the long flight.

In that respect, Kian wasn't much different from Turner. Both men were inept at social interactions, mainly at casual conversations. The difference was that Kian was emotional, sometimes overly so, while Turner was not.

Except, Bridget suspected that wasn't entirely true. Turner didn't lack the capacity to feel, he actively stifled it. The only question was whether he did it consciously or subconsciously.

The why was pretty damn obvious.

He would benefit from a few sessions with Vanessa, but the chances of that happening were slim. Victor was stubborn, and it had taken bribery combined with pressure for him to agree to chemotherapy.

One battle at a time.

The cancer had to be dealt with first.

CHAPTER 30: KIAN

*H*er expression somber, Annani remained quiet during all of Bridget's abbreviated presentation, listening intently but not offering comments or asking questions.

It wasn't like her. She almost looked subdued, which greatly unsettled Kian. His mother was a force of nature who didn't know the meaning of accepting defeat or even slowing down her forward movement.

"What are your thoughts, Clan Mother?" Bridget asked when she was done.

Annani sighed. "If you are asking me whether I am shocked, I am not. This is nothing new. Women and girls have been exploited throughout history. It saddens me on many levels, but fighting this phenomenon is larger than the clan, larger even than the capabilities of superpowers. I still believe that the only way to cure humanity's maladies is more education, more progress, and more innovation. Redirecting our resources to a Sisyphean effort is not going to solve this problem or any of the others."

Fuck, Kian had been so sure that Annani's soft heart would make her an enthusiastic supporter of their undertaking. The one time he was counting on it, his mother decided to respond with her brain rather than her heart.

Deflated, Bridget sank in her chair. "Does it mean you'll oppose it?"

Annani re-crossed her legs and leaned forward. Taking one of Bridget's hands in both of hers, she smiled. "This is a very big and ambitious plan you have hatched. We need to take it apart and address each section separately. Perhaps some are less costly than others. Unless you can show me that none of the other projects we are working on will suffer as a result, I cannot support this effort."

Bridget cast Kian a pleading look, but there was not much he could help her with. Annani was right.

Still, he was not going to give up so easily. "Several of our businesses are just for profit and have nothing to do with innovation. We can sell a couple to finance this project."

Annani arched her brows. "I know that, Kian. But I also know that we need those profits to finance our technological and educational agendas."

She got him there.

Annani rose to her feet and walked over to him. "Do not look so despondent, my son. You just have to work harder to find a solution. If you can increase profits while maintaining the current trajectory of progress, I will consider approving a less ambitious plan."

Easier said than done. It wasn't as if he was idling and not dedicating every moment to achieving just that. How the hell was he going to increase profits enough to finance such a huge project? He'd already stretched the clan's finances by building the new village. They were operating on a bare-bones budget.

It was impossible.

"I'll prepare a financial plan for you to look at."

What that plan was going to be eluded him, but he wasn't going to admit he had nothing.

"Very well. When you are working on it, I want you to

concentrate on education and increasing awareness. Those are not as costly as some of the other things Bridget mentioned."

"If I may," Bridget interjected.

Annani waved her on. "By all means."

"This is not as clear cut as it seems. We need the old Guardians back. The keep and the new village are not safe with only nine of them serving. The problem is that in peacetime they don't have much to do. Training only takes up so many hours of the day and it's not enough to give them a sense of purpose. Rescuing enslaved girls will give them that. I believe most will come back if given a good enough reason."

Annani nodded. "There is something to that."

Encouraged, Bridget continued. "The Guardians' salaries represent a big portion of the budget, but we would have been paying those regardless of the project just to maintain the force in case we needed it. I think we can take it out of the cost projection and apply it to the security budget, which needed fortification regardless of anything."

Kian regarded Bridget with even greater appreciation than before. It didn't matter that the money to pay the Guardians still came from the same pocket, which wasn't as deep as he would've liked it to be. Perception mattered. If they took the salaries out of the projected cost of the project, the budget would be much more palatable to the clan members.

The cost of security was at Kian's sole discretion, and he didn't need to get the clan's approval for it.

Annani sat back in her chair and readjusted her floor-length gown. "I think the two of you still have a lot of work to do before the big assembly. First of all, clean up from the budget all the items that do not belong in it, like the salaries. It will make it easier for you to sell your plan. Then reevaluate everything based on what will bring the most bang for the money and discard the rest. Also, I want that financial plan before the assembly begins. Preferably several hours before so I will have time to go over it."

"Of course." Kian stood up only to kneel in front of Annani. "Thank you, Mother."

She leaned and kissed his forehead. "You are welcome, my son. And next time you come, I want you to bring your lovely wife and stay for a few days."

"I will." Once he surfaced for long enough to take a breath.

Mothers were not the most rational of people. Or maybe it was just his. Annani had just dropped a huge chunk of work in his lap but was still expecting him to take time off to visit her.

Back on the plane, Kian dove right into the financial reports. It would take days to go over everything and figure out where the money would come from. The bottom line was that he needed to find a way to make more of it.

"You've been awfully quiet during this trip," Bridget said.

Kian lifted his head, but it seemed she was talking to Anandur. The guy hadn't said much during the meetings, but he usually didn't butt in during those. Except, he hadn't said a word on the plane ride either, which was unlike him.

"Did Syssi tell you about her dream?" Anandur asked.

So that was his problem. Again, Kian lifted his head but the question had been addressed to Bridget, and he decided to keep his mouth shut. Syssi's dream could've meant anything.

"No, she didn't. Was it a prophetic one?"

"Maybe. She dreamt that I was comforting a crying young woman. But she didn't know what the girl meant to me."

"It can be anything," Bridget said. "You hang around clubs where a lot of young people go, and there are bound to be dramas. Someone says something offensive, a breakup, a lost purse, there are plenty of reasons for tears. Not every tear is shed over a catastrophe."

"I know. But Syssi never dreamt about me before. That's why I think it must mean something."

"Not necessarily," Kian butted in. "She dreamt about a little boy and thought he was ours, but he was Eva and Bhathian's. Her visions are real, but the problem is interpreting them. I wouldn't lose sleep over this."

"Listen to the boss," Bridget said.

Right. When it was convenient, he was the boss. Which reminded him that he hadn't complimented Bridget on her quick thinking yet. A good boss should offer praise when it was due.

"You did well in there. I would've never thought of the Guardian angle."

"Thanks. Though I should have realized that earlier and removed it from the budget. Without the sticker shock, we might have gotten Annani's approval."

Kian shook his head. "Annani is more shrewd than she lets on. I thought we had it in the bag. But apparently, she only gets emotional when it suits her agenda. She was all business today."

Bridget chuckled. "Who would have thought, huh?"

Kian closed his laptop and leaned back in the comfortable seat. He was exhausted. "I should have known better. With all her drama-queen antics, it's easy to forget who we are dealing with. Annani wouldn't have achieved all that she has by being soft and emotional. Her remarkable journey has required smarts and unyielding determination."

CHAPTER 31: LOSHAM

"Money makes the world go around," Losham said.

"Indeed it does." His assistant poured him a shot of whiskey and sat down in the other armchair.

The table between them was set up for a chess game, but they would not be playing tonight. He needed to think aloud, and Rami was an excellent sounding board.

Losham took a small sip and put his glass down. The Lagavulin was good, but it wasn't on par with what Losham was used to. A shame he'd had to give up the good stuff for the sake of appearances.

Navuh had demanded budget cuts, and one of the first things to go had been fine spirits. It wasn't as if Losham couldn't get whatever he wished; he was Navuh's son and was exempt from many of the rules and limitations others in the organization were subject to, but he had to set a good example.

"The clubs are doing well," he said.

"Yes, sir. We are opening another one in Copenhagen."

"They could be made more profitable."

Rami picked up his yellow pad. "How so, sir?"

"Paid services to club members. We are now providing

them per request by collaborating with local escort services, but we could double and triple the clubs' income by having our own in-house escorts, catering to the various tastes of our members."

"An excellent idea, sir. I'll contact the managers and tell them to start recruiting." He scribbled on his yellow pad.

"The structure should be twenty and eighty. The girls get twenty percent, the house gets eighty."

"Naturally, sir." Rami added the numbers to his notes. "The escort services offer a better split, sir. It would make it difficult to lure service providers to our clubs."

Losham took another sip and grimaced at the inferior taste. "We don't have to lure them from other places. We could do what we do on the island."

Rami lifted a brow. "They have nowhere to go on the island. It's not the same in the big cities."

The man was still so naive after all the years he'd worked for Losham.

"That's why they will get twenty percent and not work for tips only like they do here. Don't worry about that. It's quite simple to get quality young flesh for low pay. Between threatening their families if they refuse to cooperate and offering them compensation that is more than they ever dreamed of making, they will do what they are told."

Rami nodded. "What should I tell the club managers? How should they proceed?"

"We will take care of the supply for them. They will get the girls after they are already fully trained. In fact, we will need one more person on staff who will be in charge of managing them."

"Any ideas where we could find the appropriate people for the job?"

Losham smiled. "We have plenty right here under our noses."

Rami looked doubtful. "Lord Navuh will not agree to allocate warriors to civilian jobs."

"That's where you are wrong, Rami. Lord Navuh's instructions are to make money generation a priority. The warriors' thralling ability would come in very handy while managing a bunch of reluctant prostitutes."

"Yes, sir." Rami still sounded unconvinced.

"The world is changing, Rami, and we need to adapt. Sending our warriors to instigate conflicts and assist allies is getting more and more difficult given the surveillance cameras and drones and satellites. Besides, the new wars are not fought on the battlefield using swords or rifles, they are fought in dark rooms behind computer screens. Whoever controls the technology, controls the world."

Rami shook his head. "Then we are in trouble. The clan is decades ahead of us when it comes to technology."

Losham took another sip, then put the glass down. "True. But that doesn't mean we cannot catch up or perhaps surpass them. Even with the recent setback of losing our biggest client, we still command more resources and certainly more manpower. It will take years, maybe even decades, but with the right focus we can beat them at their own game."

"We need better education for our men," Rami said. "They are trained as soldiers, not software developers or even simple operators."

"Precisely. That's where we need to start."

Rami tapped his pencil on his yellow pad. "The breeding program favored the strong and ruthless, not the smart. I'm not sure our men can rise to the task."

Losham sighed. Since the very beginning, he'd been trying to tell Navuh that the program was producing inferior specimens and that better quality humans should have been used to breed the Dormants. But Navuh had been short-sighted and insisted that a mighty army that was easy to control was better than a smart army that wasn't.

"That is true, Rami. But we have many men. I'm sure we can find a few who are more than goons with muscles. Look at you. You're the product of the program, but you're smart."

Rami dipped his head, "Thank you, sir."

"I hope Lord Navuh will reconsider the parameters of the program. All those influencers we get in here can be used for more than politics and information. They can help us breed a better stock."

"So no more warriors?"

Losham laughed at Rami's alarmed expression. "There is always a need for soldiers, Rami. All I'm suggesting is some diversification. We need both the brains and the muscles. Unfortunately, they don't usually come in the same package."

CHAPTER 32: TURNER

"*R*ight this way, sir," the hostess said as she led Turner to the table.

"Thank you." He took off his suit jacket, hung it on the back of his chair, and sat down.

"Could I offer you something to drink while you wait for the rest of your party?" the hostess asked.

"Water, please."

"Of course." She handed him the menu and left two others for Douglas and his fiancée.

Looking at the familiar menu, Turner thought about how different this trip was from the many previous ones he'd taken to meet his son.

Usually, when flying to the East Coast for their semi-annual get-together, Turner stayed for a couple of nights, using the opportunity to visit with some of his Washington contacts. This time, however, he'd scheduled only one dinner appointment and was taking the redeye back to Los Angeles.

It wasn't that he had some pressing business to attend to back home. He just couldn't stand the thought of being away from Bridget any longer than was absolutely necessary.

Was that need to be with her what people called love?

If it was, it was nothing like what Turner had imagined.

This wasn't about a storm of emotions, or about an all-consuming passion, or an uncontrollable longing. There was nothing irrational about what he felt for Bridget.

The best description he could come up with was that he was comfortable with her. Perhaps to others that would have seemed too trivial of a feeling, but to him it meant more than all the craziness people associated with love put together. For the first time in his life, he felt completely at ease with another human being, well, an immortal being, but that was semantics.

With Bridget, he was no longer alone in the world, and that meant everything to him.

Naturally, the passion and attraction were there, but they were merely a bonus and not the most important components of what made his relationship with Bridget unique.

Turner had been attracted to plenty of women in his lifetime, but he could think of none of them as a potential life partner. In fact, the thought was as appealing as being strapped to a chair and getting tortured.

"Here is your water. Would you like a basket of bread?" The waitress smiled sweetly.

"No, thank you." To maintain his physique, Turner had to watch his carb intake, especially given that his training routine had shrunken to a third of what it used to be before he'd met Bridget.

Was cohabiting with a woman the reason married men grew flabby middles?

Given the many jokes floating around about the misery of marriage, Turner would have thought the opposite should have been true. If someone was unhappy at home, an evening training session was a good excuse to get out and spend a couple of hours away from the wife, not to mention that physical activity was a constructive way to release aggression. But since that was obviously not happening, the jokes must be a lie, and most married men must enjoy staying home with their wives and their kids.

He wondered at the source of those jokes. Perhaps men viewed home life as unmanly and therefore pretended they were suffering through it.

Glancing at his watch, Turner confirmed that Douglas was late.

As a foreboding déjà vu washed over him of another restaurant where he'd been waiting for two people who hadn't shown up, Victor had to remind himself that he'd called Douglas back and verified where and when they were meeting.

This time it hadn't been an imposter calling to invite him for a deadly rendezvous.

A few minutes later, Douglas and his fiancée entered the restaurant.

His son hadn't changed much from the last time Turner had seen him. He was still the same stocky young man with a friendly smile, though he must've stepped up his weight-lifting regimen because his biceps were bulging. The sleeves of his T-shirt were straining to contain them.

The girl was exactly the type Turner would have imagined with Douglas. Early twenties, short, a little on the chubby side, with a pretty round face and flushed cheeks. It wasn't cold outside, nor hot, so the flush must be due to anxiety. Meeting the scary future father-in-law was the probable cause.

Turner stood up and plastered a smile on his face. "Melanie, it is so nice to meet you." He offered her his hand.

"Same here." The flush deepened. She cast a nervous glance at Douglas, then took the offered hand, shook it, and a moment later threw her arms around Turner's neck. "I'm so excited to meet you."

Looking at Douglas for help, Turner patted her back awkwardly.

"Come on, Mel. I told you my dad doesn't like hugs. Let him go."

The girl dropped her arms, but even though her cheeks

were blazing red, she smiled sheepishly. "We are family now. A little hug never hurt anyone."

Gutsy girl. Turner liked her. She didn't let her natural shyness stop her from going for what she wanted.

As always, once the hellos were over, Turner and Douglas sat in awkward silence.

"How is your mother?" Turner asked though he wasn't really interested.

"She is fine."

"And your post? Are they treating you right?"

Douglas shrugged. "I love it despite all the inconsequential bullshit."

"I don't," Melanie said. "I don't know what he does, but if he can't talk about it, it must be dangerous."

Douglas wrapped his arm around her shoulders. "Mel, we talked about this."

"Yeah, we did." She sighed. "What can I do? I fell in love with Rambo."

Douglas picked up a napkin, folded it, and tied it around his head. "Don't be scared, little lady," he imitated Stallone. "Your man is invincible."

Turner chuckled. "Aren't you too young to even know about Rambo?" Melanie hadn't been born when the movie came out.

She waved a hand. "It's a classic, or so my dad says. My brothers agree."

"How many siblings do you have?" Turner asked, glad to have something to talk to his future daughter-in-law about.

"I have three brothers. Two older and one younger."

"What about your parents? What do they do?" Again, he had absolutely no interest in finding out, not unless they were criminals, in which case she wouldn't want to talk about them.

"They both work for the school district. My dad is a basketball coach, and my mom teaches chemistry. They teach in the same high school where they met. Isn't that cute?"

"It is." He meant it.

Given her facial expressions and her tone of voice when she talked about her family, Melanie loved her parents and got along with her siblings. The girl came from a good home —parents who were still married to each other and held respectable jobs. It didn't get much better than that.

"Did you guys decide on a date?" Turner asked.

The flush in Melanie's cheeks deepened. "We did." She cast a worried glance at Douglas.

His son looked sheepish. "Yeah, about that. The wedding is in a month. I wanted to tell you about the engagement first."

Melanie's flushes suddenly took on a new meaning. "Is there anything else I should know about?"

Douglas nodded. "We would've gotten married anyway."

Turner rubbed a hand over the back of his bald head. He was going to be a grandfather. It shouldn't have come as such a shock. After all, Douglas was a grown man. Except, the thought had never crossed Turner's mind. He had a hard time internalizing being a father, let alone a grandfather.

What the hell was he supposed to do now? There was only one thing he'd done well for Douglas, and that was supporting him financially. He knew how to do that.

"Did you reserve a place for the reception?"

Douglas nodded. "I put down a deposit."

"I'll pay for the rest. Just tell me who to write the check out to, and I'll mail it as soon as I get back."

His son seemed offended by the offer. "Thank you, but we got it covered."

Melanie smiled. "That's very generous of you, but we have money saved up to pay for the wedding."

Melanie's parents didn't have high-paying jobs and had raised four kids. Turner doubted they could finance even part of the cost. It made perfect sense that the young couple had to use their own money.

"If you don't want me to pay for the wedding, that's fine. But I'm buying you a house."

Douglas opened his mouth to protest, but Turner lifted his palm. "Don't argue. It's a done deal."

Melanie gaped at him as if he were Santa Claus. "I don't know what to say. Thank you. Douglas and I never expected that." She lowered her eyes and picked up her napkin. "I don't want you to think that we invited you today because we wanted you to give us stuff. I just really wanted to meet you."

"I know. I'm doing this because it makes me feel good to provide you with a solid start. Not having to deal with a mortgage for the next thirty years will make things easier for you. I was never much of a father to Douglas. This is the best way I know how to show both of you and my future grandkids that I care."

"Thank you, Dad." Douglas got up and pulled Turner into his arms for a crushing hug. "I always knew you cared."

"*N*ow, that was some news you got, Grandpa." Bridget held the phone between her chin and shoulder as she fed coins into the vending machine.

Turner was freaking out in classic Turner style. His tone of voice was devoid of any emotion, and he was telling her the news as if it pertained to someone else.

"Not yet. I need time to get used to the idea. I don't think of myself as a father. A grandfather is an alien concept to me."

"And yet, you offered to buy them a house." She selected a muffin and put in the corresponding number and letter combination.

"At least I'm good for one thing."

Bridget fed more coins into the machine for the Danish Julian had requested. "You're good for much more than that."

"Like what?"

She collected both pastries, stuffed them in her lab coat's pockets, and lifted the phone to her ear. "If Douglas or his wife or any other family members need rescuing, you're the man."

He chuckled. "Yeah, that about sums it up."

"You can also deliver a riveting speech at their wedding."

"Why would you think I'd be good at that?"

"I can write it for you. After working on the presentation, I've become an expert on writing emotional speeches." She entered the elevator and pressed the clinic's floor.

"You can do better than that. You can come with me to the wedding. And don't you dare come up with an excuse for why you can't."

"Of course, I'll come. What gave you the idea I wouldn't want to?"

Turner sighed. "You didn't want to come today."

"It's not the same. Today was about you meeting Melanie. But if you want, we can go visit them before the wedding so you can introduce us. That way there will be no awkward moments at the reception. Unless you expect Douglas's mother to act wonky."

"No, she won't mind."

Bridget wasn't sure about that. Having a child bound people together whether they wanted it or not.

"You never told me her name."

"I didn't?"

"Nope. Subconscious reluctance?"

He chuckled. "Her name is Nancy."

"Maybe we should meet up with Nancy and her husband. What's his name?"

"Peter. Peter Grohovzski."

"That's a mouthful. I hope Douglas uses your last name." She'd wanted to ask before but felt awkward doing so.

"I'm registered on his birth certificate, and he goes by my last name."

Bridget reached her lab, took out the Danish from her pocket and handed it to Julian. "Do Nancy and Peter have other children?"

"No. Nancy encountered difficulties conceiving again."

"That's unfortunate." Poor Peter must have been disappointed.

"Speaking of names. Do you go by anything other than Bridget?"

She sat down and put her legs up on her desk. "I have to have a last name to put on official documents. But it's meaningless. We pick up common last names at random and keep them for fifteen years until new documents are needed. This time I chose Ward."

"As good a name as any."

"I guess. Did you check your arrival time in Los Angeles?"

"It's still six am. Why, do you miss me?"

"Terribly." She threw a muffin crumb at Julian who was making kissy faces.

"I miss you too."

"Let me pick you up from the airport." The stubborn man insisted on taking a taxi.

"It's an unnecessary schlep during morning traffic. I scheduled a service."

"I'll wait for you with breakfast."

He laughed. "Are you going to be awake that early? I've been fantasizing about finding you still in bed and slipping in to cuddle against your warm body."

Across from her, Julian stuck his fingers in his ears and started humming a tune.

She cleared her throat. "Julian is here with me, and he's acting very immature."

"Got it. I need to go, but just so you know, I'd rather skip breakfast."

"I'll take it under advisement."

Bridget ended the call and looked at her son. "You can take your fingers out of your ears."

He did and sighed dramatically. "That was awkward."

"Oh, grow up, Julian, you're not twelve."

"I'm not?" He looked down at his long torso. "I guess, I'm not."

"How is living with Robert?" she asked to change the subject.

"I like him. He is very quiet, tidy, and he likes to cook. The perfect roommate."

"How are things going with him and Sharon?"

"Looks good. I try to give them as much privacy as I can without disobeying Kian's instructions, so I can't tell you much about what's going on."

She arched a brow. "Since when are you a stickler for the rules?"

"I'm not, but Robert is. He is terrified of Kian. Robert is not a risk taker."

"He took a huge risk for Carol."

Julian nodded. "That's different. I'm not a risk taker either, but I can see myself doing the same thing to save someone from unimaginable torment. Especially a female."

"I think he did it for love."

"No, he didn't. She was a stranger to him. How could he have loved her? He saved her because he is a decent guy."

"Imagine what kind of a man he could've been if he weren't raised in the Doomer camp."

Julian chuckled. "A saint?"

"Maybe, or maybe not. Sometimes the pressure makes a diamond out of coal. Maybe without all that he went through Robert would have still been just a dark lump."

Julian raked his fingers through his hair in a move so similar to Kian's it was eerie. "You have a way of seeing the good in people."

She arched a brow. "Are we still talking about Robert?"

"I'm talking about Turner. He is not exactly a lovable teddy bear."

A laugh bubbled up from her chest. "A lovable bulldog is more like it."

"The operative word is lovable. Do you love him?"

Did she?

If love was the need to spend every waking moment with someone then yes, she did love Victor Turner.

"I like being with him," she admitted.

"It's more than that."

She arched a brow. "I like being with him a lot?"

Julian waved a dismissive hand. "Who is acting immature now? Do you need a flower to pluck the petals and ask; he loves me, he loves me not?"

To give herself a moment to think of an answer, Bridget lifted her muffin and took a big bite.

"Do you want coffee to wash that muffin down with?" Julian asked.

She nodded enthusiastically, glad of the reprieve he was offering her.

"I'll be right back." He stood up and walked out of her office.

When he came back, she was no closer to an answer than she was before.

"I've never been in love before. I love you with all my heart, and I love many members of our family, but that's a different kind of love. I love Turner's quick mind and all the fascinating information he has stored in it. I love talking to him, and we have passion. But is it love? Frankly, I don't know."

Julian shook his head. "You're living in denial. It is obvious to anyone who knows you that you love him and he loves you back. Not every love is explosive like Fourth of July fireworks; some loves are like the steady warmth of a fireplace."

"And you would know that how?"

He shrugged. "During my residency, I've spent a lot of time with humans and was exposed to all kinds of love. If you ask me, I'd rather have the fireplace than the fireworks."

CHAPTER 34: TURNER

$\mathcal{A}$t five o'clock, Turner turned off his computer and decided to call it a day.

It had been a week since he'd started chemo, and it wasn't going well. It was becoming more and more difficult to put in full days at the office, and even more difficult to actually get anything done.

His brain was foggy, he was nauseous, and his coordination was shit. He'd stopped training and was spending his evenings in front of the dumb tube because he lacked the energy to do anything else.

Even his sex drive was practically gone.

Bridget kept promising that it would get better, that his body would adapt, and the side effects would lessen with time, but he doubted it. Not everyone reacted well to chemotherapy, and apparently, he was one of those unlucky ones who couldn't tolerate it.

In the meantime, he needed to find a way to put in some work. Maybe if he could set up shop at home, he could take rest breaks in between short bouts of work.

Even driving was becoming challenging, and he'd taken to using the shuttle service for his commute to work and back. Naturally, he still used his evasive maneuvers, going to one of the malls first and taking another service from there.

When the shuttle dropped him off half a block away from the keep, he went into the office building, waited until the guy drove away, and then shuffled the thousand feet or so to the keep.

He was exhausted by the time he entered the elevator, but instead of going up to Bridget's, he went down to William's lab.

"Hey, Turner, what's up?" Roni greeted him.

"I want to set up shop at Bridget's, and I was wondering if you guys can hook me up with some equipment. I don't need it for long. A couple of weeks to a month." By then all his current projects would be done, and in preparation for his attempted transition, Turner wasn't taking on any new ones.

William lifted his head and adjusted his glasses. "What do you need?"

"I need a secure and independent network similar to what I had at home. I have a list." He pulled the piece of paper out from his suit jacket and handed it to William.

The guy scanned it in seconds. "Elementary stuff. I can have all of it installed in a day, two max."

"I need it to be impenetrable. My clients expect nothing less."

William waved a hand. "Don't worry about it, I got you covered."

"You'd better check with Kian first," Roni said. "He likes to know everything that's going on in the keep."

Even though it had nothing to do with Kian and the clan, the kid had a point. "I'll ask him right now."

He pulled out his phone and dialed Kian's number.

The guy picked up almost immediately. "Turner, what can I do for you?"

"I'm in William's lab. I need him to hook me up with a secure network at Bridget's. Roni suggested I get your approval first."

Kian was the only one other than Bridget who knew about the chemo. The question was whether he'd make the connection.

"No problem, you can tell William it's okay. Take it easy, Turner." Apparently, he did.

"Thanks." Turner put the phone back in his pocket. "You heard the boss."

"Why did he tell you to take it easy?" Roni asked.

The kid could make a good agent. He paid attention to small details, things that most people ignored.

"I'm an old human. That's why."

"Right." Roni snorted. "I'm a young immortal and look at me." He lifted one scrawny arm and flexed. "You can easily beat me at arm wrestling."

"You need to stop spending your days sitting in a chair and start exercising. To build muscles, you need to use them."

Roni grimaced. "I hate weight training, it's boring, and so is running like a gerbil on a treadmill. The only reason I did it before was to look good enough to get laid. Now I don't have anything to motivate me."

William chuckled. "Be careful. Sylvia might lose interest."

"She loves me, you dickhead. She doesn't care that I'm the weakest dude in the keep."

"Yeah, keep telling yourself that."

Roni looked as if he had some more choice words for William, but decided to keep his mouth shut. Smart. William seemed like an easygoing fellow, but antagonizing him wasn't going to do Roni any good. After all, he was sitting in the guy's lab and not the other way around.

"Is there any physical activity that you enjoy?" Turner asked.

Roni leaned back in his huge executive chair and steepled his fingers. "I liked Anandur's fake martial arts class."

"Fake?"

"Yeah. Andrew and Anandur set up this fake class as an excuse to get me out of the agency. Andrew convinced the boss that I needed physical activity to keep my brain sharp. Sylvia and her friends distracted my handler, while Anandur and Andrew tried to activate me. Long story short, it didn't work because I got sick and they ended up sneaking me out of the hospital. But in the meantime, I sort of enjoyed the fake training. Anandur had based his lessons on what he had learned from YouTube, pulling the rest out of his ass."

An idea started to form in Turner's mind. He could no longer participate in the advanced classes, but he could teach a beginner one. At least he would get to move his body a little and not let it deteriorate completely while undergoing chemo. The best part was that it would give him something to do that didn't involve staring at a screen.

"I can train you and teach you the real thing. I'm a black belt in several disciplines."

"That would be awesome. Just you and me?"

Turner shrugged. "I don't mind if others join the class. You can bring Sylvia."

Apparently, that wasn't what Roni's question had implied because he shook his head. "No way. It will be too embarrassing. Until I get in reasonable shape, I don't want Sylvia to watch me make a fool of myself."

"No problem. One on one it is. Where do you want to do it?"

Roni took a look around the lab. "Can we do it in here? There is always someone in the gym, and as I said before, I don't want anyone to see me train while I still suck."

The room was big, but the equipment was too valuable to mess with.

"Not a good idea. Not with all this equipment."

"No one is using the room next door. It's empty," William said.

"Perfect. Tomorrow at seven?"

Roni nodded. "Do I need to get any special clothes?"

"Anything that doesn't restrict movement is fine."

Roni stood up and offered his hand. "Thanks, man. I

appreciate it. I'm sure you have better things to do than train me."

"Right now I don't."

Surprisingly, Turner found that he was looking forward to spending time with Roni. According to Bridget, the kid was one of the best hackers in the world. It should be a rare pleasure to talk to someone that bright, and having a super hacker owe him was always good.

Dimly, he was aware that there was more to it than he was willing to admit. From what Bridget had told him about Roni's history, the kid was a kindred spirit. There couldn't be many of those in the world.

CHAPTER 35: RONI

"How long until you're done?" Roni glanced at Sylvia.

"Five minutes. Why?"

"I think I'm done for the day. This stuff depresses me."

For the past week, he and Sylvia had been collecting information on human trafficking, which meant that for the first time ever Roni wasn't looking forward to starting his workday. What they were doing was important, but he would have rather been doing anything but that.

Sylvia leaned back in her chair. "I have an idea that is going to cheer you up."

"I'm listening."

"How would you like to leave the keep and go for a ride? Maybe visit the beach? Go to a restaurant?"

"I would love to. But I can't. They are still looking for me. It's not safe."

"What if I give you a makeover? I think you'll look great with spiky blond hair. That, a few fake piercings, a pair of dark sunglasses, and you can rock the beach bum look."

Roni wasn't crazy about changing the color of his hair, but freedom was worth the sacrifice. He'd been cooped up in one building or another for years. "When?"

"Yay!" Sylvia jumped out of her seat and did a little dance. "I'm going to the nearest drugstore to get the hair color and the sunglasses. I'll meet you upstairs."

"What about the thing you needed to finish?" He pointed at her computer screen.

"It can wait until tomorrow. I'm too excited to stay here for another minute." She grabbed her purse and stopped by his chair to peck him on the cheek. "I'll be back in ten minutes. Close up your station and go home."

"Yes, ma'am."

As Sylvia rushed out with her hair billowing behind her, Roni swiveled his chair to face William. "What do you think? Am I going to look good as a blond?"

The guy shrugged. "If you don't like it you can always cover it up with a hat."

"Good point."

An hour later, Roni looked at his reflection in the mirror and grinned. "I look like a plucked chicken, but I don't care. My own mother would not recognize me."

"Wait until I spray you with the self-tanner."

He lifted his arms. "Go for it, baby."

Clad only in his boxer shorts, he stood patiently as Sylvia applied the spray first to his face and then the rest of his body.

"Pull down your boxers," she instructed.

Roni hesitated. "I don't think I want that stuff on my privates. What if it's a carcinogen?"

"Don't be silly. You're an immortal now. Besides, I'm not going to spray your junk, only your upper thighs and your ass."

"Hey, don't call it junk." He didn't appreciate his manhood being referred to in such a derogatory manner.

Sylvia rolled her eyes. "Your crown jewels. Is that better?"

He pushed the briefs all the way down. "Much. But I prefer scepter and orbs."

"Yes, your majesty." Sylvia mock bowed while spraying his ass. "What do you think?" she asked when she was done.

"I look orange."

Placing the can on the vanity's counter, Sylvia regarded him with a critical eye. "Give it a few minutes. The color will get deeper. In the meantime, get dressed."

Roni pulled up his boxer briefs, then stepped into the board shorts Sylvia had found in the drugstore. The muscle shirt was next.

"You got to be kidding." He looked ridiculous. "I'm going to get a regular T-shirt."

"Why? You look awesome."

Despite being an immortal, the woman must have had bad eyesight. He lifted his arms and turned in a circle. "You think?"

Sylvia grabbed him by the shirt and pulled him to her. "You're nineteen, Roni. You look like any other guy your age who doesn't spend half his day in the gym. Stop being so hard on yourself."

He wanted to point out that Jackson, who was about the same age and as far as Roni knew didn't spend hours lifting weights, looked like an underwear model.

The lucky bastard.

She kissed him hard, nibbling on his lower lip and then sucking on his tongue. "I can't wait for your fangs to be fully grown."

That made two of them. The suckers hurt as if they were going through rapid growth, but every time he checked, they seemed the same to him. Thank God for the meds Dr. Bridget had prescribed him, or he would not have been able to work.

"Can you see any difference?" He opened his mouth wide.

Sylvia peered at his teeth, then patted them with her index finger. "They are definitely growing, that's for sure. And your gums are swollen."

He sighed. "I hate all this waiting. First, it was the transition, and now those fucking fangs. Why does everything have to go so slow for me?"

Poking him in the chest, Sylvia smiled. "So you'll appreciate the good stuff more once you get it."

"Talking about good stuff, I'm ready to go."

"Give me a moment to put my bathing suit on."

He hoped it was a bikini. "Take all the time you need."

It was beside the point that he saw Sylvia naked regularly; it wasn't the same as seeing her in a bikini. Roni hadn't seen her or any other girl wearing a swimming suit other than on the pages of *Sport's Illustrated* or online or on television. If he'd been to the beach as a child, he'd forgotten.

A few moments later Sylvia emerged from the walk-in closet wearing a sundress and flip flops. She was holding out a pair of men's flip flops for him. "I got you these too. Put them on."

Down in the garage, she led him to a red convertible. "Your majesty." She opened the passenger door for him.

"I didn't know you had a convertible."

"It's not mine. I borrowed Rachel's. I figured your first excursion should be done in style with the top down."

Roni was touched. He'd only told Sylvia once about his road trip in a sports car fantasy. "Thank you."

She got behind the wheel, turned on the ignition, and leaned to give him a quick kiss. "You're welcome."

With the push of a button, the roof retracted and folded in the back.

"Let's get this baby on the road, shall we?"

Roni put his sunglasses on, leaned back, and put his hands behind his head. "Full speed ahead, Mr. Sulu, maximum warp."

CHAPTER 36: ROBERT

*T*he room was dark, the bed was warm, and the woman in Robert's arms was sleeping peacefully with her head on his chest, her arm resting next to it, and her leg thrown over his.

Frozen in the same position, he'd been awake for hours, listening to Sharon's even breathing and steady heartbeat while waging war with his conscience.

According to Julian, as long as Robert used condoms, Sharon couldn't turn. But that wasn't a foolproof method. There was no reason to believe that it was more effective at preventing transition than it was at preventing unwanted pregnancy.

Julian had suggested waiting until Robert was sure of his feelings for her, and hers for him. But what if a condom failed and Sharon transitioned without being told?

It was wrong. Turning a Dormant without her knowledge was dishonest.

They'd been seeing each other almost every day for the past two weeks, but it was not long enough to make such life-altering decisions. After all, he and Carol had been together for much longer than that, and things had ended between them.

The difference was that Carol had never claimed to have feelings for him other than gratitude. On his part, he'd been convinced that he loved her, but with the perspective of time and distance, he'd realized that he'd been more in love with the concept of finding an immortal mate than with Carol herself. She was a beautiful woman, sensual and passionate. And she was kind, despite what everyone thought of her after she'd kicked him out. But she wasn't his one and only.

Was Sharon?

Robert was afraid of even entertaining the thought. What if he was convincing himself they had something special the same way he'd done with Carol?

Except, this time, the consequences of his mistake could be dire. If he weren't Sharon's fated mate, he'd better stand aside and let the right man step up.

The rage that thought brought about was as startling as it was terrifying.

It had been ages since Robert had felt the impulse to kill. He despised that dark part of himself, that monster that had time and again burst out of him, providing the edge he'd needed on the many battlefields he'd fought on.

He refused to be that guy, that unthinking, vicious killing machine. How many children had he orphaned? How many women had he widowed?

Those thoughts had always come haunting him after the killing was done. But never in the heat of the battle. That was why he never wanted to be a soldier again. The monster inside him was still there, buried deep, but always at the ready to emerge in the right circumstances.

The thing that terrified him the most was that the killing frenzy would emerge somewhere other than the battlefield. Like it had now at the thought of Sharon with someone else.

She stirred, turning to the other side and pulling the blanket up to her nose. Robert tucked it under her to keep her warm.

In the next room, he heard Julian get out of bed. A

moment later he heard him in the bathroom, flushing the toilet and turning the shower on. It was easy to imagine Julian standing under the spray, lifting his too handsome face to the water and flexing muscles no doctor should sport.

He was the type of male any female craved. Not only was Julian good-looking, smart, and well-educated, he was also young and untarnished by a dark past. Robert envied the guy's easy smile and cheerfulness, an attitude only someone who'd never endured or witnessed horrors could hold on to.

What if Julian was the one for Sharon?

As the uncontrollable rage seized Robert again, he shifted sideways and got out of bed without disturbing the mattress. It wasn't safe for him to remain in the apartment while the monster lurked so close to the surface. The best way to subdue it was to exorcise it by exhausting the body.

After a quick visit to the en-suite bathroom, Robert pulled on a pair of loose exercise pants, a T-shirt he intended to later discard, and running shoes. He wasn't supposed to leave the apartment once he got there after work, but he was only hitting the gym.

After all, he'd used that route every morning when going to his office in the underground and later returning home. Because this level wasn't occupied by the clan, the corridor and the guest elevators were all rigged with cameras. He had no doubt he'd been followed on the monitors every time he made his way to and from work.

Stepping outside, he waved at the camera, pointed to his running shoes, and mouthed, "Going to the gym."

He took the guest elevator to the lobby, where he ducked through the hidden door to the other elevator bank that served the clan and took one down to the gym level.

Thankfully, at four in the morning, the place was deserted, and there was no one to watch him demolish a punching bag.

CHAPTER 37: BRIDGET

"*R*elax, you're going to be great." Turner squeezed Bridget's hand.

She was so nervous her neck was sweaty, and her blouse was sticking to her back. "I need to change clothes. I'm covered in sweat."

"There is no time."

"I know."

He glanced behind her at what was definitely a big wet stain on the silk. She was an idiot for choosing this outfit, thinking only about how good she looked in it instead of practical things like absorbent fabric in a dark color.

"You should put the jacket on."

"Then I'll be even hotter."

"It's not hot in here, and the jacket will cover the wet spots. Just knowing that will help you relax, and you'll stop sweating."

"Can you grab it for me? I left it over there." She pointed at the chair she'd left it on.

Everything she was wearing was new. The black skirt suit, the white silk blouse, the black pumps. With her dark red hair, which she had decided at the last moment to leave unbound, Bridget didn't need more color on her to distract

175

people from paying attention to her presentation. She would look professional in the pencil skirt and tight fitting jacket, with only the collar of her white blouse peeking out. She was going to sweat even more, but at least no one would notice.

Crap, she'd forgotten about the cameras. Her speech was going to be broadcast live at the Alaskan and Scottish keeps. The strong lights directed at her would make her even hotter. Not to mention the worst part—the close-ups. Everyone would be able to see the perspiration gathering on her temples and her upper lip.

Turner came back with her jacket and helped her put it on. "Take a deep breath." He massaged her shoulders. "Another one," he said. "Pretend that your audience is comprised of children. Speak slowly, enunciate, and pause between segments. You want to give them time to process. Don't forget that you've been living and breathing the subjects for weeks, and what is by now self-explanatory to you might baffle your audience."

As his hands kept massaging, Turner's calm voice did to her nerves what his hands did to her shoulders—eased the tension.

"And remember," he continued. "Everyone likes you and respects you. This is your family, not a bunch of strangers." He gave her shoulders one last squeeze before giving her a push toward the stage.

Victor had made the same comments before, which resulted in a major rewrite of her presentation. Before, it had sounded like an elegant speech prepared for a doctors' convention. The new version reflected the way Bridget talked to her friends. Simple, direct, and without a lot of fluff.

Plastering a smile on her face, Bridget walked up to the podium with her head held high and her back straight.

"Good evening, everyone. I'm honored to have the privilege of speaking in front of the big assembly. Thank you for coming." Bridget took a deep breath and plunged into the presentation she had practically memorized.

"Human trafficking is a more palatable way of referring to sex slavery. But I prefer to call it as it is. Most of the victims are young women and girls. In Third World countries, twelve-year-old girls and younger are sold into prostitution. Countless lives are ruined, and no one is doing anything about it. It goes unchecked, unpunished, and is rarely talked about or reported in major media outlets. Instead of a public outcry, there is silence. It's an ugly subject no one wants to touch."

There were three large screens on the stage. On the one to her left, Bridget could see the Scottish assembly with Sari sitting in the first row. On the one to her right, she could see Annani and her much smaller group.

The screen right behind her was dedicated to the presentation. Visuals were often more powerful than the spoken word. Bridget had prepared a number of charts, pictures, and several short video clips.

"Let's start with some numbers." She clicked on her remote, and the first chart appeared on the big screen for everyone to see. The next several minutes were dedicated to showing the extent of the worldwide phenomenon.

Her audience reacted as she'd expected—murmurs of surprise and outrage, tight lips and heads shaking, and even a few gasps. When she moved to the personal stories segment, there were also tears.

Bridget had debated long and hard whether to include them or not. On the one hand, she wanted to stay away from the dramatic, which might have been perceived as manipulative, but on the other hand, people needed to internalize the personal tragedy and the devastation, which could not have been achieved by talking about the problem at large.

The third segment, which she'd named 'hope,' was dedicated to what could be done. Her audience looked excited, the sad expressions replaced by determined ones.

So far so good.

The big question was how they were going to react to the fourth segment that talked about the financial burden.

"Our long-term goal is, and always has been, to help humanity evolve by encouraging education and innovation and pushing the ideas of freedom and equal opportunity to all. We are making good progress, but we are decades if not centuries away from achieving that goal. In the meantime, we cannot watch the suffering without doing something about it. I know it's a deviation from the way we've done things since Annani set us upon this journey, and I know tremendous resources are needed to make even a small dent in this problem. I know we cannot do this alone. However, I believe that if we give this boulder its first push, the momentum will carry it the rest of the way."

Bridget glanced to her right, searching Annani's face for her reaction. Earlier, Kian had emailed the goddess the revised budget and the much less ambitious plan they'd devised as per her instructions. Hopefully, it was enough.

When Annani finally nodded, Bridget felt faint with relief. Half the battle was already won. From now on it was going to be easy.

Joining her on the stage, Kian raised his hand to quiet the murmurs. "It's time to vote. All those in favor, please rise and raise your hands."

The first to stand were the council members and acting Guardians of both keeps, followed by about one-third of the audience.

That wasn't good enough. They needed a unanimous vote, and there was only one way it was going to happen.

Everyone's eyes turned to Annani.

With a smile, the goddess rose to her feet, but instead of raising her hand, she started clapping.

A moment later, all three assembly halls were roaring with claps, and every clan member who was old enough to vote was standing.

Mission accomplished.

Almost.

Bridget saved the call to the Guardians for last. The success, or conversely failure, of this part was almost as pivotal to the plan as the financial one.

CHAPTER 38: TURNER

*T*urner was honored by Kian's invitation to witness the clan's big assembly vote on the proposed plan, and grateful for the opportunity to observe the democratic proceedings.

He'd gotten several suspicious looks before Anandur had taken him under his big wing, seating Turner in the front row between himself and a council member named Edna, who'd been gracious enough to explain that the clan didn't operate as a pure democracy. Not every decision needed a vote, but then even the goddess couldn't overrule the big assembly's vote on those that did.

It was a hybrid system, which Edna assured him had withstood the test of time.

Turner listened intently to the councilwoman's explanations until the moment the two big screens flanking the podium lit up, and he'd gotten his first look at the goddess. No one had to point her out to him; he knew right away who she was, and not because of Bridget's Little Mermaid story.

When whoever was filming the goddess, and the group of immortals living with her, zoomed in on her impossible face, Turner's breath caught in his throat. Ancient eyes in a youthful face that was so beautiful he could not look away.

There was a glow around her, and it was nothing like the halo artists depicted above angels' heads. Every exposed part of her body seemed to emit a soft light.

He wondered whether it was safe for a human to be exposed to her. Had the men she'd seduced in order to have children died following the encounter?

Had it been worth it?

He had a feeling it had.

"The Clan Mother has this effect on people," Edna whispered in his ear. "Even on us who are familiar with her. I've seen Annani countless times, and I'm still awed every time anew."

Turner could do little other than nod in agreement. His eyes refused to leave the incredible sight.

"She can dim the effect when she wants," Edna said. "Otherwise she could've never interacted with humans."

"Is it dangerous to be near her? For a human?" Turner asked without looking at Edna.

"Not unless you anger her. She might look like love personified, but Annani has a temper, and she is impulsive."

Curious to find out more, Turner finally forced his gaze away from the goddess and looked into Edna's kind eyes. "Does she hurt those who anger her?"

Edna smiled. "She can give a verbal lashing like any other irate female with a diva complex. But nothing more dangerous than that. Annani is compassionate. Overly so, if you ask me. She never uses her power to do harm."

Interesting.

The way the councilwoman talked about the goddess, openly and without fear, one would think she was gossiping about a beloved aunt. Edna had respect and genuine fondness for Annani, but she didn't worship her as a deity, and she also didn't hesitate to poke a bit of fun at the most powerful being on earth.

It spoke volumes about Annani's character and made him even more eager to meet her. To have so much power and not abuse it required incredible strength, an unyielding moral code, and a clarity of purpose. It seemed as if her only flaw was a bit of a diva attitude, but in his opinion, she was wholly entitled to it.

Turner would've given away his entire life savings for an audience with Annani. Regrettably, there was no chance of her granting it unless he transitioned, and even then there was no guarantee she would.

"Good evening, everyone." Bridget walked up to the podium, and everyone hushed.

Looking at her, no one would have suspected how anxious Bridget had been only moments before. The woman on the podium looked confident and professional.

He was so proud of her.

Bridget's presentation lasted about forty-five minutes and went without a hitch. Her audience ate from the palm of her hand, responding exactly as she wanted them to.

Well, that remained to be seen. Until the voting was done, nothing was guaranteed.

Then the moment of truth arrived, and Turner watched with dread as only about a third of the clan supported the initiative. Bridget would be devastated.

Hell, she wouldn't be the only one.

He'd been hoping to get the ball rolling before attempting his transition. If he died, he would check out peacefully knowing that he'd accomplished something important.

On the big screen, the goddess stood up and started clapping, and soon everyone was on their feet and clapping along.

The noise was deafening, but it was the best sound Turner had ever heard. Annani had backed their initiative, and the clan followed.

The clapping continued as Shai, Kian's assistant, counted the votes.

"We have a unanimous vote," he announced.

"Thank you, Shai," Bridget said, trying to look professional and not show the tremendous relief she was feeling.

"I have one more item on my agenda for tonight."

The room fell quiet, as did the other two, and people sat back down. She clicked her remote, and a slide with about a hundred names appeared on the screen behind her.

"I'm sure you recognize the names." She pointed at the screen. "This is a list of every Guardian who's ever served. The first eighteen names are those who are currently active. Nine here at this keep, six in Scotland, and Annani's three. That leaves seventy-six retirees."

Snickers and backslaps resounded throughout the room, as those seated next to ex-Guardians laughed at the term.

He and Bridget had debated which one to use, vacillating between those that were more flattering and those that sounded somewhat offensive. Eventually, they had settled on retirees as something in between.

"We need you," Bridget continued once the noise settled down. "These girls need you. They need powerful men like you to be their champions, their heroes, to show them that there are men who are not like the ones who took them and abused them, and to show the world what a few good men can do."

She paused, letting her words sink in.

"You have a chance to make a difference, to make the world a better place. Isn't that why you joined the force in the first place?"

She looked at the people sitting in front of her and then turned to those on the two screens flanking the podium.

"We need our army back to protect the clan when needed and help those who no one else will help."

She switched to the next PowerPoint presentation, showing slide after slide of the new village Kian had built for his people. "This beautiful place is remote and well protected, and yet close to all the amenities a big city like Los Angeles can provide. This is where you will be living."

She smiled and lifted a hand. "Before all of you hurry to pack your suitcases, I want to remind you that Sari needs you as well and that some of the brothel raids are going to be happening in her territory. So please, talk among yourselves and decide who stays and who comes here."

This was another tactic they'd discussed—assuming the win.

Bridget put back up the list of names. "I would love to get an answer from each one of you, either yea or nay, over the next several days. After that, I'm going to call those who are still facing difficulties leaving their current occupations and offer any help I can."

Turning toward Annani's screen, Bridget bowed. "Thank you, Clan Mother, for your support." She then turned to the other screen and bowed again. "Sari, thank you for helping organize this event." Lastly, she faced her live audience. "Everyone, thank you for your selfless support of this important cause. I'm proud to be a member of such an amazing family." She put her hand over her heart. "My clan. My people."

That last part hadn't been rehearsed.

Bridget's heartfelt gratitude was genuine, and everyone hearing it recognized it as such. The crowd erupted in applause, everyone present and those on the screens standing up as Bridget bowed again and then wiped tears from the corners of her eyes.

Turner clapped until his palms stung. *Well done, my lady, well done.*

*B*ridget's face hurt from smiling. Everyone wanted to congratulate her personally, ask questions, and give her hugs. It was amazing and exhausting, and she braced herself for spending several more hours doing the same.

After all, she couldn't refuse anyone, not after they'd unanimously approved her proposal.

Victor stood to the side, partially hidden behind one of the screens and trying to avoid the immortal stampede. As he was the only human present, she couldn't fault him for being cautious, but she longed for his embrace. This was his victory as much as it was hers. They had both worked hard to make this presentation a success.

He deserved to be in the spotlight just as much as she did.

Bridget cast him an apologetic smile, but he seemed satisfied remaining in the shadows. That was where Victor felt the most comfortable. It was obvious he didn't want the attention. Even if he were an immortal and part of the clan, he would have done exactly what he was doing now.

Bridget didn't mind one way or the other. She didn't crave the attention or shy away from it. But it would have been nice to get out of there, kick off her high heels, and relax with a drink.

It had been a long and intense journey that had culminated in an emotionally charged performance, and she was exhausted.

"You've done great." Kian pulled her into a hug, which was a rarity for him. The guy wasn't into displays of physical affection except with his wife. On the few occasions Bridget had interacted with the couple in a social setting, she'd been embarrassed for Syssi because Kian insisted that his wife sit in his lap, and he kept stroking her back as if she was his comfort blanket.

In a way she was. Syssi had a calming effect on Kian, for which everyone in the keep was grateful. Without her, the guy would have been intolerable.

"Thank you." She made a move to push away from him, but Kian wrapped his arm around her shoulders and held on.

"If I don't get you out of here, you're going to fall down on your face from fatigue," he whispered, but it was loud enough for those standing close to them to hear.

He waved a hand in a shooing motion. "Let the good doctor rest after the tremendous job she's done. Bridget is tired and needs to go home. Whatever you want to tell her or ask her can be done via text or email tomorrow. She is done for tonight."

"Thank you again." She leaned her head against his bicep as Kian walked her out of the assembly hall. Turner followed a step behind them, walking in Kian's big shadow.

"Come up to the penthouse. Otherwise, you'll get accosted in the elevators. Syssi is making cappuccinos."

"What I need now is a drink, not a cappuccino," she said as they entered the penthouse's dedicated elevator.

Kian let go of her as soon as the doors closed. Bridget leaned against the wall and extended her hand to Victor. "I need a hug."

Turner glanced at Kian, then embraced her for about two seconds, clapping her back and murmuring, "I'm proud of you."

Her guy wasn't into public displays of affection either.

Syssi, on the other hand, had no such qualms. "You were awesome," she squealed and pounced on Bridget as soon as Kian opened the door to their penthouse.

"Thank you. It was exhausting."

Syssi led her to the couch. "I can imagine." She pushed the ottoman closer. "Take off your shoes and put your feet up. They must be killing you after standing up for so long."

"They are." Bridget followed Syssi's advice.

To her great surprise, Turner sat on the ottoman, lifted one of her feet into his lap, and started massaging.

The groan she emitted sounded like she was having a mini orgasm.

Victor chuckled. "Better?"

"Yes. Please don't stop."

Kian walked over to the bar, where Syssi got busy with her cappuccino machine. "What would you like to drink, Bridget?"

"Something sweet but strong. I need to unwind."

"You can make her my version of a Moscow Mule," Syssi suggested.

"Sounds interesting. What's in it?"

"Ginger ale, ginger paste, fresh lime juice, and mango-flavored vodka."

"Yummy. Just don't skimp on the vodka."

"For you, Turner?" Kian asked.

"Whatever you're drinking."

"Scotch?"

"Sure."

Victor switched to her other foot, eliciting another inappropriate moan.

"We have a guest room you can use." Syssi handed Bridget her drink and sat on the couch next to her, a cappuccino cup cradled between her palms. "The problem with you Scots is that you all like your alcohol so much. Hardly anyone wants to taste my cappuccinos, which are amazing if I do say so myself. I think I make the best ones in town."

"Don't brag." Kian handed Turner a glass, eyed the spot next to Syssi on the couch, then sighed and sat on one of the armchairs. "Before you know it you'll be running the new café in the village. You'll get sick of making cappuccinos in no time."

Bridget stifled a giggle. Syssi was just saved from sitting in Kian's lap again.

Except, a moment later the woman rose to her feet and went to sit on her husband's lap anyway. As she settled against him, his hand went to work stroking her back, and his facial muscles relaxed.

Did Syssi know she had such a profound effect on Kian?

Probably. Or maybe she just enjoyed the closeness as much as he did.

"That was a clever move on your part to show the Guardians pictures of the village," Syssi said. "The place is beautiful, and the individual houses are such a big departure from the almost communal living we have here in the keep, and at the two other strongholds. It's a powerful incentive."

Bridget sighed and let her head drop back on the couch's down-filled cushion. "I threw in everything I could think of. If that doesn't work, we are screwed because I'm out of ideas."

"It will work," Victor said. "I was watching the expressions on the faces of some of the men. I think you will have a good turnout."

"I agree with Turner," Kian said. "When you finished the segment with the personal stories, the guys I watched looked ready to kill. And when you finished the segment about what can be done, they looked excited."

Bridget took a sip of the Moscow Mule. It was good, so she took another sip, and then another, until most of the drink was gone. It wasn't enough alcohol to affect her, but it tasted great. She could go for another.

"We will know by tomorrow."

Syssi cast her a worried look. "Will you be able to sleep?"

"Oh, yeah, like a baby." Bridget waved a hand. "I've done my part to the best of my ability, and I have no regrets. The rest is up to the Fates."

CHAPTER 40: TURNER

By the time they had left Kian's and got back to
their own apartment, Bridget was swaying on her
feet. Holding on to her, Turner wondered whether the
culprit was fatigue or alcohol. She'd ended up drinking three
of Syssi's vodka and ginger ale concoctions.

Bridget kicked off her shoes the moment they crossed the
threshold and, not bothering to pick them up, headed down
the corridor to the master bedroom. She shrugged off her
jacket, letting it fall on the floor, then pulled her blouse over
her head and let it drop too.

With a smile, Turner collected the discarded items of
clothing and followed her to the bedroom. The trail
continued into the bathroom, where he found her standing
naked and looking at the shower's faucet as if it were an alien
contraption she had no idea how to operate.

Bridget was definitely drunk.

"Would you like me to draw you a bath?" He picked up
the rest of the garments, put the suit and blouse in the dry-
clean bin, and the bra and panties in the delicates hamper.

She glanced at the jacuzzi tub, then back at the shower,
and again at the tub. "I can't decide."

He reached around her and turned on the faucet. "You

look too tired for a bath." Or rather too drunk, but he was being polite.

"Okay." She waited for the steam to fill out the shower enclosure before stepping inside.

Leaning against the vanity, Turner watched her stand under the spray. Should he get in there with her?

He shook his head. She was exhausted. The best he could do for her was make sure she didn't fall and then carry her to bed and tuck her in. It was good Bridget was a small woman, or he would not have trusted himself to hold her up. He felt weak, and his coordination was all messed up.

Bridget had been too frantic in the days leading up to her presentation to notice that he hadn't been himself. Not wishing to distract her attention from where it needed to be, Turner hadn't admitted the severity of his symptoms, or that he was contemplating stopping the treatments.

Bridget would be furious with him, but Turner just couldn't function like that. He would give it another week and if things didn't improve he was going to stop.

As Bridget turned the faucet off, Turner grabbed a towel and fluffed it out, then waited with his arms outstretched for her to step into it.

"Thank you," she said as he wrapped her in the towel and lifted her up.

"How is your head?"

She frowned. "My head?"

"You're drunk."

"No, I'm not. You think such an itsy bitsy amount of vodka can get me drunk?"

"If not drunk, then tipsy."

"A little," she admitted, resting her head on his chest.

"You'll be good as new tomorrow morning." He lowered her to the bed, pulled the towel from under her, and covered her with the blanket. "Goodnight." He kissed her cheek.

Bridget's hand closed around his wrist. "Where are you going?"

"To the bathroom. Do you need anything?"

A crooked smile was his answer. "Always. I'm in the mood to celebrate."

He felt his impaired libido stirring to life. "Aren't you tired?"

Bridget flung the comforter off. "Not for this." She beckoned him with a sultry smile.

Desire for her burned hot in his mind, but his body followed the brain sluggishly, the physical response diminished in intensity and speed.

Bridget had been most understanding and hadn't complained. Nevertheless, her acceptance didn't make it any less embarrassing.

It was quite ridiculous.

His sexual drive and prowess in bed had never played a major role in Turner's self-perception, and he'd been proud of the fact that unlike most men he wasn't ruled by his dick.

Apparently, that wasn't true. As soon as the chemo affected his sexual drive and performance, Turner's confidence in his masculinity had taken a nosedive.

Hell, it was much worse than that. He was losing confidence in his ability to perform his job. If he had anyone he trusted to hand over the few open cases he still had to take care of, Turner would have done it without giving it a second thought. He couldn't afford mistakes or oversights. In his field that meant unnecessary suffering at the least and unnecessary loss of life at worst.

"I'm waiting," Bridget said.

"Let me grab a quick shower first."

She frowned. "You showered this morning."

"So did you."

"What's wrong, Victor?"

"Nothing." Turner leaned, cupping a breast as he kissed her. "I want to smell good for you." He tweaked her nipple before straightening up. "I'll be quick."

"You'd better."

In the shower, Turner braced his hands against the glass enclosure and let his head hang between his outstretched arms. As much as his head wanted to get in the game, his dick had other ideas, hanging loose and useless between his legs. He couldn't even get mad at the malfunctioning appendage because it wasn't its fault.

The worst part was the loss of control over his body. He hated it more than all the actual symptoms put together.

It wasn't even about letting Bridget down. She knew what was going on and was willing to pay the price, suffering the consequences of the treatment along with him. Besides, he knew how to pleasure the woman into an explosive orgasm in other ways.

Back in the bedroom, he found Bridget asleep, the comforter covering her up to her chin and hiding her beautiful body from his eyes. A moment of indecision passed as he contemplated letting her sleep or waking her up with a kiss. The former was the coward's way out, the latter was what he wanted to do.

Hell, he wanted his mouth all over her, starting with those partially parted puffy lips, moving over to the long column of her throat, and then feasting on her luscious breasts.

He loved the way her nipples puckered at the slightest touch.

Bridget was the most responsive woman he'd ever been with. Was it because she was an immortal female who was more lustful than the average human woman? Or was it her reaction to him? And only him?

A guy could hope.

Still warm from the shower, Turner didn't feel too bad about peeling the comforter off Bridget and quickly covering her up with his body, shielding her from the room's chill.

"Hello," she murmured without opening her eyes. "This feels nice. You're like a warming blanket."

Not exactly what a man wanted to hear. Except, he knew

how to make her sing a different tune to lyrics that didn't include nice and blanket.

As he kissed her, his palms followed the contours of her body, brushing the sides of her breasts, dipping into her narrow waist, then getting a handful of her flaring hips.

Her arms wrapping around his neck, Bridget licked into his mouth, deepening the kiss.

He brought his left hand just beneath her breast and brushed his thumb over her nipple.

"Oh, yes..." she groaned as he cupped her breast.

Turner dipped his head and sucked the hardened bud into his mouth, swirling his tongue around and flicking the tip before moving to Bridget's other breast. Not to neglect the one he'd just left, he covered it with his palm, warming it up before closing his fingers around the tip and tweaking it.

With a groan, Bridget's fingers dug into his scalp and her thighs parted under him. It was an invitation he wished he could accept but couldn't. His dick was semi-hard at best, and not for lack of wanting to be inside her.

Good thing that he hadn't anticipated any miracles and was mentally prepared to remain on the giving end. Her pleasure was his.

Curling down, Victor kissed her belly button. He kept kissing and nipping until his mouth reached the top of her bare slit.

She moaned and lifted up to meet his mouth.

Denying her was out of the question.

He pressed a soft kiss to that most sensitive spot on her body then flicked it with his tongue, once, twice, before running it down her slit and then up again.

She was so wet, so ready for him.

Cupping her bottom, he lifted her up to his mouth and penetrated her, fucking her with his tongue.

Alternating his rhythmic thrusts with short flicks over the top of her sex, he was giving her just enough to stoke the flames but not enough to combust. She went wild under him, her hips churning against his mouth, her head thrashing from side to side on the pillow, the mass of her red hair all tangled and wild around her face and shoulders.

Beautiful, passionate woman. He would always be hungry for more of her.

There was no need to slick his fingers with saliva before pushing two into her welcoming heat. Bridget was more than ready.

The pulsing clenches around his fingers were echoed by the pulsing of his cock. He was getting hard.

Thank fuck.

Bridget let out a throaty moan, her hips arching up as she was gripped by the powerful climax ripping out of her, then collapsed down on the mattress when it was over. In her post-orgasmic languor, she was a vision to behold. Her porcelain white skin flushed, her ample breasts heaving with her panting breaths, her limbs lying loose on the bed, Bridget closed her eyes and sighed a content, sleepy sigh.

But he wasn't done with her.

"Are you ready for more?"

CHAPTER 41: BRIDGET

*B*ridget's eyes popped open. Was she ready for more? Of course she was. She could repay the favor. "Always."

Except, when she made a move to sit up, Victor pushed her back down with a hand between her breasts, and a moment later she felt the head of his shaft push through her wet folds.

"Ah…" she moaned as he filled her up so perfectly the sensation brought tears to her eyes. It had been a while since he'd been able to do that. Did it mean his body was finally getting accustomed to the treatment?

She hoped so, but the pleasure was too intense for her to focus on anything other than where their bodies connected in the primal dance of male and female completing each other in the most perfect way.

It was on the tip of her tongue to blurt that she'd missed this, but she still had enough presence of mind to swallow the words. The last thing Victor needed was a reminder of that.

There was no preamble, no slow buildup, Victor went fast and hard from the first thrust on, as if afraid that his erection was going to falter at any moment and wanting to reach the finish line before it did.

She wanted that too.

Fates, she hadn't realized how much she craved the feeling of his shaft swelling a moment before his seed shot out and filled her. It was about more than sex, more than pleasure, it was about the affirmation of life. Even though the chances of him giving her a child were slim to none, the possibility was there.

A miracle could happen, and she would have a piece of him to cherish forever. A little Victor or Victoria.

Damn, this was the least appropriate time for morbid thoughts.

Gripping his muscular ass, Bridget pushed up, meeting him thrust for thrust and relishing the delicious friction.

His entire focus on reaching the point of no return, Victor was breathing hard, and droplets of perspiration were dripping down his neck.

Afraid that any sound she made would break his concentration and ruin his forward momentum, Bridget clamped her teeth over her lower lip and kept pumping her hips up and down, following Victor's increasing tempo.

This wasn't about her, and she didn't care if she got another orgasm out of it or not. This was for him.

Bridget almost cried with relief when Victor threw his head back and roared his release, and when his sperm hit her channel, she let herself go and climaxed along with him. It wasn't an earth-shattering orgasm like the first he'd given her tonight, but it was so much more precious to her.

Letting go of his buttocks, she crossed her arms over his back, holding him so tightly to her, she was crushing him.

"Too tight?" she whispered in his ear when he started wheezing.

"A little. But don't let go."

She eased her hold. "Never. I got you."

Fates, she was such a damn liar. It wasn't a promise she

197

could make. It wasn't up to her, and she wasn't the kind of woman who could blindly put her faith in the Fates and hope for the best.

It was such an impotent feeling.

What if she'd dedicated her time to cancer research instead of the elusive immortal genes?

Wasn't that more important?

The guilt washing over her was irrational, her mind was aware of that, but it didn't help her heart.

Even if she'd focused her entire medical career on researching cancer, chances were she would have not been more successful than others who did it on a much larger scale and collaborated their efforts. She was a one-woman show, and what she could do wasn't enough to help her own people let alone humanity at large.

Still draped over her like a blanket, Victor croaked, "I need another shower."

Bridget doubted he had an iota of energy left. She could have lifted him and moved him aside, but that would have hurt his male ego. Instead, she gave him a light push. "Roll over, lover. I'll get us some washcloths."

He chuckled as he did what she'd asked. "I like it when you call me lover. Makes me feel manly."

"You are all male, Victor." She rolled the other way and got out of bed. "You don't have an ounce of femininity in you."

"Are you saying I'm not in touch with my feminine side?" he said as she headed for the bathroom.

Bridget laughed. "I'm afraid not." He wasn't in touch with his inner self, male or female, but that was a talk for another time.

Wetting a few washcloths, she wiped her herself clean before returning to the bedroom with the rest.

"You're pampering me," he said as she wiped his chest and then his neck.

"I love doing so. In fact, I should be doing it more often."

Victor was so self-sufficient, it was easy to forget that pampering was not about fulfilling a real need but about showing affection. However, in Turner's case, it might have been a real need.

He'd lived such a solitary life. The man was probably starving for someone to care for him and not even aware of it. Bridget suspected he'd suppressed all such yearnings a long time ago.

Victor looked at her with guilt in his blue-gray eyes. "You're tired. I should be the one taking care of you."

"Next time. It's my turn tonight. I'm fully awake. It must be the adrenaline pumping me up."

Fortunately, he seemed too spent to argue.

Bridget put the second used up washcloth away and picked up a fresh one. "Turn around. I want to wipe down your back."

He did as she asked, and a minute or so later fell asleep, his deep rhythmic breaths causing her eyelids to droop.

When she was done with the fourth washcloth, Bridget dropped it on the nightstand, lay down next to Victor, and covered them both with the comforter.

"Good night, lover," she whispered in his ear.

There was no answer.

CHAPTER 42: ROBERT

*A*fter Robert had fed her, Sharon walked into the living room, sat on the couch, and put her feet on the coffee table. He liked seeing her so comfortable in his home. Unless she had an evening assignment, Sharon was coming over every day after work and staying most nights.

It was fortunate that she worked and lived in the same house and didn't have to worry about changing clothes in the morning.

"Robert, come watch with me. There is a new episode of *Altered Carbon*." She clicked the television on.

He followed her to the couch and handed her the Diet Coke she'd asked for. "Can't you watch it later?"

"Sure. It's Netflix. Do you want to watch something else?"

Sitting next to her, Robert cradled a bottle of Snake's Venom. One of Julian's many good qualities was stocking the fridge with a fresh supply of the beer whenever they ran low. Another reason not to kill the guy in a jealous fit.

Lucky for Julian, Sharon seemed indifferent to him, and the guy made every effort possible to make himself scarce when she was there.

"I'm not a fan of television." Robert popped the cap and took a gulp.

"I've noticed." She clicked the screen off. "Is it watching stuff in general, or is it just the shows I like to watch?"

Sharon was a big fan of science fiction and fantasy. Which was good. Her mind was open to the unusual. She wouldn't freak out when he told her.

"Fiction in general. Reality is stranger than anything people can imagine. It's more complex. I can see the plot holes in every episode, and it irritates me."

"Do you like reading?"

He nodded. "I can skip the parts I find boring or unrealistic."

Sharon chuckled. "Fiction is supposed to be unrealistic. If I wanted reality, I would watch the news."

It was his turn to chuckle. "Most of it is fiction as well."

"How so? Aren't they reporting the facts?"

"It's possible to report the exact same event in so many ways that the people watching one news outlet will be convinced it's black and the other that it is white and so on. They can show only the fragments that support whatever that outlet's agenda is, or their backers. They can interview supposed experts that will put the appropriate spin on the story, and so on. Bottom line is, it is very difficult for the common people to get the bare facts and draw their own conclusions when what they are reading and watching is the equivalent of a dramatized version."

She eyed him with curiosity in her eyes. "How do you know all that?"

He could've told her that he'd been at the center of some major events, and what had been reported had born little resemblance to what had happened on the ground. Instead, he chose the easy way out.

"You can go downstairs and buy three different newspapers, each following a different agenda, you can then read the leading story in all three, and you'll see what I'm talking about."

"Do you actually do that? Do you compare stories?"

He nodded. "I do that almost every day. I pick up several newspapers at the café and read the headline news, then I choose the story I want to get all the angles of. Sometimes you can piece together what really happened by reading opposing views."

Sharon leaned her head against his shoulder. "You're a dinosaur. No one reads actual newspapers. You can get it all online."

Small things like that gave away his real age. The young generation of humans didn't read anything on paper if they could help it. "I know. I like spreading the big newspaper and hiding behind it, so my coworkers don't bother me on my lunch break."

Sharon cast him an amused glance. "I bet those pesky coworkers are all female."

Mostly, but he wasn't going to admit it, or she would go into full-blown interrogation mode. Sharon was possessive of him, if not outright jealous, and he loved that she was. It meant that she valued him and that she considered him as hers.

The thing was, she had nothing to worry about. His life as the keep's gigolo was officially over. None of those females could compare to Sharon, and it wasn't as if he was speculating. He'd been with most.

"Your silence is as good as an admission. Tell them you're taken." She looked up at him and smiled. "Can I tattoo it on your forehead?"

"Tattoo what?"

"I belong to Sharon." She made air quotes.

"What if you dump me? I'll be stuck dating only girls named Sharon."

She cupped his cheeks and brought his face down for a kiss. "I'm never going to dump you. You're mine, so you'd better get used to the idea. I'm the only Sharon you'll ever date."

"I can live with that."

Her mouth gaped. "Really? That's what you have to say in response?"

Robert was confused. "What was I supposed to say?"

"How about that I am yours? Or that you want to tattoo your name on my ass?"

"I don't want to sound presumptuous."

Sharon rolled her eyes. "This is not our first date. You can tell me what you really think."

His mouth suddenly feeling dry, Robert lifted the bottle of Snake's Venom and took a long gulp. If he told her how he really felt she would get up and leave. Or maybe not. She'd been pretty blunt about her feelings.

"You sure you're ready for it? Because what I feel is pretty damn scary."

Nodding eagerly, she beckoned with her hand. "Give it to me, baby."

"I feel like I'm capable of killing any man you show interest in. So if you don't want to be responsible for anyone's untimely death, please ignore all other males."

She sighed. "Oh, that's so sweet."

Her reaction was not what he'd expected. Instead of being appalled by his murderous inclinations, she thought them sweet? Something was wrong with the girl.

He shook his head. "You're strange."

By the grin spreading across her face, she'd taken it as a compliment. "I know. I wouldn't go as far as killing anyone you dared ogle, but I could think of a nasty thing or two I would like to do to them." She pointed a finger at him. "Some girls might not mind their men's eyes straying, but if I catch you staring at another woman for more than a couple of seconds, you'll be in big trouble, mister."

"Come here." He lifted her and deposited her in his lap. "You have nothing to worry about. I have eyes only for you."

CHAPTER 43: SHARON

*F*inally, Robert was admitting his feelings. It wasn't as good as him telling her he loved her, but it was progress.

"Let's go to the bedroom," she whispered in his ear and wrapped her arms around his neck in anticipation of what was coming next.

Robert lifted her up as if she weighed nothing, which was unfortunately not so. She could lose fifteen or twenty pounds, five of which, at least, she'd gained because of him insisting on feeding her.

He cooked her dinner every time she came over, claiming he did it primarily for Julian and himself, but she knew it was Robert's way of showing her he cared. The table was always set up for a romantic dinner for two. Julian never ate with them, notoriously disappearing into his room within a few minutes of her arrival. His excuses were quite lame, either that he'd already eaten, or that he was taking a plate to his room to eat while watching a sports game.

It was weird that the hunky young doctor never went out or had a girl over himself. And it was also strange that Robert never took her out on a date. His excuses ranged from claiming that restaurant food was unhealthy, to him wanting her all for himself, and to his newfound love of cooking.

It might have all been a load of bull crap to cover up for some financial trouble he was in, but Sharon couldn't care less.

The guy was cooking for her. What was not to love about that?

Holding her up with one hand, Robert flung the comforter aside before lowering her to the bed and quickly covering her up. It was so sweet of him to remember she hated being cold. Not that Sharon really suffered from a particular sensitivity to it, but she preferred to get undressed under the blanket and didn't want to admit the real reason.

"Thank you."

"What for?" he asked.

"Remembering that I don't like being cold."

He looked puzzled, as he often did when she thanked him or complimented him on something. Robert either didn't think small things like that deserved her appreciation, or he wasn't used to compliments.

If there was one thing Sharon knew about relationships in general and men in particular, it was that taking the good for granted and only reacting to the bad was a sure way to get less of the former and more of the latter. She wasn't going to make this mistake with her most important relationship to date.

Robert was a keeper.

"I remember everything you tell me about what you like or don't like. I want you to be comfortable, and I want you to be happy. I'm not always sure what the best way to go about it is, but the least I can do is listen."

Definitely a keeper.

"That's one of the many things I love about you, baby."

Seeing the dumbstruck expression on his face, Sharon realized how what she'd said could be interpreted. Was

Robert one of those guys who ran at the mention of the word love?

Did she love him, though?

It was a bit too early to tell, especially since Sharon had never been in love and didn't know what it should feel like.

Let's see.

Handsome? Check.

Smart? Check.

Has a good job? Check.

Is hard working? Check.

I like being with him, in bed and outside of it? Check.

Can I imagine having babies with him? Check.

If that wasn't love, she didn't know what else was.

Robert still looked like a fish out of water. He opened his mouth to say something then closed it and frowned.

Her lips twitching with stifled laughter, Sharon asked, "Are you shocked?"

He rubbed his hand over his jaw. "I'm not sure. Should I be?"

She shrugged. "Not really. There is a lot to love about you, Robert. I knew that even before you took me to bed and showed me what great sex is like. Loving you is easy."

Robert plopped down on the bed as if suffering a fainting spell.

Sharon giggled. "Should I bring the smelling salts?"

"What?"

"You look pale."

Not amused at all, he pinned her with a hard stare. "Please don't joke about a thing like that. I'm a tough guy, and I can take a lot of beating, but I don't think I can take you telling me you love me and not mean it."

Wow. She must've hit a nerve.

It was one of the few times in her life Sharon was rendered momentarily speechless. Dropping the comforter, she got up to her knees and embraced Robert.

"I would never joke about a thing like that. I meant every

word. I've never been in love before, so I can't say this is it for sure, but what I feel for you is a hundred times more than I ever felt for any other guy." She chuckled. "I even thought that I would like to make babies with you, and I never thought about making babies before."

Robert let his head drop on her shoulder. "We need to talk," he mumbled in her ear.

Oh boy. So he was one of those guys who ran off when the word love was uttered, and she'd scared him away.

"Why?" she asked in a small voice.

"There are things you don't know about me, and if things are getting serious between us, I can't keep hiding them from you."

The big guy was trembling in her arms. What could be so horrible that it scared him so?

Did he suffer from PTSD?

Asking him straight up if he did might offend him, but she could go about it in a roundabout way. "I don't care about your military past. I know soldiers are sometimes forced to do things that leave them feeling guilty. If that's what is bothering you, I want you to know that I understand and accept whatever you had to do. But if you feel so horrible about it, maybe you should talk to a therapist. They can't reveal anything you tell them, so I think the army will be fine with you talking to one."

He shook his head. "That's not it, or rather it's only a small part."

Crap. She'd have to ask straight up. "Do you have nightmares about your time in the service?"

"It's not that either."

What else?

There was one more possibility. Potentially the worst one.

Sharon dropped her arms and moved back on the bed, distancing herself from Robert. "You're married."

That would explain why he never wanted to take her out,

or why he was strapped for cash. If he was living with Julian, he was probably separated from his wife but was still paying the bills.

Her heart sinking, Sharon tried to convince herself that it wasn't the end of the world, not if Robert had already left his wife before meeting her.

She wasn't a home wrecker.

He lifted his head. "What? No, I'm not married, and I've never been married."

"You have a bunch of illegitimate children."

"Where do you come up with this nonsense? No, I don't have any children." He rubbed the back of his neck. "At least not any that I know of."

Sharon rolled her eyes. "What am I to think when a guy gets all pale and tells me there is stuff about him I should know? The most common things are wife and children, the other thing is a drug addiction, which I know you don't have, or a gambling problem. Do you have a huge gambling debt or something? Is that why you never take me out? Because you have no money?"

Robert snorted. "I wish it was something as mundane as that."

Now he was scaring her. What could be worse than that?

"Do you have AIDS?"

"No. Will you stop asking ridiculous questions and let me talk?"

"I'm sorry. I'm too scared of what you're going to say. That's why I'm trying to guess."

"It's nothing bad. At least I don't think it is."

Well, that was a relief. "Okay, I'm going to shut it and listen."

"Let me pour you a drink. You might need it."

Way to alleviate her fears. A revelation that required a drink couldn't be good news.

CHAPTER 44: ROBERT

*A*s Robert poured a glass of wine for Sharon, he debated whether he was doing the right thing. By telling her the truth, he was disobeying Kian's orders and taking a considerable risk. If this was discovered, it could have dire consequences for him.

Could he trust Sharon to keep this a secret?

As a detective in training, she was accustomed to confidentiality and was aware of its importance. Eva, who knew her well, trusted her, which was another point in her favor.

Except, Sharon was a young woman and as such easily excitable. She could change her mind about him the next day or the next week or the next month, and he would be in a worse position than he'd been after leaving the Brotherhood. At least then he had Carol's support and the clan's gratitude. If Sharon left him and revealed what he'd told her, the loss would be catastrophic. Kian would lock him up and throw away the key, or put him in stasis like he'd done with the other Doomers the Guardians had captured.

Not executing them was a mercy, but only to an extent. Stasis was death, just not permanent.

Robert rubbed the back of his neck. Did immortals dream while in stasis?

He'd read that some humans dreamt while in a coma. But stasis seemed like an even deeper state than a coma. His guess was that there was no brain activity other than the minimum required to keep the body's systems from shutting down completely.

Perhaps he could ask Julian about that. Except, his questions about the Doomers resting down in the keep's catacombs might raise suspicions as to his intent. Not a complication he needed.

With the wine in one hand and another bottle of Snake's Venom in the other, Robert walked back into his bedroom to find Sharon in exactly the same position he'd left her.

She looked up at him with worried eyes. "Perhaps we should have this talk in the living room?"

He shook his head while closing the door behind him. It was better for Julian to assume that they were getting busy in the bedroom so he would put his noise-canceling headphones on.

Handing Sharon the wine glass, Robert sat next to her on the bed. "You know all those science fiction shows and those about paranormal stuff that you like to watch?"

She lifted a brow. "What about them?"

"Not all of it is fiction."

"Well duh, I know that. Paranormal phenomena are real, and I'm sure we are not the only intelligent living beings in the universe. Believing that is as absurd as believing that earth is a flat disk. Just because we can't see them or communicate with them doesn't mean they don't exist."

As he'd expected, Sharon had an open mind.

"There is more to it than just inexplicable phenomena and alien life on other planets." He looked into her eyes as he continued. "A divergent humanoid species has lived among humans since the beginning of history. In fact, according to legend, this divergent species created humanity, or rather jump-started its evolution."

"You mean the God myth? The one about creating Adam and Eve?"

"Gods. Plural. Did you ever read about the Sumerian gods?"

If she had, Sharon was much better informed than he'd been up until recently. History lessons hadn't been part of his education in the Doomer camp. It seemed that Lord Navuh preferred his warriors as ignorant as possible even about their own origins.

Most of what Robert now knew about immortal history he'd learned from Carol, like the fact that the Doomers and the clan had shared ancestry. He hadn't known that. There were rumors, of course, most of them so misleading and absurd that they were most likely planted on purpose to further confuse the soldiers and keep them from asking questions.

She shook her head. "I've read a little about the Egyptian pantheon, but I'm more familiar with the Greeks and the Romans." She tilted her head. "Is this what you wanted to talk to me about, or are you stalling?"

"I'm not stalling. I'm providing background."

"About mythology?"

Perhaps it was the wrong place to start. "Have you noticed anything strange about Eva?"

Sharon regarded him as if he had a screw loose. "Talk about a random subject change. But yeah, I've noticed a lot of strange things about my boss."

"Like what?"

Sharon took a few sips of her wine and then put the glass on the nightstand. "She looks like she is in her late twenties but talks and behaves like she is in her fifties. She is secretive, but that is probably because of what she does for a living. She used to disappear for days without telling us where she was going, and it wasn't on any jobs we knew of. But after she met Bhathian, she stopped doing that. There are many other little things. She's just odd."

211

"In all the years you've known her, did she change at all?"

Sharon waved a hand. "She must have damn good genes. Not even one wrinkle. And that body, you'd think she exercised every day to maintain that figure, but she doesn't. I don't know how anyone can eat the junk she eats and not gain weight. I'm green with envy."

Robert was taken aback. "Why would you envy her? You have a beautiful body."

Sharon patted his knee. "You're sweet. But please don't lie to me just to make me feel good. I could lose a few pounds."

Robert shook his head. Human females were obsessed with being thin. It hadn't always been like that. There had been times when voluptuousness was appreciated. With her slight feminine padding, Sharon would have not even qualified as such.

But that wasn't what this conversation was about. He needed to steer her back to the subject of Eva's ageless appearance.

"Would you say that Eva looks exactly the same today as she did when you first met her?"

Sharon nodded. "Except, she is happier now that she has Bhathian and is expecting a baby."

He'd been building up to this moment, but now that it was time for the punchline, Robert lost his nerve. Lifting the beer, he gulped the rest of it and then wiped his mouth with the back of his hand. "Eva didn't change at all during all the years you've known her because she is immortal. And the reason she often sounds and behaves like a grandmother is that she is probably older than yours."

Sharon snorted. "Good one, Robert. But you need to work on the delivery. A joke is not funny if it takes more than a minute to set up."

He took in a deep breath. "I'm not joking. Eva, Bhathian, Nathalie, Amanda, and everyone else Bhathian has introduced you to all immortal. I'm one too."

Reaching for the wine glass, Sharon picked it up, threw

the rest of the liquid down her throat, and then put the glass back down.

"I knew you were too good to be true. Delusional much?"

It wasn't going the way he'd thought it would. Sharon didn't believe him.

"If I showed you proof, would you believe me then?"

"What proof?"

"Kiss me, and I'll show you."

He'd planned on getting to the part about fangs and venom last, letting her absorb all the possible benefits of immortality before scaring her with his vampiric transformation, but this was the best proof he could provide.

She grinned. "I knew it was a drawn-out joke. Okay, I'll play along."

Up until now, he'd always controlled the kissing, not letting Sharon's tongue pass his lips. She was in for one hell of a surprise.

Used to Robert's mild dominance, Sharon didn't expect him to retract his tongue from her mouth and invite hers to follow. A long moment passed before she responded, but when she did, it was with gusto.

Climbing onto his lap, she plastered herself against his chest and kissed him while grinding her bottom into his groin.

His glands and fangs' response was predictably quick, and Robert braced for the moment Sharon would discover that.

"Ouch." She pulled away as her tongue scraped against one of his fangs. Focused on her injury, Sharon didn't look at him as she touched a finger to the bleeding spot and lifted it up to look at it. "I think you should see the dentist. You must've chipped a tooth."

"Look at me, Sharon," he slurred.

CHAPTER 45: SHARON

*H*er dream guy was turning out to be a toad. First was that stupid joke about immortals, and now he was drunk on all that Scottish beer he'd been gulping as if it were water. She'd read the label—the stuff had an alcohol content to knock out a horse.

With an exasperated sigh, Sharon licked her finger clean and lifted her eyes. "Holey moley!" She leaned away at the sight.

Robert had put in a pair of gleaming white fangs. "Shit, these things look realistic. And they are sharp too." She licked her finger again. "They should put a warning label on the packaging. No kissing with those babies in."

With a groan, Robert closed his mouth, not all the way because the prosthetic fangs protruded over his lower lip. "I never expected you to give me so much trouble over this," he said while scratching his head.

His words had come out slurred, but at least now she knew it was the prosthetics' fault and not the beer's.

"I think I'm being a very good sport about all this." She waved a hand at him. "Are you and Julian planning a costume party?"

Robert clasped her hand. "Look into my eyes and tell me

what you see. Then try to pull one of my fangs out."

His eyes were glowing.

Sharon looked around for the source of the reflected light, but couldn't find any. She looked again. Robert's eyes were still glowing.

What the fuck?

Had he put something in her drink and she was hallucinating?

Reaching with her finger, she touched the top part of a fang. It was smooth, exactly the same as tooth enamel. She leaned closer and patted the gums above the fang. If this was a prosthetic, it was excellent quality.

Robert lifted her off his lap and put her down on the bed so her back was propped against the pillows. "It's not a fake. My fangs elongate when I'm aroused or when threatened. I have venom glands that produce venom. The composition of the venom is different when I bite during sex than when I bite to incapacitate an opponent, so you don't need to worry about harmful effects. What you get is a powerful dose of aphrodisiac and euphoric. It also has healing properties."

He was dead serious. "Look at my mouth and watch my fangs retract."

The fangs were shrinking in front of her eyes or rather receding into the gums. No prosthetic could do that.

There was still the possibility that Robert had drugged her, but she didn't really believe he had. Her mind was clear and she wasn't woozy. Besides, what did he have to gain by drugging her? She was already in his bed.

"Start from the beginning, and please talk slowly because the circuits in my brain are not ready to accept what you're telling me. You weren't kidding about reality being stranger than my shows."

Robert sighed in relief. "I'm glad you finally believe me. Otherwise, I would have had to cut myself to provide further proof."

"Why?"

"Immortals heal very quickly. If I made a cut on my forearm, the wound would have closed while you were watching and after a few moments not even a scar would've remained."

"Fascinating. What else can you do?"

"I'm stronger than a human male, and all my senses are enhanced. I can see better in the dark, I can hear what is being said in the next apartment, and I can smell strong emotions like fear and arousal. I can also thrall humans and make them forget things or remember things that never actually happened."

So he could've made her see fangs that weren't there, but being able to do that was even stranger than having fangs. "You don't suck blood with those, do you? Because I've seen you eat regular food."

"I'm not a vampire."

"Right. Can you teleport?"

He chuckled. "No. But I can make a human believe that I do."

"You keep saying you can do all those things to humans. Does it mean you can't do that to other immortals?"

"Correct. Immortals can't manipulate each other's minds." He seemed impressed with her logic. "When you decide to listen, you actually pay attention to the details."

"Duh, I'm an assistant detective."

Was it really such a huge leap of faith to believe a divergent humanoid species lived on earth along with regular humans? If she could accept that aliens existed, why not have them living on earth?

The hardest part was getting used to the idea that Robert was one of them.

He smiled. "A detective should know which questions to ask, and you didn't ask the most important one."

"Which is?"

"Why am I telling you this?"

That seemed obvious. "You want to come clean, right? Get it off your chest?"

He shook his head. "If it were only about getting it off my chest, I would've never told you any of this because I'm not supposed to. Keeping our existence secret is a top priority for immortals. In fact, I can get in a lot of trouble if the others discover that I revealed who I am to you. I trust you to keep it a secret and pretend you don't know anything, which will be difficult around the other immortals."

Sharon waved a hand. "Being a great actress is part of my job. No one will suspect a thing."

"Good."

"So why are you telling me this?" She hoped the answer was that he loved her and wanted no secrets between them.

"A tiny fraction of the human population carry dormant immortal genes. The venom of an immortal male can activate those genes in a Dormant. They can become immortals."

"What about an immortal female's venom?"

Crap, did Eva grow scary long fangs when she got horny? No wonder she'd never dated before meeting Bhathian.

"Immortal females don't have fangs or venom. Only the males do."

"That's not fair." Sharon crossed her arms over her chest.

"On the other hand, these special genes are only transferred through the mothers. Which means that if you are a Dormant and you have a child with a human, that child will carry the immortal genes. If I have a child with a human, that child will not carry them."

That evened the score. Although she would've loved to have fangs. It would've been cool.

"Wait a minute. How do you know I'm a dormant carrier? Did you take a blood sample from me?" She narrowed her eyes. "Did Julian?" After all, he was a doctor, and if he was rooming with Robert, he was probably an immortal too.

Robert shook his head. "I wish it was that easy to identify Dormants. There is no blood test, and even genetic screening doesn't reveal anything. One hypothesis was that Dormants have paranormal abilities, and some of them do, but some don't. We go by a hunch. Eva is sure every member of her crew is a Dormant. Tessa, by the way, has already transitioned."

Sharon sat up straight. "What?" What kind of a detective was she that this had happened under her nose and she hadn't had a clue? Though in her defense, how the hell could she have suspected something that was completely in the realm of fiction up until now?

"Remember when she got sick? That was the start of the transition."

"Jackson is an immortal."

Robert nodded.

"Did he tell Tessa before?"

"I don't know. They don't tell me everything." He chuckled, but it was without mirth. "In fact, they don't tell me anything. I'm an outsider, a former enemy who crossed over and is still not fully trusted. For some reason, though, Amanda liked me and decided to give me a chance with you. Or maybe she thought we fit. I don't know. I'm just grateful that she did. That is the real reason why I can't take you out on dates. I'm not allowed to leave. Not without someone to keep an eye on me, that is." He lifted his arm with the odd piece of jewelry he always wore. "This is a locator cuff. If I try to leave they would know."

It angered her that he was treated like that. Robert was a good man. "It's not fair that they keep you locked up and still expect you to work for them." Unless he'd lied to her about his job.

"No, I like to work, and I'm getting paid for it. Eventually, I'll gain their trust." He put a hand on her thigh. "I was supposed to wait until I was sure what we have is real, and only then tell you. The thing is, once I did, you would have become a prisoner in here just like me. After you transition and become part of the clan, you'll be trusted to walk around with the secret of immortals' existence. But I didn't want you imprisoned while we waited for that to happen."

"Thank you. I appreciate that. I would have hated being locked up. And I hate that they are doing it to you."

"It's okay. I don't mind. Or rather I didn't mind until I met you."

Damn, and she'd kept pushing him when he couldn't have done anything about it. "I'm sorry about giving you a hard time over that. I figured you were strapped for cash or something like that."

"I'm not. As I said, they pay me well, and I have very few expenses. I save most of my pay."

"That's good." Sharon fiddled with a corner of the comforter, pulling out loose threads. "So let me get it straight. If I am a Dormant, and you bite me, your venom mojo is supposed to activate my immortal genes?"

"Yes."

She touched her neck at the spot she now knew he'd bitten her. She'd thought it was a phantom bite. There was a lingering memory of the sensation but no physical mark. "You bit me here."

He nodded.

"So why am I still human? Maybe Eva is wrong, and I'm not a Dormant?"

Robert rubbed a hand over his chin, which meant he was uncomfortable. If what he'd revealed before didn't bother him, whatever he was about to say next was probably devastating.

Sharon braced for the worst.

"We've used condoms. To activate a female Dormant, the biting has to be done together with insemination. I felt it wasn't right to turn you without your consent. Now that you know, you can decide if you want to become an immortal or not."

Sharon couldn't help the giggle that escaped her throat. "So the only thing standing between me and immortality is a rubber?"

"Basically."

That was it. The laughter that burst out of her sounded hysterical and for a good reason.

This was the craziest thing she'd ever heard, and yet in her heart and in her gut, she knew it was all true. Hell, on some level Sharon had always known that she was different. There was a reason she couldn't stick with any guy until Robert came along, or that the only people she'd ever felt truly comfortable with were Eva, Nick and Tessa, and later Bhathian and his gang.

They were her people.

CHAPTER 46: KIAN

*T*he Guardians were coming back, and the keep was buzzing with excitement.

A blackboard had been hung on the wall across from the clan's private elevator bay, listing the names of those who were coming back within an hour or two of him getting notified.

Waiting for the council members and Guardians to arrive, Kian wondered who was the source of the leak. Most times Anandur was the usual suspect, but this time Kian was betting on Shai.

A day after Bridget's presentation there were already forty-two names up there, and the list was still growing. Kian wanted to commend whoever was leaking the news. The morale at the keep had never been higher.

Hell, he hadn't felt so optimistic about the clan's future since the day they'd leveled the Doomers' camp in Ojai and rescued the women that had been imprisoned there.

One more milestone on the road that had led him to this date.

The Fates had been pushing Kian to do something about the slave market for a while now, but he'd been slow to connect the dots.

Perhaps it had taken him so long to realize where all of this was leading because he was a skeptic and an iconoclast. Kian had scoffed at his mother's belief in fate. He'd regarded it as nonsense, a comforting illusion created by people to explain the inexplicable and to make sense of a chaotic world.

Annani was well aware of his dismissive attitude toward her beliefs, and yet she hadn't been offended by it. She'd known the day would come when he would be forced to accept that there was some higher power at work.

He still didn't believe, not fully, but he could no longer dismiss it either. Even if he could somehow convince himself that the chain of events leading up to his intervention in the abhorrent sex trade was random, he could not do that in regards to the Dormants.

Suddenly, after centuries of searching, they were popping up one after the other. Even a skeptic like him could not in good conscience call it a coincidence. Especially since it seemed it wasn't the result of Amanda's efforts. Callie had no paranormal abilities, and neither did Tessa. There had been nothing to indicate that they were Dormant other than their mates' reaction to them.

He wished the reaction could be measured or quantified, and that it could be used to search for more. Except, the reaction was subjective. Brundar hadn't reacted to Tessa, and Jackson would not have reacted to Callie. Bottom line, searching for Dormants was futile. As much as he hated the thought, it seemed that the Fates decided when and who.

"Penny for your thoughts," Amanda said as she walked into his office and took the seat to his right.

"I can't believe you're the first one to arrive."

"That's what you were thinking so hard about?"

"No. I was thinking about Dormants and how we have to rely on the fucking Fates to find them."

Amanda slapped his back. "Shush, you idiot. Do you want to provoke their wrath? You should be thanking them

222

morning and night for Syssi." She grinned. "And me too. I was the matchmaker."

"Thank you, yenta."

She kissed his cheek. "You see? That wasn't so hard."

Despite calling her a yenta, he could not have made Amanda happier if he'd invited her mate to sit on the council. Not that Dalhu would've ever accepted the position. The ex-Doomer had become an artist and loved what he was doing. If needed, Kian had no doubt Dalhu would fight by his side as he had at Ojai, maybe even relish the rush of excitement, but otherwise Amanda's guy was satisfied with his solitary artistic endeavors.

Dalhu had earned his nirvana.

As the last participants were seated, Kian motioned to Shai to start the recording. He was no longer opening the sessions by announcing their number. There was no need. Shai added the necessary tag later while editing the footage.

This wasn't a regular council meeting though. Turner, a human, was present, as was Vanessa who wasn't on the council. The therapist was the first clan member Bridget invited to be part of the team she was putting together.

"Brandon, you're first." Kian addressed the media specialist who was now wearing two additional hats—a fundraiser organizer, and a permit facilitator with the various municipal agencies, expediting the clan's latest building project.

"I got a retired movie star, Belinda Rochester, if any of you remember her, excited about the project, and she is helping me organize the charity ball, by which I mean she took the project over. I trust her since she's done many of those in the past, successfully I might add. She freed up my time for all the other things I need to do. Like stroking the ego of Santa Barbara's mayor."

Kian arched a brow. "Why would you need to do that?"

Brandon leaned back in his chair and flashed his toothy smile, looking like a very well-dressed shark. "Do you want to rebuild the monastery in three months or in twenty-four?"

"It's impossible to do in three months."

Brandon's grin widened. "It is if we use the original plans, which should be fine to start with. I convinced the mayor that allowing an expedited process to restore what used to be a historical building, while at the same time providing a school for the girls, would be great publicity and help with his reelection."

"Was the building a historical site?" Edna asked. "I wasn't aware of that."

"No, but I claimed that it should've been. It was an old building. One of the first to be built in Ojai."

"Good work, Brandon," Kian said.

"Thank you. Now you need to find a fast crew to build it."

The fastest crew he'd ever had the pleasure of working with were the Chinese. It was good they didn't have another job lined up, a rarity for them, because he needed them to stay and build a new section for the village. All those Guardians needed a place to stay, and they had been promised houses in the village. The question was whether they could split up and rebuild the monastery as well. Perhaps they could bring in more people.

"I have a fast crew."

Brandon crossed his arms over his chest, stretching the fabric of his designer jacket. "The Chinese? Don't you need them for the new village?"

"It's not a new village, it's an extension of the old one. I will ask if they can bring more crews."

"But people are about to move in," Bridget said. "What about secrecy and security?"

Kian waved a dismissive hand. "It's not going to be a problem. I told the contractor we needed to protect the current occupants from the dust and the equipment of the new construction, and he suggested we build a tall, temporary fence separating the completed section from the new one."

"Do we have enough land to build on?" Amanda asked.

Onegus answered before Kian had a chance to. "We have the whole mountain and the area around it. We can build a city if we want to. Originally, the plan was to use only a small portion of the land for the village, and the rest was supposed to act as a buffer. But since we are supplying our own utilities and are not limited by municipal restrictions, we can add as many homes as we want."

Amanda chuckled. "At this rate, we will soon need to change the name from The Village to The Metropolis."

That earned her a few chuckles. Calling the new place The Village was already an exaggeration, but it had a nice sound to it.

"What are we going to do with the girls we rescue until the monastery is ready?" Vanessa asked.

"I'm in the process of acquiring an old hotel. I plan to demolish it and build a new one, but until the monastery is ready, we can use the building to house the girls."

"Is it safe?"

"The hotel is still open for business. So yes, it's safe. Just ugly and small. The location is good, and I expect a new boutique hotel to do well there."

"Wonderful. I have great news that will save us a small portion of the budget. I know you're looking for ways to minimize expenses," Vanessa said.

"Any savings would be welcome."

"I talked with the other therapists who work in my building. Each of them is willing to donate half a day of work a week to help with the girls, provided the commute is not too long. I hope they don't think of Ojai as too far away."

"If it is, do you think they will agree to one full day every other week instead?"

She nodded. "I'll have to ask again."

"Thank you. You have no idea how much I appreciate all

that you're doing for this cause."

Vanessa had agreed to head the rehabilitation portion of their rescue plan, and she was dividing her current caseload between several of her colleagues in order to free up her time. She was sacrificing a practice that she'd worked long and hard to establish.

She nodded. "I gave it a lot of thought and decided that this is what I need to be doing. I entered the field to help people deal with traumas and other issues and improve the quality of their lives. I now have an opportunity to do it on a much larger scale."

"Nevertheless, thank you. On another note, what about confidentiality? Did you talk with your colleagues about keeping quiet? I know they are not allowed to disclose confidential information about their patients, but that is not the same as keeping a lid on the whole program."

Vanessa lifted her hands. "I did. I warned that the girls' safety depended on it and was promised silence. But I can give you no guarantees. I wish we had someone who was good at compulsion. That would solve a lot of problems for us."

Indeed. Kian would sleep much better at night knowing people were compelled to keep secrets rather than relying on their good characters and judgment. Interaction with humans in general could be less restricted if those humans were compelled never to reveal the clan's existence.

But wishing it wasn't going to make it so. If they were lucky, a child would be born to the clan who possessed this rare ability. The only other option was to have Annani do that, but that wasn't an option at all.

The Clan Mother needed to remain in her Alaskan retreat, safe and secure. An occasional short visit was fine, even though it meant more sleepless nights for him worrying about his mother and her disregard for her own safety, but it was unavoidable. She wasn't a prisoner, and it was important for her well-being to get out of there once in a while.

"*W*hy didn't you tell me before?" Bridget glared at Turner.

The guy had a lot to learn about being in a relationship. Not that it was news to her, but still, he could have said something about his upcoming trip to South America and not waited until the last minute.

Well, three days to be exact, but it felt sudden nonetheless. He'd known about this trip for weeks.

Victor had made such a big fuss about going to see Douglas and being away from her for just a little over twenty-four hours, but he hadn't thought he should have informed her that he would be gone for four days?

"It wasn't a done deal until yesterday, and you've been busy."

True. The Guardians had taken her up on her offer and had been calling to let her know they were coming. Each one of the men deserved to be heard and encouraged and congratulated and not reprimanded for forgetting to check the time difference between the continents. She was asking them to make a major life change. The least she could do was give them her undivided attention even if it was two in the morning in Los Angeles.

Bridget rose to her feet and started collecting the empty containers of Thai takeout they had eaten for dinner. "Does it have anything to do with the ambush?"

Turner picked up their plates and followed her to the kitchen. "It has everything to do with that. I can't just leave it be. I have to get to the root of this. Besides, my client wants an outsider to check his network and find out the breach."

Bridget dropped the empty containers in the trash and turned around to face him. "You're not a tech person."

"I'm taking one with me."

Leaning against the counter, Bridget crossed her arms over her chest. "I feel uneasy about this. If the breach is in your client's network, it means that whoever ordered the attack on you is there as well. It's dangerous."

He shrugged. "If you want someone safe you should have picked an accountant. My work comes with certain risks that I'm well aware of and that I take the appropriate precautions against."

"I would've felt better if you had a couple of burly bodyguards with you. Maybe I can ask Kian to lend you a Guardian or two?"

Victor walked over to where she was standing and put his hands on her waist. "I don't think he can spare any at the moment, and I don't think my client will appreciate me showing up with bodyguards. It's offensive to someone like him. It's like suggesting that his security is shit."

"Apparently it is."

"It isn't, but even if it was, I can't disrespect him like that."

"You told me that he doesn't go anywhere without a cadre of goons. Why would he mind if you did it?"

"Because he is an important political figure and I'm just a contractor providing a service. We are not equals. Not in his eyes."

Bridget huffed. "Male posturing. That's all it is."

"Politics. A woman holding the same position would have been no different."

She sighed. "Just promise me to be careful."

When she'd first met him, Victor had looked like a man who could handle himself in a brawl. Not that his fighting skills were a guarantee of safety, as proven by the ambush and the potentially lethal knife wound he'd sustained, but it was better than having none. The problem was that Victor wasn't doing well on the chemo, and his body was weakened.

His skin, which had been pale before the chemo, was now so pasty it looked grayish. He lacked energy, and he wasn't as focused as he used to be.

Naturally, she pretended that nothing was amiss and encouraged him to keep going for treatments. The side effects were unfortunate but there was no way he could stop them. Hopefully, his body would adapt and the adverse reactions would diminish.

In the meantime, though, he was supposed to rest as much as possible and not go on long trips to Third World countries.

He kissed her forehead. "Always."

With a sigh, she dropped her hands and pushed off the counter.

Victor wasn't going to change his mind no matter what she said. Besides, she shouldn't try to stop him from doing what had to be done. Finding out who was behind the attack was important not only to his client but for Turner's safety.

Understandably, Victor had been in a crappy mood ever since he'd started the chemo. Some good news would cheer him up.

"Come, let's sit in the living room." She took his hand and pulled him behind her. "You wanted an update on what's going on with the Guardians."

As they sat on the couch, he wrapped his arm around her shoulders and pulled her to him. "Don't think that I'm going willingly. I'm going to miss you, and I can't even ask you to join me. First of all, because you're up to your ears in work, and secondly because it's not safe. Or rather the other way around."

She lifted a brow. "Are you admitting that it's not safe?"

"Not safe enough for you. The moment the culprit finds out I have my girlfriend with me you become a target. He would think you're the weak point and could be easily taken."

"The jerk would be in for one hell of a surprise." She looked up at him. "Are you sure you don't want me to come? I can be your secret weapon."

Bridget wasn't a violent person, but she found the idea of taking out the scum behind the attack on Turner extremely appealing. Perhaps she could take a leaf out of Eva's book. If a detective could become a novelist, a doctor could become an assassin. Just once. When it came to protecting her loved ones, Bridget had no qualms about doing a little cleanup job.

"Not going to happen, Dr. Bridget, so wipe that evil smirk off your pretty face and tell me about the Guardians."

Yeah, it was a nice little fantasy. She would make a shitty assassin.

"We have fifty, and I expect more phone calls in the coming days."

"That exceeds our best estimates."

"It does, and they are starting to arrive soon. Kian is expediting the move to the Village to make room for them in the keep. Nathalie and Andrew are moving as are Amanda and Dalhu. Brundar and Callie have to stay because of Brundar's job. All the current Guardians are staying to welcome the newcomers and start training them."

Turner frowned. "That's not a good strategy. He is leaving the Village unprotected. Some of the Guardians should move with the first wave."

"I'll mention it to him. Unless you want to?"

As much as Kian appreciated her input and respected her opinion, he would be quicker to take Turner's advice on matters of security.

"You're the expert. You should talk to him."

"I will."

"I wish Eva and Bhathian could move. Between the two of them, they can protect the others."

"Why can't they?"

"Because Eva refuses to leave her crew behind. She is convinced they are Dormants and is waiting for them to transition."

That sparked Victor's interest. "Do they have special abilities?"

"Nothing definite, quite iffy if you ask me. Supposedly Sharon is an excellent judge of character, like in infallible, and Nick is a whiz with electronics."

"The girl's ability might be paranormal, but what is special about being good with electronics?"

Bridget shrugged. "He managed to infiltrate the keep's security system, and he is not a super-hacker."

Victor whistled. "Now, that's impressive. My hacker is excellent but had no luck breaking in here. That guy must be special."

"You tried to hack into the keep?"

"Did you expect anything less from me?"

She chuckled. "Right. The keep was another mystery you just had to solve. I'm surprised you didn't succeed."

"I was surprised too, and impressed."

"How about disappointed?"

He waved a hand. "Nah. It would've been more disappointing for me if I succeeded. Besides, it was a much-needed dose of humility. I was reminded that I'm not omnipotent."

Bridget gasped dramatically. "You're not?"

"Sorry."

"Don't sorry me, mister. Come to bed, and I'll show you that you're plenty potent for me."

"Yes, ma'am."

CHAPTER 48: TURNER

"Come on, Alfred, hurry up," Turner said.

Herding his hacker through the airport was like trying to herd a goat with an attention deficit disorder. The guy gawked at everyone, stopping to take a better look at anything from a pretty face to fancy luggage. It was like observing someone who'd been just released from jail and was seeing people for the first time in years.

Most hackers didn't get out much, but Alfred was married with three small kids. There must've been trips to the supermarket, and the preschool, and all the other places parents shuffled their kids to and from. Even if he wanted to, Alfred couldn't hide in his cave without surfacing once in a while.

Thanks to the TSA fast pass, they had gone through the security check in no time, but then the guy took forever to get his things organized. Turner watched Alfred fumble with his belt, then look for an appropriately-sized pocket for his wallet, another pocket for his passport, and lastly the miscellaneous shit he'd pulled out of his pockets and had placed in the bin.

"I hate flying," Alfred said once they were seated.

"You're not flying yet. Besides, a first class seat is hardly a hardship." With Sandoval footing the bill, Turner could be magnanimous.

"Are the drinks free?"

Turner nodded.

"Good. I'm going to get shitfaced and sleep until we get there."

"No, you're not. I'll give you a sleeping pill. A hangover is the last thing you need while working on Sandoval's system. It's not like you can take a day or two to rest before you start. You sleep on the plane and start working the moment we get there."

Alfred snorted. "I told you before. I don't know why you're dragging me all the way out there when I could've done it from home."

Turner slapped the guy's back. "Stop complaining. It'll do you good to get out of the house from time to time."

Sandoval agreed with Turner's assessment that the breach in security was on his side. Arturo's people assured him that his network was as safe as it could be and was protected by the best security protocol money could buy. Wisely, the guy wanted an outsider's opinion.

Listening to the recording of the message he supposedly had left for Turner, Sandoval insisted that it hadn't been an actor imitating his voice, but a piecing together of snippets of his phone conversations.

Turner had never told Sandoval what exactly had happened at the restaurant, leaving the details out so Arturo would think that he'd handled it. First of all, he'd wanted to gauge the guy's response, and secondly, it wasn't something he could admit without losing face. An operative like him should have never been caught with his pants down, so to speak.

Unless Sandoval had intel on the incident, which would cast suspicion on his involvement in the ambush, Turner wasn't going to volunteer the information.

"I don't like being away from the house overnight." Alfred

hunched his shoulders, looking and sounding like a schoolkid on his way to detention.

"That's the power of habit, buddy. The longer you succumb to it the harder it is to break. Your comfort zone is sitting in your gaming chair and manipulating data. You're good at that, but it's not good for you."

"It pays the bills."

Making a career out of a hobby was great, but it had a few downsides. Passion often turned into an obsession to the exclusion of everything else. The intense focus was good for attaining incredible skill, but not for relationships, health, and fitness, which usually got neglected.

He was one to talk.

Achieving the desired results for his clients was so important to Turner that he was sacrificing his health to deliver what he'd promised, maybe even his very life.

In order to restore his mind to the top level machine it used to be, he had stopped the chemotherapy. It had taken several days until the fog had cleared. Now that his brain was back to functioning the way it had before, Turner was adamant about never undergoing treatment again.

The thing was, he hadn't told Bridget yet, and with each passing day, the lie by omission was getting bigger and heavier. He'd even resorted to faking tiredness.

The old Turner would have kept it a secret, pretending for a few more weeks that he was getting treated while pushing for the transition as soon as he closed all of his open cases.

The new Turner knew that lying to Bridget was wrong. She was too smart and too observant not to figure it out on her own. He had to man up and tell her before that happened. If he told her, the worst that could happen was a bit of a tantrum followed by her trying to convince him to resume treatment.

The woman had a temper and was not afraid to use it.

But if she found out before he told her, she was going to kick him out, lock the door, and never let him in again.

"It's not about the habit," Alfred said as the plane started to move on the runway. "Well it is, but that's not the main reason. You don't have kids so you don't know how it feels."

None of Turner's associates knew about Douglas. But the truth of the matter was that he wouldn't know how it felt because he'd never done any actual parenting.

Turner rubbed the back of his neck. "You're right, I don't. But I assume parents need a break from a bunch of noisy kids from time to time."

Alfred chuckled. "I dream of it every day, especially when they fight and the screams are loud enough to bring the house down. But when I'm forced to leave, especially on a plane, I have this fear that something will happen to me, and my children will be left fatherless. Who will take care of them?"

Turner patted the hacker's shoulder. "These fears are irrational. Statistically, you're safer on a plane than driving your car. Are you afraid of going to the supermarket?"

"Of course not. I look forward to it."

"You do?"

"I work from home, and my wife drives the kids to and from wherever they need to go. In the evenings, my time belongs to the family, and after the kids are in bed, I usually put in a few more hours of work. Going to the supermarket is the only break I get."

Poor guy. Alfred didn't have much of a life.

On second thought, that wasn't true.

What was life all about?

Life was about a lot of things, but trips abroad and even work well done were not what defined one's life as worth living or not.

Turner considered himself lucky.

His work was about rescuing people. He was needed, his

services were vital. There weren't many operators like him in the world, and he was entitled to think of himself as indispensable. So even if he had nothing else in his life, this was enough to fill him with a sense of purpose and pride of achievement.

Except, since he'd met Bridget and Kian had allowed him almost unlimited access to the clan, Turner's worldview had shifted.

Life was about family first and everything else second.

CHAPTER 49: SHARON

"Stop!" Sharon called after Julian, who once again was ducking into his room within thirty seconds of her arrival.

He turned around. "Yes?"

"You are eating dinner with us, and I don't want to hear any excuses about you not being hungry or watching a game in your room. You make me feel like I have a contagious disease or something." Not that he could catch it even if she had it, but Julian didn't know that Robert had spilled the beans about them being immortal.

What an emotional rollercoaster.

When he'd first told her, his very real fangs had convinced her that he was telling the truth. It had been a week ago, and they'd been going at each other like rabbits ever since, without condoms, but nothing had happened.

It hadn't taken long for her to start doubting what she'd seen, until yesterday she had Robert cut his arm to provide further proof. Sure enough, the small cut had closed within a minute, and after two there had been no trace of it.

Bottom line, Robert really wasn't human, and she wasn't a Dormant.

If she were, she would've transitioned already. Robert was

a bit fuzzy about the details, but he thought that three or four bites should do it. There had been quite a few more. If not for his saliva or the venom itself healing the puncture wounds, she would've looked like a pincushion.

Julian glanced at Robert who shrugged.

"You heard the lady. I wouldn't argue if I were you."

Smart man.

Sharon was in a bitchy mood and was just looking for an excuse to tear into anyone who dared annoy her.

Bloody damned period.

Why couldn't she be one of those women who breezed through it?

Sharon was the unlucky one who suffered through every symptom possible and even some that no one had heard of, like colorful spheres dancing in front of her eyes. Her doctor claimed it was part of the migraine headaches that attacked her during that time of the month, but she'd talked with enough migraine sufferers to know it was different than the corona they described.

Add to that mood swings worthy of a split personality, debilitating stomach pains, and leg cramps, and she was a peach to hang around a day before her monthly ordeal and throughout.

Poor Robert was coping as best he could, being an angel and tolerating her outbursts of bitchiness. It was good that she'd given him fair warning that his good-natured girlfriend was about to turn into a Godzilla. Otherwise, he would have thought she'd gone nuts.

Julian planted a grin on his too-handsome face and sauntered to the dining table. "It seems I will be joining you for dinner after all." He winked at Robert. "What did you make today?"

"Brisket, baked potatoes, spinach, and a green salad."

Smacking his lips, Julian unfolded the cloth napkin and put it over his knees. "Did I tell you already that I love you, man?"

Robert carried a tray loaded with the aforementioned dishes and put it in the center of the table. "You love my cooking."

"Yes, that is true, but they say that the way to a man's heart is through his stomach."

Sharon snorted. Whoever invented that saying was an idiot. The way to a man's heart was through his dick. That was all they thought about every minute of the day. Except, she was too much of a lady to say it out loud in front of Julian. The guy had such refined manners for someone so young. Perhaps he needed them because he was a doctor and had to be polite around his patients.

"Save it, Julian. I'll feed you even if you don't profess your love for me." Robert cut a big chunk of the brisket and dropped it on Julian's plate. "You must forgive me." He glanced at Sharon. "I'm serving him first because the only way to shut him up is to fill his mouth with food."

She waved a hand. "You're forgiven."

Poor guy was walking on eggshells around her. He was such a mensch, not making fun of her grumpiness and being so kind and understanding.

Cursing her hormones, Sharon wiped away the tears that had pooled in the corners of her eyes. She was a physical and an emotional mess.

Robert eyed her with concern written all over his face but wisely refrained from commenting as he put a small chunk of the brisket on her plate.

She hadn't failed to notice that he'd chosen the best cut for her. "Thank you, that's very kind of you." As more tears threatened to spill, Sharon reached for the potatoes.

"You're very welcome." Robert loaded his plate with brisket and spinach while waiting for her to be done with the potatoes.

"This glass dish is so heavy," she said. Her hand was trembling from the effort of holding it up.

Robert took it from her. "It's the potatoes. I overloaded it."

It made sense, but when she lifted the salad bowl, and her hand trembled again, Sharon wondered if a migraine was coming on. She was used to the strange symptoms preceding it, like confusion, dancing color spots, and forgetfulness. A tremor, though, was a new addition.

Watching her hands, Julian asked with a frown, "Does it happen often?"

She shook her head. "Only when I have a high fever. It weakens me, and everything feels like a huge effort. But I don't have a fever now." She touched her forehead.

"Do you mind if I check?" He put his napkin on the table and pushed his chair back.

"I'm probably getting a migraine. All kinds of weird shit happens when it's on the way."

"I'll be right back," Julian said as he ducked into his room.

Did he have a thermometer there? And if he did, what for?

It wasn't as if his patients were getting fevers. Come to think of it, why did immortals need a doctor at all?

A moment later Julian came back with one of those contraptions they used in the doctor's office. "Would you mind pushing your hair back?" he asked.

Tucking a few strands behind her ear, Sharon tilted her head to give him access. On the other side of the table, she heard Robert making a noise in his throat that sounded like an angry dog about to attack.

Julian put the tip of the device in her ear and lifted a hand toward Robert. "It will only take a second."

As the thing beeped, Julian removed it and looked at the display. "Ninety-nine point five. You have a low fever. Anything else going on?"

Damn, it was embarrassing. True, he was a doctor, but he was also a young, handsome guy. "I'm on my period."

She wasn't sure immortal females had them. Maybe she

should explain? But without being obvious because she was not supposed to know.

"I get all the worst symptoms women experience with menstruation. Migraines, cramps, mood swings. It's not fun."

Julian nodded. "No, it's not. Do you take something for the symptoms?"

She grimaced. "I take Motrin. It helps with some of the aches."

"The fever might be caused by your period, or you might be coming down with something."

"Right, I forgot to mention that I usually get sick right after. It works like a charm. The period ends and a cold or the flu starts. Do you think menstruation lowers my immune system?"

"Absolutely."

"So it's not a case of bad mood causing illness."

"The body and mind are one system. If one is not doing well, the other is affected."

Well, duh.

"That being said, the menstrual cycle is known to affect the immune system in some women."

When the guys were done scarfing up the last of the food, Sharon picked up her plate and pushed away from the table.

Robert took it out of her hands. "Julian will help me clean up. You can sit on the couch and put your feet up, and I'll bring you coffee when we are done. Or do you want tea?"

The freaking tears were back. She couldn't help it. This man was just too kind, too understanding, too everything.

"Okay. Thank you." She rushed to the living room before he could see the stupid tears.

After kicking her shoes off, she put her feet up on the ottoman, leaned back, and closed her eyes. The clunking of dishes and low male murmurs coming from the kitchen were oddly soothing. Sharon felt the irritation that was her constant companion during her menses start to ease. Even her stomach stopped cramping as much, which it usually did more after eating a heavy meal, not less.

Was it a psychological effect?

Could kindness and understanding cure menstrual pain?

It didn't seem likely. On the other hand, according to Julian, the mind and body were like a self-feeding loop. If one was doing well, the other was affected, and the other way around.

The guys were so nice to her.

But she wasn't sick, not really, and she shouldn't be sitting on her butt while they did all the work. She should help in the kitchen. Robert had done the cooking, so he shouldn't be doing the dishes and making coffee as well. It wasn't fair.

If it were her, she would've been pissed if anyone treated her like that.

With a sigh, Sharon put her feet down and pushed up off the couch. She must've risen too fast because her vision blurred and those damn rainbow-colored circles started dancing in front of her eyes.

Leaning her shins against the couch, she waited for the sensation to pass, but then one of the guys decided to dim the lights.

Sharon opened her mouth to yell at whomever had that bright idea, but no sound came out of her throat. A split moment later even the dim light flickered out, plunging her into darkness.

CHAPTER 50: ROBERT

"*H*ow are you holding up?" Julian asked in a near whisper.

Robert loaded the last plate into the dishwasher and turned around. "What exactly are you referring to?"

Julian tilted his head toward the living room. "Who, not what. Sharon is cranky as hell. It's not easy to deal with someone who suddenly is not the same person you've grown to care for."

It seemed Julian had never had to deal with difficult people, or he would've known that Sharon's irritation was nothing to get worked up about.

"The irritable mood will pass. I've dealt with much worse. My ex-commander was a monster. He could turn from charming to murderous in a blink of an eye."

Robert wiped his hands with a dishrag and leaned against the counter. "On the one hand, Sharim--or Sebastian, the name he'd adopted for that mission--was good to us. He took the time to get to know each of his soldiers and provided us with perks whenever he could. But he was unpredictable, and we never knew what would trigger his anger. His soldiers were afraid to breathe the wrong way around him."

Julian chuckled. "I know the type. My chief at the hospital

was like that. Not the murderous part, though he had the power to kill a resident's career."

First World problems, Robert thought.

As the coffee machine announced it was done brewing with a loud beep, Robert filled up three cups and handed two to Julian. "Take these to the living room."

"Yes, boss."

The third cup in one hand and the creamer in the other, Robert followed Julian to the living room where they found Sharon asleep on the couch.

"The meat must've been too heavy for her." Robert put the cup on the coffee table.

Julian's two were still in his hands as he stood and stared at Sharon. "Take the cups, Robert." His tone, which was serious and commanding at the same time, implied something was amiss. The guy wasn't serious about anything other than his profession.

"What's wrong?" Robert asked as he took the cups from his hands and placed them on the coffee table.

Julian knelt next to Sharon and touched two fingers to the pulse point on her neck. "The way her body is arranged suggests she fainted rather than fell asleep. But her pulse is strong, so that's good."

Could human females lose too much blood during their menses and faint because of that? Robert felt like an idiot for not knowing and debated whether to ask Julian or not.

The guy pulled out the thermometer from his pant pocket and checked Sharon's fever again. "It's gone a bit higher."

"Should we wake her?" Robert asked.

Julian nodded. "Could you bring her a cup of water?"

"Sure." He hurried to the kitchen.

"Sharon, wake up, honey," Julian said softly. When there was no answer, he touched her shoulder and repeated, "Sharon, wake up, sweetheart, I just want to make sure you're okay, and then you can go back to sleep."

Sharon groaned and turned to the other side.

Julian took the glass from Robert and then turned to Sharon. "I need you to open your eyes, Sharon."

Under normal circumstances, watching Julian leaning so close to Sharon, listening as he talked to her in that soothing tone of his that was way too intimate, Robert's jealousy would've roared by now. But something was wrong with her, and Julian was a doctor and could help her.

"I felt dizzy," she murmured. "It started with those colorful spheres, and then I blacked out." She opened her eyes. "I don't remember lying down on the couch."

"You probably fainted and just dropped sideways. Let me help you get more comfortable." He lifted Sharon's feet, which were still on the floor, and put them on the couch, then tucked a pillow under her head.

"Would you like a drink of water?" Julian asked.

"Yes, please."

"I can do that." Robert snapped the glass off the coffee table, gave Julian a slight shove, and crouched next to Sharon. "Here you go, love." He propped her head gently.

"Thank you." She smiled. "But I think I can hold the glass up by myself." She reached for it.

"As you wish."

Sharon took a few small sips and handed him the glass back. "Any idea why I fainted, Julian? That never happened to me before."

Smart man that he was, Julian took a couple of steps back so as not to crowd them. "It was probably because you ate a large dinner. It can be caused by postprandial hypotension, low blood pressure in layman's terms, or low blood sugar. The first one is more common among older folks, so low blood sugar is the more likely culprit. You should get it checked."

"Can you do it for me?"

"I don't have a lab here. You should have your regular doctor run some tests."

Robert held his breath. Sharon knew where Julian

worked. The question was whether she'd remember she was not supposed to know that.

"But you have a thermometer," she said.

Robert's shoulders sagged in relief.

Julian chuckled as he pulled the device out of his pocket again. "This thing? It's a present from my mother. I'm not taking it with me to work."

"Speaking of work." Robert looked into Sharon's eyes. "I want you to call Eva and tell her you're sick. And I want you to stay here tonight and tomorrow and rest."

"But you and Julian are going to be gone all day. What am I going to do all alone in here?"

"I work in the building and Julian works nearby. Both of us can be here on a moment's notice."

"I'll come and visit you during the day," Julian offered. "With Robert," he added quickly when Robert glared at him.

"You guys are fussing over me as if it's a big deal. I'm a little sick because of the freaking period, that's all. No reason to skip work."

"I can give you a sick note for your boss," Julian said.

"It's not like Eva is going to be mad because I missed one day. We are not all that busy lately. But I like working and hate doing nothing."

"I have every episode of *Game of Thrones* on DVD," Julian said. "You can binge watch it. If you're up to it, that is." He arched a brow, issuing a challenge.

"I've seen them all, but I don't mind watching again. Jaime is hot."

"Then it's settled. I'll bring it here." He turned and headed to his room.

"Who is Jaime?" Robert asked.

"A character from the series." She reached for him and cupped his cheek. "But you have nothing to worry about. You're much hotter than the actor playing him."

"Good, you just saved that poor schmuck's life."

Sharon laughed. "I see that Eva is rubbing off on you."

He had no idea what she was talking about. "And you're saying this because?"

"You said schmuck. That's something Eva would've said."

Robert rubbed his jaw. "Isn't it part of the English language?"

Sharon laughed again. "I guess it is."

CHAPTER 51: TURNER

*D*ripping with sweat had never felt so good.

In his hotel room, Turner pushed through the last set of sit-ups, then moved to the after-workout stretching routine.

Regrettably, there wasn't enough free space in the room for martial arts katas, but old-fashioned lunges, sit-ups, and pushups provided enough of a workout to produce a good sweat.

There was plenty of space to practice in the suite of rooms Sandoval had reserved for him and Alfred, but naturally, Turner and his hacker weren't staying there, even though Sandoval assigned two goons to guard them. With how easy it had been to slip by them, they weren't the guy's best. And if they were, it would explain why Sandoval's network was leaking like a sieve and why his nephew had been snatched with such humiliating ease.

If he could take on new assignments, Turner would've sold Sandoval more of his services, performing background and security checks on the guy's personnel.

It could have lined Turner's pockets nicely. But until he attempted transition and either emerged immortal, unchanged, or dead, he wasn't going to take people's money for a job he wasn't certain he would be around to deliver.

Done with the stretches, Turner wiped his face with the hotel towel and headed for the shower.

The workout had been invigorating, physically and mentally.

It seemed that his mood had been improving at the same rate the side effects from the chemo were diminishing. Regaining mastery of his body felt great. Turner felt sharp, strong, and ready to take on the world.

He was back to his old self.

Including the sex drive.

The problem was that Bridget was thousands of miles away, and transporters were still in the realm of science fiction. It could have been great to get himself beamed over to Bridget and then return to his hotel room in the morning.

As it was, they could only talk on the phone.

Hey, he hadn't had phone sex yet.

The idea excited him. But before he got comfortable in bed and dialed Bridget's number, he needed to check on Alfred. The guy might decide to come in for a chat and ruin the mood.

Dressed in a pair of sweats and a T-shirt, Turner stepped out into the hallway and knocked on the door of the next room over, using a short sequence of taps and raps to let Alfred know it was him.

"Yes, boss?" The guy opened the door after several moments of fumbling with the lock bar and disarming the portable alarm Turner had brought for each room.

It was a precaution he always used while traveling. Both he and Alfred slept with a handgun under the pillow, and if an intruder opened the door while they were asleep, the alarm would wake them up and the lock bar would give them a few seconds to get to their weapons.

"Everything okay?"

"Yeah. I was in bed already."

It seemed Turner had interrupted virtual sexy time for Alfred. He knew no one had come into the hacker's room because he had two hidden cameras out in the hallway monitoring it. Alfred was either sexing up his wife on the phone or watching porn.

"I just wanted to say goodnight and see if you need anything."

"Thank you. I have everything I need. Goodnight, boss."

"Don't forget to put the alarm and the lock bar on the door."

Alfred chuckled. "Don't worry. I might forget that my glasses are on my nose but not this. Your two-step blockade is the only reason I can sleep at night in a place like this."

He meant the country in general, not the hotel which was modest but decent.

"Good to know. Goodnight, Alfred."

Back in his room, Turner checked the time. It was a little after eleven at night, which meant it was after seven in the evening in Los Angeles, and unless there had been a medical emergency, Bridget should be back in her apartment.

Their apartment, he corrected himself. Even though he knew he was welcomed, Turner still didn't feel like the keep or Bridget's place were home because they weren't. It was a temporary arrangement. Soon they would be moving into his renovated apartment. He couldn't wait. Finally, he would have his privacy back. It bothered him that his comings and goings were being monitored by security cameras that were not his.

Hopefully, Bridget would feel better about moving in with him than he felt about moving in with her.

Picking up his secure sat phone, he got in bed and dialed her cell phone.

"Hi, Victor," she answered on the first ring. Had she been waiting for his call? It made sense that she'd expect him to call at the same time he'd called her last night.

"How was your day?" He got comfortable on the bed.

"Great. Brandon's ball is going to bring in lots of donations. He was lucky to get Belinda Rochester on board. They are expecting over a thousand guests."

Turner whistled. "Impressive."

"Very. Other than that, I spoke with a couple of Guardians who are arriving within a week because they just sold their startup to a larger company for a solid half a million."

"Software?"

"Naturally. What else brings in that kind of money?"

"And they are willing to go back to being humble Guardians?"

Bridget chuckled. "Humble? There is nothing humble about Guardians. They think they are the best of the best and that the entire clan owes them a debt of gratitude."

"I guess they're entitled to that."

"True, but they don't need to be so cocky about it."

"Are you back at the apartment?"

"Yes. Why?"

"Are you alone?"

"Yes…" As always, Bridget caught on right away.

"Can you get in bed?"

"I sure can."

"Get naked."

"I'm not sending you a nude pic even if we are on a secure line," she teased.

"I don't need you to send me a picture. All I have to do is close my eyes, and I can see you. I have every little detail memorized. Last night, I masturbated while imagining I was with you." Hopefully, he wasn't giving himself away by admitting that. She might guess he'd stopped the chemo.

He heard the rustle of clothing. "Really? Your client didn't push beautiful bimbettes at you?"

"He gave up. Probably thinks I'm gay."

"Why, did you ogle one of his bodyguards? I bet they are handsome. Big and muscular."

She was teasing him, he knew that, and yet the idea of Bridget thinking of any man as handsome or desirable irritated him.

"They are big and muscular, like overgrown apes with brains to match."

"Ugh, that totally spoiled the image for me."

Turner smirked evilly. "That was the intention. I don't want you thinking about any other males but me."

"Victor, Victor, Victor. Are you jealous?"

"Yes." There was no point in denying it after he'd just admitted as much.

"I'm so proud of you."

"Say again?"

"Jealousy is a strong feeling. You're opening up emotionally."

She was right. How had he missed that?

It had been happening so gradually that he hadn't noticed the change until Bridget voiced it.

Compared to a few weeks ago, he was feeling many things he hadn't before, or perhaps just hadn't allowed himself to feel. Most of them weren't positive, though. Jealousy and possessiveness were not good traits to have. He would've expected that from Sandoval's goons, but not from himself.

"Are you there?" Bridget asked. "Did I stun you into silence?"

"I was thinking that jealousy is nothing to be proud of. It's a primitive feeling."

"True, but so what? I'm a jealous woman. Do you think I keep asking you about bimbos just to tease you? I keep imagining you surrounded by gorgeous Latinas in bikinis, and even though I trust you, I can't help but get mad. It's irrational, but it's part of our makeup. Humans and immortals alike. In fact, I think immortals are worse than humans when it comes to their mates."

Turner sighed. "It's sad. On the inside we are chimps."

"Why sad? Look at the bonobos. These chimps know how to live the good life."

CHAPTER 52: ROBERT

*L*ike every morning, Robert woke up early. But unlike other mornings, the first thing he did was to put his hand on Sharon's forehead and check whether her fever had risen or subsided overnight.

It seemed the same to him, but a hand wasn't a thermometer. Julian should be up already. Maybe he could borrow the guy's device. It seemed easy enough to use, just point it at the ear and press a button.

The doctor was an early riser like him, and most mornings they hit the gym together, but not today. Robert wanted to stay with Sharon as long as possible.

Kissing her forehead, Robert got out of bed and rushed to pull on his training pants. He then headed to the kitchen hoping to catch Julian before the guy left for the gym.

"You're just in time for coffee." Julian took another cup out of the cupboard and poured the fresh brew into both. "Here you go, buddy. How is Sharon doing?"

"Still sleeping. I wanted to ask if I can borrow your thermometer. I don't think her fever has risen, but I want to make sure."

Julian put his coffee cup down. "I can do it."

Robert lifted a hand. "No. She sleeps naked." For the past

two days, she'd left her panties on because of the menses, but the rest of her beautiful body was bare. He wasn't letting Julian anywhere near her.

"You're aware that I'm a doctor. Right? I see people with no clothes on all of the time. I'm immune to it."

Right. Like being a doctor meant that he wasn't a man, and getting an eyeful of a beautiful nude female was not going to affect him.

"Not going to happen. Can I borrow the thing or not?"

Julian shook his head. "You're a strange fellow, Robert. I was sure you were the mellowest, non-confrontational guy I've ever met. I couldn't figure out how you could've been a Doomer. But that's just a façade, is it not? Underneath there is a whole different man who is hard as steel."

Robert rubbed his jaw. "It's not a façade. I'm both. When nothing important is at stake, I'm very happy following the rules and doing what I'm told. I like order. It gives me peace of mind. But I'm more than capable of fighting for what's important to me. Sharon is important to me."

"Obviously." Julian was still eyeing Robert as if he was a puzzle the guy wanted to decipher. "I'll get the thermometer."

"Thank you."

It took less than a minute for Julian to explain how it worked.

"I'll wait for you to be done. Just remember. Anything under a hundred and two is considered mild."

"Understood. And don't worry, I'm not going to damage the thing. I'll leave it on the counter when I'm done."

Julian waved a hand. "I don't care about that. I meant that I'll wait for you to go down to the gym with me."

"I'm not going. I want to stay with Sharon."

"Are you taking the day off? Because I'll have to stay with you."

"Right." Robert smoothed a hand over the back of his neck. "I'm not taking a day off, but you can't go to the gym if

I'm not going. I apologize for making you miss your workout."

"No problem. I can go through a basic routine in here."

Robert was grateful for Julian's easy-going attitude. "I planned to do the same. We can do it together in the living room."

"You're on." Julian slapped his back.

Robert palmed the thermometer. "Just give me a moment to check Sharon's fever."

Back in the bedroom, he found Sharon sleeping in the same position he'd left her—on her back, her lips slightly parted, her wavy dark hair spread over his white pillow.

Beautiful.

He hated to disturb her peaceful sleep, but it needed to be done. As gently as he could, Robert put the tip in her ear. He sighed in relief when she didn't wake.

The display said one hundred and one.

It was a little higher than last evening, but not high enough to cause worry. According to Julian, it was considered mild.

He glanced at the floor where Sharon's clothes had been haphazardly dropped last night and fought the urge to pick them up and fold them for her. But Julian was waiting for him in the living room, and Robert didn't want to make him wait any longer than needed.

He grabbed a muscle shirt and his athletic shoes from the closet, a pair of socks from the pile of clean laundry, and then tiptoed out, taking one last look at the woman sleeping in his bed.

A big mistake.

Not watching where he was going, Robert tripped over one of Sharon's shoes, knocking a vase off the dresser as he tried to steady himself. Naturally, his quick reflexes were good enough to prevent him from falling on his face, but the damn vase slipped from his grabbing fingers and shattered on the floor.

"Fuck." Now he had to clean the mess up.

As he started collecting the larger pieces, it occurred to him that the noise of breaking glass and his loud curse hadn't woken Sharon. He rose up and glanced at her.

She was still sleeping in the same position.

Sharon wasn't a heavy sleeper.

Something was wrong.

Dropping the shards he'd just collected, Robert rushed to the bed.

"Sharon, sweetheart, wake up." He nudged her shoulder.

When she didn't respond, he repeated the words and shook her.

Nothing.

Panic setting in, he bellowed, "Julian! Get in here!"

A split second before the door burst open, he remembered to cover Sharon's naked breasts. Not that it mattered to him anymore. But she would've expected him to do so.

"What happened?" Julian looked down at the floor and the glass shards strewn about. "Did you cut yourself?"

As if he would've screamed for the doctor because of a cut. "Sharon didn't wake up from the noise. I shook her and nothing. She is unconscious."

In a blur of movement, Julian was at Sharon's side. "Pulse is fine, and she is breathing normally." He narrowed his eyes at Robert. "You didn't use the condoms like I told you, right?"

Robert shook his head. There was no point in denying it.

"She is most likely transitioning. According to my mother, fever and loss of consciousness are the most common symptoms. We need to take Sharon to the clinic and call Bridget."

Stupefied, Robert nodded.

"You should put some clothes on her."

"Right."

"I'll go get the gurney. Unless you want to carry her?"

"I'll carry her."

CHAPTER 53: TURNER

"What do you think?" Turner asked Alfred. After two days the guy should have found the leak.

Alfred pushed his glasses up his nose and leaned back in his chair. "The network is well protected. It's one of the best protocols money can buy. We are either dealing with a super-hacker or an inside job. My bet is on the second one."

Turner had been leaning toward this conclusion as well. Sandoval wasn't going to like it. No one wanted to believe they had a traitor in their midst. Truth be told, though, Sandoval hadn't been the target of the attack. Turner had. It was still a betrayal, but not as painful.

It was either a personal vendetta for whoever that guy Xavier was, or a test to gauge Sandoval's reaction to an attack on another person in his network of close associates.

Except, after the nephew's rescue, which Turner had organized, and the deadly blow the kidnappers had suffered, there should have been at least some period of quiet. Once the rumors subsided, and the repercussions were forgotten, another organization of thugs might try something again.

It was the nature of the beast.

A massive show of force brought peace, but it lasted just as long as the losses were remembered.

Besides, Turner was a sub-contractor, not a member of Sandoval's family. Arturo's people needed to be checked. Andrew Spivak's lie-detector skills would have come in handy for a quick and efficient interrogation.

"What about tracing inter-network communications? Can you find out who could've been tapping Sandoval's conversations from the inside?"

Alfred shook his head. "The network is not the only way to access communication. If we assume it was an inside job, then whoever did that could've been planning something for a while and planted well-hidden bugs. Sandoval would be smart to order a sweep of the place."

"Good thinking." Turner clapped the hacker on his back.

Alfred was a smart guy whose outside-the-box thinking wasn't limited to computers. There might be better hackers out there, but Alfred brought other skills to the table.

The computer room where Alfred worked was located in the sprawling mansion's basement, protected by massive concrete walls that could withstand bombing from above and ground explosives. Turner hadn't been granted access to the other rooms down below, but he could guess their uses. Some were luxurious shelters for Arturo and his family, others were probably holding cells for his enemies.

As Turner headed to Arturo's office, he had to stop by the two goons guarding the thick door to the stairwell. The thing was not only fireproof but resistant to most explosives. Whoever wanted to get in when the thing was locked was better off blowing a hole in the wall.

There were no elevators. There was no need. Above ground, the mansion was only two stories high, and below there was only one sublevel. Besides, all the reinforcements Sandoval introduced to the place would have been rendered useless by an elevator shaft. It was a vulnerability he was better off without.

"What do you have for me, my friend?" Arturo pointed Turner to an armchair, then joined him, sitting in the other one.

It was a show of respect, which Turner appreciated.

"Your protocol is sound. I believe that you're dealing with an inside job. I suggest sweeping for bugs."

If Sandoval were taken aback by Turner's suggestion, he didn't show it. There was very little the guy revealed unintentionally. The fatherly charm was a great façade for a ruthless politician.

Leaning closer to Turner, he smiled. "I had many bugs planted throughout my compound. Spying on my people is necessary for my survival."

"I know about your bugs." Turner was the one who had suggested them, but it seemed Sandoval thought it had been his idea and Victor wasn't about to set him straight. "It makes it very easy for someone on your staff to add a few of their own."

Smoothing his hand over his short beard, Sandoval leaned back. "That is true." He looked around his office. "Not in here. I check the place myself every morning before I start my workday."

"Some of them are so small I doubt you can find them."

There was alarm in Sandoval's eyes. "If this is so easy, why am I spending so much money on cybersecurity?"

"It's very difficult to guard against insiders who have access to your offices, or even your private residence. I can refer you to someone who can install additional hardware to detect unauthorized transmissions, but even that is not foolproof. If the goal is to listen in on you and your dealings and maybe record a few conversations, no outside transmission is necessary."

"So what am I supposed to do?"

"We can start by sweeping this office. I'll show you what to look for, and you can continue in other rooms or have people you trust do that."

Sandoval waved a hand. "I don't trust anyone. There isn't a single person who can't be either bought or blackmailed or threatened."

He should know. Sandoval probably did all three on a regular basis.

"Then you have to do it yourself. Which, frankly, I would've made my standard operating protocol. Choose one room to conduct business from and check it every morning like you do now."

"What about my staff?"

"Instruct them to watch what they are saying and to whom. Most of what they do is legit." Turner smiled coldly. "The rest gets outsourced."

"True." Sandoval smoothed his hand over his beard again. "Not that I know what you're talking about." He winked.

"Of course. I'll come back tomorrow morning, and we will clean up this office."

Arturo chuckled. "I haven't done any cleaning up since my college days. I have maids to do that."

"You need to screen them too, and not based on how hot they look in the uniforms you make them wear."

The man didn't go as far as cladding his service staff in naughty French maid costumes, but the uniforms weren't the standard issue either. They were formfitting in a way that must made working in them uncomfortable, but the length was modest, coming to just above the knee, and there was no cleavage showing. After all, Sandoval had a wife and three teenage daughters living in the house, and a reputation to keep up. Not that fidelity was valued in these parts, the opposite was true, but keeping appearances did matter.

"Why not now?" Sandoval waved a hand at his sprawling office.

The place was bug heaven, with almost limitless potential for concealment. The plush couch with matching armchairs, the heavy drapery bordered with tassels, the elaborately carved frames, the tapestries. It would take an entire day to go over every inch of wall, fabric, and furniture.

Turner wasn't looking forward to it.

It was a tedious job that should have been relegated to underlings. Except, he'd already committed himself and couldn't back down.

"It will take several hours. Are you sure you don't want to assign it to someone who has proven trustworthy? I'm sure there must be more than one staff member who qualifies."

Sandoval shook his head. "Maybe for the other rooms, but not this one. Knowledge is power, my friend, and the more I can learn the better. I have no aptitude for computers and no time to become an expert, but I can dedicate one day to learning how to exterminate bugs, and I can't think of anyone more qualified to teach me than you."

CHAPTER 54: ROBERT

"*T*ell me what happened," Bridget said, or rather commanded.

Sitting on the other side of her desk, Robert felt like he was in a disciplinary hearing. The consequences of that wouldn't be as severe as they had been in the Doomer camp, but the anxiety was the same.

"She complained about seeing colorful bubbles dancing in front of her eyes, then we ate dinner, and she went to sit on the couch. At some point, she fainted."

Bridget shook her head. "I heard all of that from Julian already. What I need to know is how likely it is that she is transitioning. Did you have unprotected sex?"

He nodded.

"Didn't Julian tell you to wait until you were sure about Sharon?"

"I'm sure. She is the one for me."

"Once you were sure, you were supposed to tell her and give her a choice. The condom wasn't supposed to come off until then."

"I'm sorry. I just didn't want her to be locked up in here until she transitioned. Sharon loves her job, and she can't do it from an office. She is the one who goes out and collects

263

intel for Eva." Robert was doing his best to be truthful without revealing his transgression.

Bridget narrowed her eyes at him. "I'm not happy about this. I need to collect blood samples before and after."

"I'm sorry." He wasn't. He'd done what was right by Sharon, and that was his number one priority.

"No, you're not. But what's done is done. I'm going to stay down here and watch her. This is Julian's first transition, and he is not ready for that. This is a good learning opportunity for him."

"Thank you." As much as Robert liked Julian, he didn't trust the young, inexperienced doctor with Sharon's life.

Bridget's eyes softened. "Would you like to stay here with her?"

"Yes, please. Very much so. But I have to ask Kian if it's okay for me to take time off from work."

"I'm sure it is."

They all kept forgetting that he wasn't one of them. It was nice to feel accepted, but it wasn't his reality. "I need to ask."

"Of course. Would you like to use my phone?"

He shook his head. "I'll go over to his office. Sharon will be okay for a few minutes without me, right?"

"Don't worry about a thing. I'm here, and I'm watching the monitors. See?" She turned her laptop around so he could see the screen. "All of Sharon's vitals are on display here. I even take it with me to the bathroom."

He pushed to his feet. "Thank you. I won't be long."

Unless Kian refused his request.

There was no reason for the regent to do so, but in Robert's experience leaders didn't always do what made sense. Sometimes it was more about power play than about actual work that needed to be done.

Kian might get angry for the same reason Bridget had and retaliate by not letting Robert watch over Sharon through her transition. It would be a cruel punishment, but not undeserved.

After all, Robert had deliberately broken the rules.

"Come in," Kian said as Robert was about to knock on his door.

He walked in and stood in front of Kian's desk. "I have a favor to ask. I need a day off."

Kian arched a brow. "Because?"

"Sharon is transitioning."

A wide grin, full of white gleaming teeth, split Kian's face. "Congratulations." He rose to his feet and pulled Robert into what Anandur called a bro hug.

Standing stiffly as a telephone pole, Robert didn't know how to react. Was he supposed to slap Kian's back in return? But what if he did it too hard? Not hard enough? What was the protocol for those manly embraces?

Kian let go with a chuckle. "I guess Doomers don't go around embracing each other."

"No, sir."

"You'll get used to that. I'm not a big fan either, but some of life's events are important enough to merit them. And yes, of course you can take a day off, even two or three if needed. Your place is by your woman."

"Thank you, sir."

"Drop the sir, Robert. You're not in the military camp anymore."

Damn, why did he have to say the same thing Sebastian had? Robert wanted no reminder of his former commander. Especially not coming out of Kian's mouth. He respected the guy too much.

"I'll do my best."

Kian patted his shoulder. "Old habits are hard to break, and they have a tendency to reemerge in times of stress. They provide reassurance and stability in an unstable world. Once the crisis is over, I know you'll loosen up."

This was very unlike Sebastian, and the reason Robert held Kian in such high regard. This man loved his people. He was a strong leader and a demanding one, but he was also fair.

"Thank you. I appreciate your patience with me."

Kian arched a brow. "Patience has nothing to do with it. If you're more comfortable calling me sir than using my name, I don't have a problem with that. I don't care either way. I just want you to feel safe here."

"I do."

"You still walk on eggshells around me."

"Out of respect."

Kian arched a brow again.

"And a little fear. After all, my future is in your hands."

CHAPTER 55: TURNER

"*C*ome on, Turner, don't be such a stick-in-the-mud," Alfred whined. "This strip club is so famous it's a tourist attraction."

"That's why we shouldn't go. A tourist attraction is a perfect target for thieves and thugs and muggers and every other conceivable scum. I stay away from places like that on principle."

Alfred crossed his arms over his chest and pouted like a toddler. "I can go by myself."

Right. As if he would let the guy out at night in a city where tourists were advised not to venture out after dark. Alfred was going to get robbed or kidnapped or worse.

"No."

The toddler attitude continued. "You can't tell me what to do. We are not in the army, and you're not my commanding officer. You're not my wife or mother either."

That gave Turner an idea. "Does your wife know where you want to go?"

Alfred put his hands on his love handles and leaned forward. "Yes, she does. I told her it's on my bucket list of things I want to do before I die. I promised not to touch anyone or anything."

"Since when is it on your list? If it were, I'm sure you would have mentioned it before."

"Since I found it last night on the internet and added it to my list. I sent a link to Janet, and she told me to go for it."

The guy's wife must be the most understanding woman ever. Either that or she was so sick of his whining that she agreed to him going to the famous strip club just to shut him up.

But that was beside the point.

The club was on Alfred's bloody bucket list, and it didn't matter that it was a later addition. What were the guy's chances of ever revisiting Cochabamba?

"Take your gun."

Alfred dropped to his knees. "Thank you!"

"Stop the theatrics. And don't forget the silencer."

The guy pushed up and saluted. "Yes, sir."

As Turner got dressed, he debated whether he should call Bridget and tell her that he was going to a strip club. But that was too much like asking her permission. It wasn't as if he was going to do something morally wrong. After all, he was only going as a favor to Alfred.

Besides, he couldn't risk her telling him not to go and look like an idiot in front of Alfred, or conversely go anyway and deal with Bridget's temper later.

Not a good idea.

He'd tell her later tonight when he called her, and they would have a good laugh about Alfred and his bucket list.

After a quick phone call to the transport service he used while staying in the city, the two of them headed to the hotel's small lobby and waited for the car to arrive.

It was a reputable establishment he'd vetted extensively the first time he'd done work for Sandoval, but that only meant that it was better than the alternatives. He'd been using it safely for years, so perhaps there was nothing to worry about.

Right. He was alive today because he always worried,

always searched for potential threats, and always took precautions.

Except, none of his carefully planned and executed evasive maneuvers had prevented the ambush in his own hometown. The only thing that had saved him was luck, or fate as Bridget called it. That event could've ended much differently.

As the transport dropped them off in front of the club, Turner relaxed. It was located on one of the city's better streets, and the crowd outside was mainly comprised of tourists, and not all of them were men. To his great surprise, Turner saw couples standing in line. Not what he'd expected, but then as someone who'd never been to a strip club he hadn't known what to expect. It just seemed logical that men would want to watch pretty women dance naked on stage. Weren't there strip clubs that catered to women?

"I'm so excited," Alfred said, bouncing on his feet.

"Let's see that we are getting in first."

If he wanted to ensure that Alfred got to put a check mark next to this item on his bucket list, he'd better bribe the bouncer to let them in.

"Come on, Alfred."

A folded Benjamin in the bouncer's hand put a toothy smile on the big guy's face, and they were let in through the VIP entrance.

"Sweet," Alfred said. "I owe you for this."

"Dangerous words to say to someone like me. I'll collect."

"Anything, man. Other than my first born, that is. But I don't think you'd want the brat."

"No, thank you. You can keep him."

When the show began, the hacker's jaw dropped and stayed like that until it was over. He only closed it to sip on the soft drink Turner ordered for him, then the thing dropped again.

Ridiculous.

"Let's go, Alfred."

"It's not over."

"We are not staying for the lap dances. You promised your wife no touching."

The guy sighed. "Yeah, I did."

Leaving early meant that there was no crowd in front of the club. The bouncer stood with his back to the street, watching for disturbances inside the club.

Turner pulled out his phone and called the transport.

Alfred tucked his hands into his pockets and sighed again. "They were so beautiful. It's a shame taking pictures was not allowed."

"I saw a few guys snapping away with their phones."

"I should have done the same. Fuck, I need to take a piss."

For heaven's sake, the guy was a toddler in an adult male chubby body. He probably wanted to go back and take pictures.

"Go. But do it quickly. I don't want to have to come and get you."

"No worries, boss." Alfred turned around and approached the bouncer. "Can you tell me where the men's room is?"

Glancing at Turner, the guy smiled. "I show you. Come."

Turner shook his head. Obviously, the guy remembered the folded hundred dollar bill he'd put in his hand. But if the bouncer was hoping for a juicy tip from Alfred, he was going to be disappointed.

As he watched the two wind their way in between the tightly-packed small tables, the sight of the nearly nude girls rubbing themselves against male crotches was mildly disturbing.

It was a kind of prostitution, and Turner had lost his appetite for it.

He had been with a fair number of beautiful women, and some had even danced naked for him like the beauties on stage had done tonight. Professionals, who knew all the right moves. But none could compare to Bridget's amateur performance. What made all the difference was that she'd wanted him and not the generous tip.

Preoccupied, and with the loud music blasting through the club's open doors, Turner hadn't heard a thing until the barrel of a gun was pressed against his temple. "Don't make a sound, hombre. Walk." A hand closed around his bicep, pulling him away from the entrance.

The voice sounded familiar—the barely there Spanish accent mild, the cultured tone bordering on snobbish.

Where had he heard it before? It had the same inflection as Sandoval's.

The fucking nephew?

The guy he'd rescued from a gang that had kidnapped him for ransom?

Arturo Junior was Sandoval's only nephew and the one he was grooming as his successor. Not because the kid was exceptional in any way, but because Sandoval had only daughters. In South American culture, Sandoval's options were his less than spectacular nephew or the husband of one of his daughters. The problem was that none of them was of marrying age yet.

He was stuck with Arturo Junior.

Turner needed to keep the guy talking until Alfred and the bouncer returned. The hacker wasn't a soldier, but he knew how to handle the handgun he was carrying under his suit jacket.

"Why, Arturo?"

"Why? You ask me why, you fucking idiot? You killed Xavier," the guy whispered in his ear as he pulled him toward the alley between the club and the next building. "It wasn't your finger on the trigger, but it was the same thing."

The kid's slight accent was the only indication he wasn't American. Sandoval hadn't stinted on his nephew's education, sending him to the best business school in the States.

Turner resisted. "Who was Xavier to you?"

The grip on his arm tightened. "He was everything to me.

And if not for you, we could've been living happily together far away from here. You think my uncle would've accepted a gay man as his successor? After he killed my lover, he would've had me killed to spare himself the shame."

All the puzzle pieces snapped into place.

Arturo Junior had staged his own abduction to extort money from his uncle, hoping to spend the rest of his life in comfort with his lover by his side. The question was whether Xavier had been in it for Arturo, or for the money. The gang that had staged the kidnapping hadn't been made up of amateurs. They had been major cocaine distributors.

But that wasn't what Arturo Junior needed to hear while holding a gun to Turner's temple.

What the hell was taking Alfred so long?

Turner was running out of time. He would have to disarm the nephew himself before the kid dragged him into the alley and finished what his hired goons had failed to do in L.A.

It was risky.

All the kid needed to do was pull the trigger, and Turner's brain would splatter all over the sidewalk.

A split second was all Turner needed. A little acting should confuse the guy and distract him for a moment. He started shaking. "I wish I could tell my wife I loved her one last time."

The guy shoved him harder. "You don't have a wife."

"I was about to get married. I met a wonderful lady, a doctor…" He emitted what sounded like a sob.

The grip on his arm loosened just a fraction. It was all he needed.

Dropping down, Turner grabbed Arturo Junior's ankles and pulled with all his strength. The guy went flying backward, but the gun was still clutched in his hand, and he fired.

The bullet missed.

From his crouching position, Turner kicked out, sending the weapon clattering to the pavement. The nephew flipped over and reached for it, but by then Turner had released his

272

own from the holster, sat on the guy, and held it to the back of his neck.

"Don't move."

"Do it. Shoot me. I have nothing to live for anyway."

Fucking hell. Why did he feel sorry for the kid?

"I'm not a murderer."

"Could've fooled me."

"What's going on?" Alfred said from behind them.

"You missed all the action. Say hello to Arturo Junior."

CHAPTER 56: SHARON

Sharon opened her eyes in an unfamiliar room. Robert was sitting on a chair next to her bed, his elbows propped on his knees and his head propped on his hands.

"Where am I?" She asked. "Is it a hospital?"

He lifted his head and smiled. "It's a clinic. I'm so happy you're awake."

"Did I pass out again?"

"I couldn't wake you up in the morning. You were unconscious."

"Oh, wow, that's serious. What's wrong with me?"

He took her hand, careful of the intravenous needle. "Apparently, you're transitioning," he whispered.

Why was he whispering? Was there another patient in the room with her?

Sharon turned her head to one side and then the other, but hers was the only bed in there.

"Why are you whispering?"

"You're not supposed to know about it, remember?"

"Oh, yeah. What should I do?"

"I'm allowed to tell you now, so all you have to do is act like you did when I first told you."

"Got it."

She looked at the drip tube. "What's in it?"

"Just fluids. Would you like me to raise the back of the bed?"

"Yes, please."

Robert took the remote from the side table and pressed a button. "Is that good?" He stopped when the back was inclined in close to a forty-five-degree angle.

"Perfect." Sharon pushed herself up to a more comfortable position. "How long have I been in here?"

"Since early morning. It's after midnight now. Let me get you a cup of water. You're probably parched."

"Thank you."

While Robert got busy filling a paper cup with water from the pitcher on her bedside table, Sharon made a quick calculation. Early morning by Robert's standards was around five am. She'd fallen asleep around nine in the evening, which meant that she'd been out for over twenty-seven hours.

Horrified, Sharon realized that after this long without a change of tampon meant that she was probably lying in a pool of blood.

Then another thought struck her, worse than the first. If she was being provided fluids intravenously, those fluids had to come out on the other side, which meant a catheter.

Immortal or not, she was going to die of embarrassment if Julian had inserted it.

"Um, Robert? Who put in the IV? Was it Julian?"

God, let it be a nurse. It would be freaking embarrassing even if a woman had done it, but an unfamiliar nurse was infinitely better than a young, hot doctor, whom she'd just had dinner with.

He handed her the plastic cup. "No, it was Dr. Bridget, Julian's mother."

"Thank God." Sharon slumped against the bed's raised back. "Thank you for making sure it was a woman. I would have been mortified if it were Julian." She took a few sips of water, then chugged the rest. Apparently, she'd been thirstier than she'd thought.

Robert rubbed his stubbled chin. "I can't take credit for it. With the state of panic I was in, your modesty or my jealousy were the last things on my mind. But Bridget said Julian was not experienced with transitions yet, and that he should just watch this time."

Sharon groaned. "So he was here when she did it?"

"No. She told us both to wait outside."

"Remind me to thank her for that."

"She is probably going to come in at any moment." Robert leaned up and kissed her lips lightly. "Remember to act surprised." He whispered.

A moment later there was a knock on the door, and then the doctor entered without waiting for a reply. It was a little rude in Sharon's opinion, but then in her experience doctors were strange people. Some were courteous, and some were not.

"Hello, Sharon. I'm Doctor Bridget." The woman offered her hand.

Sharon shook the woman's hand, taking the opportunity to look closely at her pretty face. "Nice to meet you. Thanks for taking care of me."

Whichever type Dr. Bridget was, the courteous or the rude, she definitely didn't look like Sharon would have imagined Julian's mom to look like. First of all, she was too young to be anyone's mom unless she went to medical school while raising a child, and secondly, the woman was tiny, and Julian was tall.

"You're welcome. How are you feeling?" the redheaded doctor asked.

"Good. Better than yesterday. No cramps."

"No sore muscles?"

"Nope."

Julian's mom frowned. "Did Robert fill you in on what's

276

going on?"

"Oh my gosh, he did." Sharon gasped dramatically and put the hand not connected to tubes on her chest. "I was sure he was pulling my leg, but then he showed me his fangs, and oh, wow. I still can't believe it." She narrowed her eyes at Bridget and then at Robert. "If those things are prosthetics and you guys are pranking me, I'm never going to forgive you." She pointed a finger at Robert, then at Julian's mom. "And if you're not a real doctor, you too."

It was a very well done performance, if she said so herself, but Bridget seemed doubtful.

Of course. They were so dumb. Could the doctor smell the lie? But then Sharon wasn't lying. She was just replaying her former reaction as authentically as she could.

Bridget smiled. "It's quite a shock to discover that humans are not the only intelligent species on earth."

"Are there more? I mean other than humans and immortals? What about shapeshifters? Or werewolves? Vampires? Angels?" She'd asked Robert the same questions, but he'd admitted to having had a very limited education. Perhaps the doctor knew more.

"Not as far as we know. But I'm not dismissing the possibility. In the same way as humans are not aware of our existence, we might not be aware of the existence of other hidden species."

"Yeah. What about aliens?"

The doctor chuckled. "You should ask Julian about that."

"I will." Her face twisted in an involuntary grimace. Even though it never happened, she couldn't banish the image of him cleaning her up before inserting the catheter.

The doctor pulled out her stethoscope from her coat pocket and turned to Robert. "Would you excuse us for a few minutes? I need to examine Sharon."

"Of course." He gave Sharon's hand a gentle squeeze. "I'll be outside."

"Okay."

Doctor Bridget waited for the door to close behind Robert. "Can you tell me what the grimace was all about? Did Julian do or say something to offend you?"

Sharon shook her head. "No way. I love Julian." She quickly added, "Like a brother. But I don't want him to handle my privates, especially when I'm on my period."

"He didn't. I did."

"I know, and you have my eternal gratitude and apologies for it. It's just that I can't stop thinking that it might have been him. I would've avoided him for the rest of my life. Ugh, what a bad time to transition. I hate having periods. I should take one of those six-month contraceptive shots and be free of them, but I'm scared. I heard there are a lot of side effects. Like gaining weight. I can't afford my ass to get any bigger." Sharon was babbling to cover her embarrassment.

Bridget chuckled. "I have good news for you. Immortal females don't get menses."

That wasn't good news. "Are you saying that I won't be able to have children?" Robert hadn't said anything about that, the asshat. What if transitioned females were rendered infertile? She would've never agreed to let him bite her without protection if she'd known that. She'd always imagined having a family.

Bridget sat on the chair Robert had vacated. "Immortal females ovulate when their body recognizes a sexual partner that is biologically compatible. A female is born with all the eggs she'll ever have. With our long lifespans, we can't afford to waste any."

"Well, that's a relief. I can't imagine life without children." She would have added something about ending Robert's prospects of fatherhood in retaliation, but that would've implied prior knowledge.

"Our long lives also mean that even when we have a compatible partner, conception is rare. It's an evolutionary balancing factor. Without it, our species would've overrun the earth a long time ago."

CHAPTER 57: TURNER

"*D*o you think he'll let him live?" Alfred asked as they left Sandoval's compound.

"Yeah, I think he will."

Turner had delivered the unconscious, hog-tied Arturo Junior to his uncle, and after the nephew had been ensconced in one of the rooms in the basement, he'd had a long heart to heart talk with the man.

Under different circumstances, he would've killed Junior on the spot. Letting compassion dictate his actions and leaving a threat alive was an amateur's move. But given Turner's impending transition and possible demise, the threat would no longer be relevant. He could afford to spare the nephew's life. Except, it didn't make sense to grant Junior another chance on life just to have Sandoval take it away.

Hence the talk.

The strangest one Turner ever had.

He'd known Latino men were not afraid to show emotions and were much less reserved than Americans and Europeans, but he hadn't been prepared for a man like Sandoval to cry openly for hours, including loud sobs and the invoking of the Virgin Mary and begging the heavens for help.

The man was as ruthless as they came, not a gentle soul.

After hearing Turner out, Sandoval had been grief-stricken, devastated worse than if Junior had arrived in a body bag.

It had taken hours to talk him into seeing that this wasn't the end of the world. The conversation had drained Turner worse than a bare knuckle match with a champion fighter. Faking empathy and compassion had stretched his acting skills to the limit, as had dealing with Sandoval's over the top emotional outbursts.

He needed to hear Bridget's calm, rational voice to regain his equilibrium.

Back in the hotel room, Turner checked the time before dialing her number. She was probably asleep, but he couldn't wait until morning to tell her the good news that he was no longer in danger.

"Hi, Victor," she answered right away even though it was late at night in Los Angeles.

"What are you doing awake?"

"Another female Dormant is transitioning. I'm down in the clinic, watching over her."

"Congratulations."

"Thank you. What are you doing awake? Or is it morning already where you are?"

"Almost. It's sunrise. But I haven't been to bed yet. I had some excitement last night."

"What happened?" Her previously cheerful tone turned somber.

He told her a shortened version of the events. "The good news is that I found who was after me and eliminated the threat."

"Did you? His uncle can release Junior tomorrow, and he'll just resume his vendetta."

"I don't think so. I had a long talk with my client."

"What did you tell him?"

"Basically, I asked him to forgive the kid. I told him Junior had thought he had no other choice, and that this was the only way for him to be with the person he loved. He knew his uncle would not accept him, and even if he had, that he wouldn't allow the boyfriend anywhere near him."

"I don't see how it solves the problem of Junior coming after you."

"I hope I convinced the uncle to give the kid another chance. I told him that he would gain Junior's loyalty by accepting him and his natural, God-given inclinations."

"God-given?"

Turner rubbed his hand over the back of his neck. "I know. That was underhanded, but I was running out of arguments. I asked him if he thought God made mistakes, which he naturally had to answer in the negative. I then convinced him that God had a plan for Junior, and that after the kid served an appropriate penance, he should restore Junior as his right-hand man. "

"I'm impressed."

He chuckled. "I don't know if you should be. I was spouting nonsense. It took hours of talking during which he didn't stop crying and bemoaning Junior never having a family or fathering a successor. In the small hours of the morning, he had an epiphany. Junior can have a wife and have kids while keeping a male lover on the side."

"I pity the future wife."

"Does it really matter if the extramarital affair is with a female or a male? Because that's the norm here."

"For men."

"Yes. I didn't say I condone it. It is what it is."

"Right. It would take longer than even an immortal's lifespan to fix everything that is wrong with this world."

CHAPTER 58: BRIDGET

"*A*re you ready for the test? Bridget asked.

Sharon nodded, her eyes wide and sparkling with excitement.

The girl was going through the process of internalizing the transition much easier than the others. Perhaps it was because of how mild her symptoms were, or perhaps she just had an open mind and didn't fear change.

"It's going to hurt a little." Bridget lifted the small scalpel off the tray.

"Go for it, Doc." Sharon offered her palm.

As she made the incision, Bridget heard Robert suck in a breath.

Sharon only winced.

Julian played the part of a fly on the wall, watching silently and not moving a muscle.

As familiar as this process was, it never failed to excite her. It was like delivering babies. No matter how many a midwife or a doctor had welcomed into this world, a new life brought joy and excitement. Well, not always, shit happened, but most of the time.

No more than a minute had passed, and yet it was enough time for Bridget's anxiety to spike. Picking up a gauze square, she held Sharon's hand and dabbed at the cut, holding her breath while cleaning the blood away.

She let out a relieved breath. The cut was closing.

"Welcome to immortality, Sharon." Bridget backed away to let Robert come forward and celebrate the good news with his girl.

"Thank you, Doctor," Sharon said through teary eyes.

"You're welcome."

"Congratulations to both of you," Julian said.

Bridget threaded her arm through her son's. "Come on, let's give them some privacy."

As they left the room, Julian closed the door behind them. "It was very moving. I didn't expect it to affect me like that."

She patted his shoulder. "It's like delivering a baby. Though in this case, the baby is immortal and fully grown."

For once, Julian hadn't retorted with a joke, which attested to his emotional state.

"I think you can manage without me from here on out. Before dismissing Sharon, give her the same instructions you would give a patient recovering from surgery."

"I got it. You're free to go."

"Call me if you need me." She removed the white coat and hung it on a peg.

Out in the hallway, Bridget stretched her arms and yawned. She should get some sleep. Turner was coming back tonight, and they were going out to celebrate at By Invitation Only. Syssi had suggested it as the best place for a special occasion and had made the reservations for them.

If the experience was as amazing as everyone who'd tried it was claiming, she might buy a membership. With Julian back and Turner in her life, she could occasionally treat her family to fancy dinners at the place. After all, she could afford it, and splurging on pampering the people she loved was never a waste of money.

CHAPTER 59: TURNER

"*W*elcome to By Invitation Only." The hostess smiled first at Bridget and then at Turner before picking up two leather-bound menus and leading them to their table.

He was still silently cursing the airline for the hour delay that had caused him to alter his plans for this evening. He'd been supposed to be home by five, which would've given them plenty of time for wild sex before getting ready for their seven o'clock dinner reservation.

Instead, to make it on time, they'd had to rush right out as soon as he'd gotten back. If it were up to him, Turner would've preferred to celebrate at home, but Bridget had had other ideas.

Naturally, he'd known all about the exclusive restaurant and the movers and shakers who bought the insanely expensive memberships for the privilege of dining on the best gourmet food outside of France. Not to mention the pleasure of having the culinary experience somewhere the paparazzi couldn't find them, which made it perfect for dining out with a mistress or a lover and other clandestine meetings.

He was intrigued. Nevertheless, Turner would have gladly skipped it for an evening at home with Bridget.

Small tables, most of them set for two, were accented by soft candlelight. It was ingeniously done, so the food was clearly illuminated but not the diners' faces. He had to squint to make out facial features, and then only when the diner bent his or her head down to scoop another morsel onto a fork.

Bridget had no such problems. Not only was her immortal eyesight sharper, it also functioned better in the dark.

When they were seated, and the hostess left them to peer over the menus, Bridget leaned closer to him and whispered, "Do you want me to tell you who is sitting where and with whom? I saw you straining to see if you can recognize anyone."

Turner would've loved to, but tonight was about Bridget and not about his insatiable curiosity.

"Maybe next time. Tonight I have eyes only for you."

That earned him a bright smile.

"In this case, how about you take me to the dance floor?"

Turner lifted the napkin off his knees, put it on the table, and pushed to his feet. "It would be my pleasure." He offered Bridget a hand up.

"You're a good dancer," she said after he twirled her expertly.

"Thank you, I took classes."

"Naturally."

"Meaning?"

She smiled. "Victor Turner has to excel at everything he does. For you, it's either not dance at all or dance like a pro. There is no middle."

He executed another twirl, then pulled her into his arms. "True. Does it bother you?"

"Not at all. It's one of the many things I love about you."

"I'm glad."

Victor held Bridget pressed tightly against him so she couldn't look into his eyes and guess his thoughts.

He could excel at many things but not at this. Not at love. He could fake it, tell Bridget he loved her too, and it wouldn't even be a lie, but it wouldn't be the truth either. Turner wished there were as many words to describe love as there were to describe the weather. Cold, chilly, or nippy, or wintery, or windy. It could be frosty or frigid or icy. Each term held a slightly different meaning.

But there was only one word for romantic love.

Fondness and the like were good to describe friendships, but not the feelings between a man and a woman, or two men in Junior's case.

Arturo Junior had no problem feeling love. As troubled as the young man was in other areas, it was obvious that he'd loved Xavier and had planned to spend the rest of his life with his partner.

Bridget pushed back a little and looked up at him. "What are you thinking about? I can almost hear the gears in your head spinning."

"I was thinking about Junior and how much he loved his boyfriend. No wonder he was bent on vendetta. I would have been too."

She grinned happily, no doubt taking his words to mean that he loved her. "I'm a doctor, so saying that I would kill someone to avenge the loss of a loved one is so wrong, but I would. At least I think so. I don't know if I'd have the stomach to actually carry it through."

"I hope you'll never face such a dilemma."

They'd already danced to the sounds of several songs, some slow, some fast when it occurred to Turner that only a week ago he would not have been able to carry on like that. If he kept going, Bridget would start suspecting that he was off the meds.

"If you don't mind, I'd rather sit the next few songs out."

"Sure. You should have told me that you were tired."

"I like dancing with you."

"We can rest a little and dance some more later."

"Sounds good to me."

Turner felt like a fraud. He needed to come clean instead of keeping up the pretense and hiding his decision to quit the chemo from her.

CHAPTER 60: BRIDGET

"*W*here are you taking me?" Turner asked.

Bridget had insisted on driving them to By Invitation Only, claiming that Victor was too tired after the long flight and she didn't trust him behind the wheel.

It was true, but only partially. She had a surprise for him.

"You'll see in a moment."

He glanced out the window. "It looks like we are going to my apartment."

Damn it. The guy was too shrewd for his own good. "Now look what you've done. You ruined my surprise."

"Which is?"

She cast him a sidelong glance. "It won't be much of a surprise if I tell you. Patience, my dear."

He crossed his arms over his chest. "It's not easy to surprise me."

"I know. Could you be a sport about it and pretend for five more minutes?"

"I don't see what's the point, but I'll humor you."

"Thank you."

Sometimes the guy was such a dry stick. Oh, well, no one was perfect.

"I'll even close my eyes."

That was nice of him. "Just don't fall asleep."

"I won't."

That remained to be seen. Flying first class, he'd had a comfortable fully reclined seat to sleep in, but the question was whether he had. The events that had preceded the flight had probably left him in an agitated state.

Knowing Victor, Bridget suspected he'd been busy replaying every move and action in his mind and trying to figure out if he could've done anything differently.

Fortunately, he wasn't snoring by the time they reached his building. "Unless you agree for me to carry you in, you need to open your eyes."

His eyes still closed, Victor chuckled. "Watching a tiny thing like you carry me inside might give the security guy a heart attack. I can't have it on my conscience."

She sighed. "So you know where we are."

"Obviously."

"But do you know why?"

"You want to show me something Ingrid had done?"

"You guessed it."

It was good Victor didn't have an immortal's sense of smell, or he would have known she was up to something.

"Close your eyes," she said as they reached his door.

"As you command."

Using the key Ingrid had dropped at her office, Bridget opened the door, and led Turner inside. "Okay, you can open them now."

Hesitantly, Victor opened one eye and then the other. "It's done."

"Surprise!" Bridget clapped her hands. "Do you like it?"

They'd agreed not to take peeks during the renovation and let Ingrid do her thing uninterrupted. As always, the interior designer delivered and then some.

"I don't recognize the place."

"Is it good or bad?"

"Good." He turned in a circle. "It feels so welcoming. Homey. I want to check out the couch."

She took his hand and tugged. "I have a better idea. Let's check out the rest of the apartment first." Meaning the master bedroom.

Victor's lips curled into a sly smile. "Lead the way."

Even the hallway was beautifully decorated with framed art hanging on the walls and sconces bisecting the space in between every two pictures. Earth tones galore, and yet Ingrid had managed to preserve some of the contemporary feel by using a light palette of colors and fixtures that were not overly ornate.

"Are you ready for the master bedroom?" Bridget paused in front of the closed double doors.

"Should I close my eyes again?"

"I didn't see it yet either. Should we both close our eyes?"

"If you want to." From his tone, it was obvious he thought the idea silly.

"Nah, let's just go in." She depressed the handle and pushed the door open.

"Wait." Victor caught her elbow. "I want to carry you in."

"That's silly." She giggled as he lifted her anyway.

"What better way to test the new mattress's bounciness than dropping you on it."

Bridget wrapped her arms around his neck. "No one is dropping anyone. I'm not letting go."

"Fine. More weight means more bounce." Holding her tight, he leaped onto the beautiful four-poster bed, turning mid-air to land on his tush.

Pretty impressive for a forty-six-year-old human on chemo. It seemed the side effects were finally lessening.

"Thank you." He kissed her.

"For what?"

"Pushing for this makeover. It's perfect in a way I couldn't have envisioned. I tried to make the place look less sterile for you. I even had Brian, my media specialist and a man of exquisite taste, come and spruce the place up a bit. But you saw the results."

"You mean the few pillows and a blanket he threw on the couch?"

Victor grimaced. "Yeah, that was Brian's work."

"But you asked him to do it." Which she thought had been incredibly sweet. He'd wanted his apartment to look nice for her.

"Well, to be honest, he suggested it, along with the wardrobe makeover."

Bridget laughed. "That explains so much. At first, you seemed so uncomfortable in these clothes, as if you were wearing a costume. But now you own the look, Mister Suave."

"You think I'm suave?"

"Indeed, and so very sexy." She lowered her voice and batted her eyelashes. "I think we should put this bed to the test."

Victor dropped back on the bed, pulling Bridget on top of him. "Kiss me, pretty lady."

CHAPTER 61: BRIDGET

*B*ridget cracked her eyes open and lifted her arm to check her watch. Crap, it was six-thirty in the morning. They'd overslept.

"Victor, wake up." She shook his shoulder.

Last night had been a night to remember. Turner's vigor and stamina were back. Even as tired as he'd been after his long flight, he'd made love to her for hours. She'd lost count of the orgasms.

No wonder he was sleeping like a dead man.

"Victor, we don't have any clothes here. You need to get back to my place and change."

He mumbled something and turned around, presenting her with his very fine posterior.

She sighed, debating whether she could fondle him a little to wake him up. But then one thing might lead to another, and before she knew it, they would be making love again. But regrettably, there was no time for that.

"Victor, you said you had a morning appointment. You'll have to cancel."

Groaning, he turned around. "Is there a chance Ingrid left a welcome home basket with coffee in it?"

"I doubt it, but I'll check the kitchen. In the meantime, get dressed."

He groaned again.

Not surprisingly, the kitchen was devoid of any food products. The cabinets were new, and even though the fridge wasn't, it was empty.

She padded back to the bedroom. "Sorry to disappoint you, but there is nothing there. We can stop on the way at a drive-through Starbucks."

Victor finished buttoning up his shirt. "No time. I need to get back, grab a one minute shower, change, and leave right away."

"I'll make coffee while you shower."

"Sounds like a plan."

They spent the drive home in silence, not because they were awkward with each other after last night's marathon sex session, or because they were too spent to summon the energy.

Well, maybe Victor was.

Bridget's excuse was more mundane. She had a hard time starting the day without a toothbrush and without a cup of coffee or two. With only a drink of water from the bathroom faucet, her mouth felt disgusting, and she wasn't in the mood to talk.

She should've planned this better. Except, the sex should have happened before the dinner date, and the trip to the renovated apartment should have been just a short visit, not a sleepover.

Back at her place, Victor rushed into the shower while she kicked off her sexy high-heeled shoes and padded to the kitchen to make coffee and a sandwich to go for Turner.

He ended up taking both to go.

"Drive safely," she called after him. "It's better to be late than get into an accident."

He waved a dismissive hand and blew her a kiss goodbye.

With a sigh, Bridget headed to the bathroom to finally

brush her teeth. It was a shame he'd scheduled a morning meeting instead of a morning cuddle with her in bed. She'd missed him when he'd been gone, especially at night when the bed felt big and empty and cold without him in it.

Soon, they would be moving into his apartment, and Bridget didn't know how she felt about it. Getting used to living outside the keep, away from her family and friends, wouldn't be easy.

On the other hand, it was exciting.

A new beginning. After all, she would be coming to work every day, so it wasn't as if she was saying goodbye. It was a good thing.

She should start packing their things.

Wrapped in a towel, she entered the walk-in closet and looked at the clothes hanging in neat rows, hers on one side, Victor's on the other. Two suitcases each should suffice.

Victor hadn't had time to unpack, and the suitcase he'd taken with him to South America lay open on the floor, its contents spilling out. It had probably unnerved him to no end to leave it like that. Victor liked his things organized.

Would he mind if she unpacked for him?

There was no reason he should. She'd handled his briefs and socks before, adding them to her laundry. He'd never voiced any objections. If she found anything that seemed like business-related material, she wasn't going to look at it, just leave it on his desk in Julian's old room where he'd set up shop.

Bridget got dressed, had another cup of coffee, and returned to the closet to take care of the unpacking. Some of the clothes went into the laundry basket, some into the dry-clean bin, and those that he hadn't used went back on the hangers. She left the few pieces of equipment that were at the bottom of the suitcase on the floor next to it, then moved them to one of the shelves.

Now that everything was organized, she would have an easier time packing for the move.

The last item was Turner's toiletries tote, which Bridget took with her to the bathroom. Toothbrush, toothpaste, a couple of unused disposable shavers, deodorant and aftershave.

That was it.

Bridget looked at the items lined up on the counter, wondering what was missing.

Duh, there was no shampoo and no conditioner.

Bridget smiled. Obviously, Victor had no use for those.

But there was something else that should've been there and wasn't. His medications.

Perhaps he'd put them in his laptop bag. It made sense. The bag was a carry on item while the suitcase went into the belly of the plane. Humans needed to keep their medications on hand.

Except, she had a nagging feeling that Victor hadn't.

Bridget opened the drawer where he kept his pills and took the containers out. To find out, all she had to do was to look at the date he'd gotten them, and multiply dosage times the number of days he should've been taking them, and then count the number of remaining pills and see if the numbers corresponded.

They didn't.

Turner had stopped taking them exactly nine days ago.

*T*urner knew he was in trouble the moment he entered Bridget's apartment, and not because he was so perceptive.

Right there on the coffee table, his pill containers were lined up in a straight row like a jury who'd already found him guilty and was just waiting to hear the judge's sentence.

The judge sat on the couch with her arms crossed over her chest and her blue eyes blazing with fury.

"When were you planning to tell me?"

"I was trying to summon the courage, but it seems I'm more cowardly than I thought." He put his laptop bag on the kitchen counter and walked over to sit next to Bridget on the couch. "Let me explain."

She dropped one of her arms to wave him on. "Please do." The arm went back across her chest.

"I couldn't function while taking these drugs. They made my brain foggy, they slowed my reflexes, and they killed my sex drive. I had to stop, or I would've gone insane."

"You're aware that you have no chance of going through the transition while you're sick, right? Even if you're a Dormant, it won't start until you get healthy."

As she turned to look at him, her eyes were no longer full

296

of fury, just sad. Which was much worse. "You know Roni's transition was delayed because he was sick. He only transitioned once he was healthy enough to endure it. You're a rational man, Victor. I can't understand why you expect irrational results."

"There must be another way. I can't deal with the chemo."

"Can't or won't?"

"I can't. Foggy brain means mistakes, and I can't afford to make them. Lives are at stake. Besides, if I kept taking the pills, I would be dead now. I would have died in that alley Arturo Junior was dragging me into. My reflexes and agility would've been impaired, and I couldn't have overpowered him."

As he'd expected, that gave Bridget pause.

She nodded. "Then I'm glad you stopped taking them. But you need to resume the treatment. Finish all your current jobs, and don't take on any new ones even if they are from old clients you don't want to lose. Tell them you're booked or something. Stay in bed if you need to, but get healthy. I need you to live." Her voice quivered, and the tears that had misted her eyes started spilling down her cheeks.

Wrapping his arms around her, he pulled her into his chest. "I really don't want to, but I'll do it for you. I'll wait until my schedule is clear, send Alice on a much needed paid vacation, and have you take care of me while the chemo sucks the life out of me."

She sniffled. "You make it sound so terrible."

"Because it is."

"I wish there was another way." She wiped the tears off her cheeks.

"There might be. Let me try an induction before I restart the chemo. You said it yourself. Every case is different, and no two Dormants transition the same way. It might work for me despite the cancer. It's worth the try. If it works, it will save me unnecessary hardship, and if it doesn't, I'll at least know that I have no choice and have to suffer through it."

Bridget looked him in the eyes. "I don't want you to ever again hide things from me, or lie to me. Is that clear?"

"Crystal."

"If you ever do that again, I'm going to kick you out and never let you back in again."

"Understood."

With a sigh, Bridget untangled herself from his arms, then took both of his hands in hers. "In the spirit of full disclosure, there are no guarantees the chemo will work, but you didn't stick with it long enough to evaluate if it has done you any good."

That was his main fear.

What if it all had been in vain?

What if his brilliant plan to escape the Grim Reaper had been flawed from the start because he hadn't known transition was not possible while the body was sick?

What if the treatment he dreaded wasn't even an option?

Unforeseen factors had the potential to derail every good plan, and regrettably, he couldn't control and manipulate nature or fate's design for him.

The thing was, Turner refused to accept that his fate was to die just when he'd found happiness for the first time in his life. He wasn't a saint, but he wasn't a bad man either.

Fate couldn't be so cruel.

Or could it?

The end... for now.

TURNER & BRIDGET'S STORY CULMINATES IN
BOOK 19
DARK OPERATIVE: THE DAWN OF LOVE

Dark Operative: The Dawn of Love is available on Amazon.

Dear reader,

Thank you for joining me on the continuing adventures of the ***Children of the Gods***.

As an independent author, I rely on your support to spread the word. So if you enjoyed the story, please share your experience, and if it isn't too much trouble, I would greatly appreciate a brief review on Amazon.

Click here to leave a review

Love & happy reading,

Isabell

JOIN THE CHILDREN OF THE GODS VIP CLUB TO GAIN ACCESS TO PREVIEW CHAPTERS, A **FREE** NARRATION OF GODDESS'S CHOICE, AND OTHER EXCLUSIVE CONTENT OFFERED ON THE VIP PORTAL AT ITLUCAS.COM

CLICK HERE TO JOIN

THE CHILDREN OF THE GODS SERIES

THE CHILDREN OF THE GODS ORIGINS

1: Goddess's Choice

When gods and immortals still ruled the ancient world, one young goddess risked everything for love.

2: Goddess's Hope

Hungry for power and infatuated with the beautiful Areana, Navuh plots his father's demise. After all, by getting rid of the insane god he would be doing the world a favor. Except, when gods and immortals conspire against each other, humanity pays the price.

But things are not what they seem, and prophecies should not to be trusted...

THE CHILDREN OF THE GODS

1: Dark Stranger The Dream

Syssi's paranormal foresight lands her a job at Dr. Amanda Dokani's neuroscience lab, but it fails to predict the thrilling yet terrifying turn her life will take. Syssi has no clue that her boss is an immortal who'll drag her into a secret, millennia-old battle over humanity's future. Nor does she realize that the professor's imposing brother is the mysterious stranger who's been starring in her dreams.

Since the dawn of human civilization, two warring factions of immortals—the descendants of the gods of old—have been secretly shaping its destiny. Leading the clandestine battle from his luxurious Los Angeles high-rise, Kian is surrounded by his clan, yet alone. Descending from a single goddess, clan members are forbidden to each other. And as the only other immortals are their hated enemies, Kian and his kin have been long resigned to a lonely existence of fleeting trysts with human partners. That is, until his sister makes a game-changing discovery—a mortal seeress who she believes is a dormant carrier of their genes. Ever the realist, Kian is skeptical and refuses Amanda's plea to attempt Syssi's activation. But when his enemies learn of the Dormant's existence, he's forced to rush her to the safety of his keep. Inexorably drawn to Syssi, Kian wrestles with his conscience as he is tempted to explore her budding interest in the darker shades of sensuality.

2: DARK STRANGER REVEALED

While sheltered in the clan's stronghold, Syssi is unaware that Kian and Amanda are not human, and neither are the supposedly religious fanatics that are after her. She feels a powerful connection to Kian, and as he introduces her to a world of pleasure she never dared imagine, his dominant sexuality is a revelation. Considering that she's completely out of her element, Syssi feels comfortable and safe letting go with him. That is, until she begins to suspect that all is not as it seems. Piecing the puzzle together, she draws a scary, yet wrong conclusion...

3: DARK STRANGER IMMORTAL

When Kian confesses his true nature, Syssi is not as much shocked by the revelation as she is wounded by what she perceives as his callous plans for her.

If she doesn't turn, he'll be forced to erase her memories and let her go. His family's safety demands secrecy – no one in the mortal world is allowed to know that immortals exist.

Resigned to the cruel reality that even if she stays on to never again leave the keep, she'll get old while Kian won't, Syssi is determined to enjoy what little time she has with him, one day at a time.

Can Kian let go of the mortal woman he loves? Will Syssi turn? And if she does, will she survive the dangerous transition?

4: DARK ENEMY TAKEN

Dalhu can't believe his luck when he stumbles upon the beautiful immortal professor. Presented with a once in a lifetime opportunity to grab an immortal female for himself, he kidnaps her and runs. If he ever gets caught, either by her people or his, his life is forfeit. But for a chance of a loving mate and a family of his own, Dalhu is prepared to do everything in his power to win Amanda's heart, and that includes leaving the Doom brotherhood and his old life behind.

Amanda soon discovers that there is more to the handsome Doomer than his dark past and a hulking, sexy body. But succumbing to her enemy's seduction, or worse, developing feelings for a ruthless killer is out of the question. No man is worth life on the run, not even the one and only immortal male she could claim as her own...

Her clan and her research must come first...

5: Dark Enemy Captive

When the rescue team returns with Amanda and the chained Dalhu to the keep, Amanda is not as thrilled to be back as she thought she'd be. Between Kian's contempt for her and Dalhu's imprisonment, Amanda's budding relationship with Dalhu seems doomed. Things start to look up when Annani offers her help, and together with Syssi they resolve to find a way for Amanda to be with Dalhu. But will she still want him when she realizes that he is responsible for her nephew's murder? Could she? Will she take the easy way out and choose Andrew instead?

6: Dark Enemy Redeemed

Amanda suspects that something fishy is going on onboard the Anna. But when her investigation of the peculiar all-female Russian crew fails to uncover anything other than more speculation, she decides it's time to stop playing detective and face her real problem —a man she shouldn't want but can't live without.

6.5: My Dark Amazon

When Michael and Kri fight off a gang of humans, Michael gets stabbed. The injury to his immortal body recovers fast, but the one to his ego takes longer, putting a strain on his relationship with Kri.

7: Dark Warrior Mine

When Andrew is forced to retire from active duty, he believes that all he has to look forward to is a boring desk job. His glory days in special ops are over. But as it turns out, his thrill ride has just begun. Andrew discovers not only that immortals exist and have been manipulating global affairs since antiquity, but that he and his sister are rare possessors of the immortal genes.

Problem is, Andrew might be too old to attempt the activation process. His sister, who is fourteen years his junior, barely made it through the transition, so the odds of him coming out of it alive, let alone immortal, are slim.

But fate may force his hand.

Helping a friend find his long-lost daughter, Andrew finds a woman who's worth taking the risk for. Nathalie might be a Dormant, but the only way to find out for sure requires fangs and venom.

8: Dark Warrior's Promise

Andrew and Nathalie's love flourishes, but the secrets they keep from each other taint their relationship with doubts and suspicions. In the meantime, Sebastian and his men are getting bolder, and the storm that's brewing will shift the balance of power in the millennia-old conflict between Annani's clan and its enemies.

9: Dark Warrior's Destiny

The new ghost in Nathalie's head remembers who he was in life, providing Andrew and her with indisputable proof that he is real and not a figment of her imagination.

Convinced that she is a Dormant, Andrew decides to go forward with his transition immediately after the rescue mission at the Doomers' HQ.

Fearing for his life, Nathalie pleads with him to reconsider. She'd rather spend the rest of her mortal days with Andrew than risk what they have for the fickle promise of immortality.

While the clan gets ready for battle, Carol gets help from an unlikely ally. Sebastian's second-in-command can no longer ignore the torment she suffers at the hands of his commander and offers to help her, but only if she agrees to his terms.

10: Dark Warrior's Legacy

Andrew's acclimation to his post-transition body isn't easy. His senses are sharper, he's bigger, stronger, and hungrier. Nathalie fears that the changes in the man she loves are more than physical. Measuring up to this new version of him is going to be a challenge.

Carol and Robert are disillusioned with each other. They are not destined mates, and love is not on the horizon. When Robert's three months are up, he might be left with nothing to show for his sacrifice.

Lana contacts Anandur with disturbing news; the yacht and its human cargo are in Mexico. Kian must find a way to apprehend Alex and rescue the women on board without causing an international incident.

Get ready for the heart pounding conclusion to Brundar and Calypso's story.

Callie still couldn't wrap her head around it, nor could she summon even a smidgen of sorrow or regret. After all, she had some memories with him that weren't horrible. She should've felt something. But there was nothing, not even shock. Not even horror at what had transpired over the last couple of hours.

Maybe it was a typical response for survivors--feeling euphoric for the simple reason that they were alive. Especially when that survival was nothing short of miraculous.

Brundar's cold hand closed around hers, reminding her that they weren't out of the woods yet. Her injuries were superficial, and the most she had to worry about was some scarring. But, despite his and Anandur's reassurances, Brundar might never walk again.

If he ended up crippled because of her, she would never forgive herself for getting him involved in her crap.

"Are you okay, sweetling? Are you in pain?" Brundar asked.

Her injuries were nothing compared to his, and yet he was concerned about her. God, she loved this man. The thing was, if she told him that, he would run off, or crawl away as was the case.

Hey, maybe this was the perfect opportunity to spring it on him.

17: Dark Operative: A Shadow of Death

As a brilliant strategist and the only human entrusted with the secret of immortals' existence, Turner is both an asset and a liability to the clan. His request to attempt transition into immortality as an alternative to cancer treatments cannot be denied without risking the clan's exposure. On the other hand, approving it means risking his premature death. In both scenarios, the clan will lose a valuable ally.

When the decision is left to the clan's physician, Turner makes plans to manipulate her by taking advantage of her interest in him.

Will Bridget fall for the cold, calculated operative? Or will Turner fall into his own trap?

18: Dark Operative: A Glimmer of Hope

As Turner and Bridget's relationship deepens, living together seems like the right move, but to make it work both need to make concessions.

Bridget is realistic and keeps her expectations low. Turner could never be the truelove mate she yearns for, but he is as good as she's going to get. Other than his emotional limitations, he's perfect in every way.

Turner's hard shell is starting to show cracks. He wants immortality, he wants to be part of the clan, and he wants Bridget, but he doesn't want to cause her pain.

His options are either abandon his quest for immortality and give Bridget his few remaining decades, or abandon Bridget by going for the transition and most likely dying. His rational mind dictates that he chooses the former, but his gut pulls him toward the latter. Which one is he going to trust?

19: Dark Operative: The Dawn of Love

Get ready for the exciting finale of Bridget and Turner's story!

20: Dark Survivor Awakened

This was a strange new world she had awakened to.

Her memory loss must have been catastrophic because almost nothing was familiar. The language was foreign to her, with only a few words bearing some similarity to the language she thought in. Still, a full moon cycle had passed since her awakening, and little by little she was gaining basic understanding of it--only a few words and phrases, but she was learning more each day.

A week or so ago, a little girl on the street had tugged on her mother's sleeve and pointed at her. "Look, Mama, Wonder Woman!"

The mother smiled apologetically, saying something in the language these people spoke, then scurried away with the child looking behind her shoulder and grinning.

When it happened again with another child on the same day, it was settled.

Wonder Woman must have been the name of someone important in this strange world she had awoken to, and since both times it had been said with a smile it must have been a good one.

Wonder had a nice ring to it.

She just wished she knew what it meant.

21: Dark Survivor Echoes of Love

Wonder's journey continues in *Dark Survivor Echoes of Love*.

22: Dark Survivor Reunited

The exciting finale of Wonder and Anandur's story.

23: Dark Widow's Secret

Vivian and her daughter share a powerful telepathic connection, so when Ella can't be reached by conventional or psychic means, her mother fears the worst.

Help arrives from an unexpected source when Vivian gets a call from the young doctor she met at a psychic convention. Turns out Julian belongs to a private organization specializing in retrieving missing girls.

As Julian's clan mobilizes its considerable resources to rescue the daughter, Magnus is charged with keeping the gorgeous young mother safe.

Worry for Ella and the secrets Vivian and Magnus keep from each other should be enough to prevent the sparks of attraction from kindling a blaze of desire. Except, these pesky sparks have a mind of their own.

24: Dark Widow's Curse

A simple rescue operation turns into mission impossible when the Russian mafia gets involved. Bad things are supposed to come in threes, but in Vivian's case, it seems like there is no limit to bad luck. Her family and everyone who gets close to her is affected by her curse.

Will Magnus and his people prove her wrong?

25: Dark Widow's Blessing

The thrilling finale of the Dark Widow trilogy!

26: Dark Dream's Temptation

Julian has known Ella is the one for him from the moment he saw her picture, but when he finally frees her from captivity, she seems indifferent to him. Could he have been mistaken?

Ella's rescue should've ended that chapter in her life, but it seems like the road back to normalcy has just begun and it's full of obstacles. Between the pitying looks she gets and her mother's attempts to get her into therapy, Ella feels like she's typecast as a victim, when nothing could be further from the truth. She's a tough survivor, and she's going to prove it.

Strangely, the only one who seems to understand is Logan, who keeps popping up in her dreams. But then, he's a figment of her imagination—or is he?

27: DARK DREAM'S UNRAVELING

While trying to figure out a way around Logan's silencing compulsion, Ella concocts an ambitious plan. What if instead of trying to keep him out of her dreams, she could pretend to like him and lure him into a trap?

Catching Navuh's son would be a major boon for the clan, as well as for Ella. She will have her revenge, turning the tables on another scumbag out to get her.

28: DARK DREAM'S TRAP

The trap is set, but who is the hunter and who is the prey? Find out in this heart-pounding conclusion to the *Dark Dream* trilogy.

29: DARK PRINCE'S ENIGMA

As the son of the most dangerous male on the planet, Lokan lives by three rules:

Don't trust a soul.

Don't show emotions.

And don't get attached.

Will one extraordinary woman make him break all three?

30: DARK PRINCE'S DILEMMA

Will Kian decide that the benefits of trusting Lokan outweigh the risks?

Will Lokan betray his father and brothers for the greater good of his people?

Are Carol and Lokan true-love mates, or is one of them playing the other?

So many questions, the path ahead is anything but clear.

31: DARK PRINCE'S AGENDA

While Turner and Kian work out the details of Areana's rescue plan,

Carol and Lokan's tumultuous relationship hits another snag. Is it a sign of things to come?

32 : DARK QUEEN'S QUEST

A former beauty queen, a retired undercover agent, and a successful model, Mey is not the typical damsel in distress. But when her sister drops off the radar and then someone starts following her around, she panics.

Following a vague clue that Kalugal might be in New York, Kian sends a team headed by Yamanu to search for him.

As Mey and Yamanu's paths cross, he offers her his help and protection, but will that be all?

33: DARK QUEEN'S KNIGHT

As the only member of his clan with a godlike power over human minds, Yamanu has been shielding his people for centuries, but that power comes at a steep price. When Mey enters his life, he's faced with the most difficult choice.

The safety of his clan or a future with his fated mate.

34: DARK QUEEN'S ARMY

As Mey anxiously waits for her transition to begin and for Yamanu to test whether his godlike powers are gone, the clan sets out to solve two mysteries:

Where is Jin, and is she there voluntarily?

Where is Kalugal, and what is he up to?

35: DARK SPY CONSCRIPTED

Jin possesses a unique paranormal ability. Just by touching someone, she can insert a mental hook into their psyche and tie a string of her consciousness to it, creating a tether. That doesn't make her a spy, though, not unless her talent is discovered by those seeking to exploit it.

36: DARK SPY'S MISSION

Jin's first spying mission is supposed to be easy. Walk into the club, touch Kalugal to tether her consciousness to him, and walk out.

Except, they should have known better.

37: DARK SPY'S RESOLUTION

The best-laid plans often go awry...

38: Dark Overlord New Horizon

Jacki has two talents that set her apart from the rest of the human race.

She has unpredictable glimpses of other people's futures, and she is immune to mind manipulation.

Unfortunately, both talents are pretty useless for finding a job other than the one she had in the government's paranormal division.

It seemed like a sweet deal, until she found out that the director planned on producing super babies by compelling the recruits into pairing up. When an opportunity to escape the program presented itself, she took it, only to find out that humans are not at the top of the food chain.

Immortals are real, and at the very top of the hierarchy is Kalugal, the most powerful, arrogant, and sexiest male she has ever met.

With one look, he sets her blood on fire, but Jacki is not a fool. A man like him will never think of her as anything more than a tasty snack, while she will never settle for anything less than his heart.

39: Dark Overlord's Wife

Jacki is still clinging to her all-or-nothing policy, but Kalugal is chipping away at her resistance. Perhaps it's time to ease up on her convictions. A little less than all is still much better than nothing, and a couple of decades with a demigod is probably worth more than a lifetime with a mere mortal.

40: Dark Overlord's Clan

As Jacki and Kalugal prepare to celebrate their union, Kian takes every precaution to safeguard his people. Except, Kalugal and his men are not his only potential adversaries, and compulsion is not the only power he should fear.

41: Dark Choices The Quandary

When Rufsur and Edna meet, the attraction is as unexpected as it is undeniable. Except, she's the clan's judge and councilwoman, and he's Kalugal's second-in-command. Will loyalty and duty to their people keep them apart?

42: Dark Choices Paradigm Shift

Edna and Rufsur are miserable without each other, and their two-week separation seems like an eternity. Long-distance relationships are difficult, but for immortal couples they are impossible. Unless one of them is willing to leave everything behind for the other, things are just going to get worse. Except, the cost of compromise is far greater than giving up their comfortable lives and hard-earned positions. The future of their people is on the line.

For a **FREE** Audiobook, Preview chapters, And other goodies offered only to my **VIPs**,

JOIN THE VIP CLUB AT ITLUCAS.COM

TRY THE SERIES ON

AUDIBLE

2 FREE audiobooks with your new Audible subscription!

THE PERFECT MATCH SERIES

PERFECT MATCH 1: VAMPIRE'S CONSORT

When Gabriel's company is ready to start beta testing, he invites his old crush to inspect its medical safety protocol.

Curious about the revolutionary technology of the *Perfect Match Virtual Fantasy-Fulfillment studios*, Brenna agrees.

Neither expects to end up partnering for its first fully immersive test run.

PERFECT MATCH 2: KING'S CHOSEN

When Lisa's nutty friends get her a gift certificate to *Perfect Match Virtual Fantasy Studios*, she has no intentions of using it. But since the only way to get a refund is if no partner can be found for her, she makes sure to request a fantasy so girly and over the top that no sane guy will pick it up.

Except, someone does.

Warning: This fantasy contains a hot, domineering crown prince, sweet insta-love, steamy love scenes painted with light shades of gray, a wedding, and a HEA in both the virtual and real worlds.

Intended for mature audience.

Perfect Match 3: Captain's Conquest

Working as a Starbucks barista, Alicia fends off flirting all day long, but none of the guys are as charming and sexy as Gregg. His frequent visits are the highlight of her day, but since he's never asked her out, she assumes he's taken. Besides, between a day job and a budding music career, she has no time to start a new relationship.

That is until Gregg makes her an offer she can't refuse—a gift certificate to the virtual fantasy fulfillment service everyone is talking about. As a huge Star Trek fan, Alicia has a perfect match in mind—the captain of the Starship Enterprise.

FOR EXCLUSIVE PEEKS AT UPCOMING RELEASES & A FREE COMPANION BOOK

Join my *VIP Club* and gain access to the VIP portal at ITLUCAS.COM

CLICK HERE TO JOIN
(or go to: http://eepurl.com/blMTpD)

INCLUDED IN YOUR FREE MEMBERSHIP:

- **FREE** Children of the Gods companion book **1**
- **FREE** narration of Goddess's Choice—Book **1** in The Children of the Gods Origins series.
- Preview chapters of upcoming releases.
- And other exclusive content offered only to my VIPs.